W9-BLA-522

DEATH AND THE SINGING BIRDS

DEATH AND THE SINGING BIRDS

Amy Myers

This first world edition published 2020
in Great Britain and 2021 in the USA by
SEVERN HOUSE PUBLISHERS LTD of
Eardley House, 4 Uxbridge Street, London W8 7SY.
Trade paperback edition first published
in Great Britain and the USA 2021 by
SEVERN HOUSE PUBLISHERS LTD.

British Library Cataloguing in Publication Data
A CIP catalogue record for this title is available from the British Library.

ISBN-13: 978-0-7278-8994-2 (cased)
ISBN-13: 978-1-78029-730-9 (trade paper)
ISBN-13: 978-1-4483-0451-6 (e-book)

All Severn House titles are printed on acid-free paper.

Severn House Publishers support the Forest Stewardship Council™ [FSC™],
the leading international forest certification organisation.
All our titles that are printed on FSC certified paper carry the FSC logo.

Typeset by Palimpsest Book Production Ltd.,
Falkirk, Stirlingshire, Scotland.
Printed and bound in Great Britain by
TJ Books Limited, Padstow, Cornwall.

ACKNOWLEDGEMENTS

Kent is known for its splendid stately homes and the area in which the fictional Wychbourne Court is situated is blessed with, amongst others, the magnificent Knole Park, Ightham Mote, Sissinghurst Castle and Hever Castle. Wychbourne Court has its own history which dates back to Norman times and earlier. Nell Drury became its chef and resident detective thanks to my publisher Kate Lyall Grant of Severn House and my agent Sara Keane, and *Death and the Singing Birds* is Nell's third case. The family and staff in this novel are almost unchanged, and the story features Mr Briggs, valet to Lord Ansley. For his existence I owe my thanks to Steve Finnis, volunteer at the Royal West Kent Museum in Maidstone, who at the beginning of this series provided such valuable information on the 10th Battalion in 1918 together with insights into what Mr Briggs might have endured as a result that Mr Briggs appeared, fully formed in my mind, to play his part in the story. Thank you, Steve. No novel should leap straight from paper or screen into print, and I am lucky enough to have Sara Porter as my editor, whose eager eyes, together with those of her excellent copyeditor, Katherine Laidler, polished the novel's rough edges. Thanks to all the above, Wychbourne Court has become a second home to me (but fortunately I don't have to rival Nell's cuisine).

WYCHBOURNE COURT

Members of the Ansley family involved in Death and the Singing Birds
Lord (Gerald) Ansley, 8th Marquess Ansley
Lady (Gertrude) Ansley, Marchioness Ansley
Lord Richard Ansley, one of their three sons
Lady Enid, the Dowager Marchioness
Lady Clarice, Lord Ansley's sister

The upper servants
Nell Drury, chef
Charles Briggs, Lord Ansley's valet
Florence Fielding, housekeeper
Frederick Peters, butler
Jenny Smith, Lady Ansley's maid

Guests, visitors and neighbours
Sir Gilbert Saddler, artist and owner of Spitalfrith Manor
Lady Saddler (Lisette Rennard), Sir Gilbert's wife
Petra Saddler, Sir Gilbert's daughter
Vincent Finch, artist
Gert Radley, artist
Pierre Christophe, artist
Thora Huntley-Doran, poetess
Lance Merryman, artist and designer
Joe Carter, Spitalfrith's gardener
Freddie Carter, Joe's son
Robin Gurney, village constable
Jean-Paul Girarde, magician

and
Detective Chief Inspector Alexander Melbray of Scotland Yard

ONE

Not again! Nell Drury groaned. Blithering bloaters, this was the third time at least she'd told Michel that the redcurrants still required more sweetening. Normally such a brilliant underchef, it was clear he had his mind on something other than preparing a summer luncheon for Lord and Lady Ansley's guests at Wychbourne Court. More accurately, they were the guests of Lady Enid – his lordship's mother, the dowager – who had, so Nell had been told, commanded that the luncheon be held here instead of at the nearby Dower House, her own home.

'It's for the new owners of Spitalfrith Manor,' Lady Ansley had explained. 'I do have misgivings about them,' she had added impulsively.

Nell had been intrigued. Rumours had been flying around Wychbourne village for some weeks, and finally a week ago, at the end of July, the new neighbours had arrived – which promptly sparked off another round of rumours. Even though this was 1926, eight years since the war had ended, villages the size of Wychbourne eyed the outside world cautiously. It amused her that she was still regarded as a newcomer even though she had been the chef at Wychbourne Court for nearly two years.

'I regret, Miss Drury,' Michel said anxiously, rushing to remedy the situation with the sugar tongs in hand.

'He's in love,' Kitty, his fellow underchef, whispered, giggling.

'No one's allowed time off for love in a kitchen,' Nell said firmly. 'So snap to it. *Now.*' At least twenty-two-year-old Kitty and Michel weren't in love with each other. Kitty was being courted by a village swain and was immune to Michel's indefatigable zest for sudden romance – usually one-sided. Michel was roughly the same age as Kitty, and Nell had noticed several nocturnal absences (judging by his late arrivals or absences at breakfast in the servants' hall).

For a moment all was quiet, apart from the clatter of saucepans, frying pans and kettles, plus the whirling whisks and mincing machines as her staff concentrated on their tasks. Not for long.

'I heard they're *artists* up at Spitalfrith,' burst out one of the kitchen maids.

'Funny ones probably.' Mrs Squires, Nell's plain cook, snorted. 'Not *real* artists. Just the sort that can't even draw what's in front of them properly. Anyway, the lady's a model, so I heard.'

'With no clothes on?' Michel asked with interest.

'Nonsense,' Kitty said indignantly. 'The gentleman coming to the lunch is a *sir.* Anyway, he's a friend of Lady Enid's, so he'd ask the lady to keep her clothes on.'

'I bet he hasn't painted Lady Enid without any clothes on.' Someone giggled.

'That's enough,' Nell commanded, suppressing a giggle of her own. 'Luncheon! Turbot ready, please.' The pace promptly quickened.

That didn't stop her wondering about the new neighbours, though. There was a splendid portrait of the dowager (or Lady Enid as she liked to be addressed) in the Great Hall, painted in 1894 by Sir Gilbert Saddler when he was a young man and she was the reigning marchioness. In that painting she was most certainly fully clad, resplendent in velvet and jewels.

Sir Gilbert was the new owner of Spitalfrith Manor, which sat in the hamlet of a mere cluster of cottages that had grown up around it on the Sevenoaks road. It was on the outskirts of Wychbourne village and, compared with the vast Wychbourne Court, its estate was small. Spitalfrith had slumbered for many years under its former owner, a widower whose only son had died young. When he himself died a year ago, the estate had been sold, including its tied cottages. Life had changed greatly since the war, even in sleepy, rural Kent. All over the country, vast estates crippled by the loss of heirs or death duties were either being sold piecemeal for all sorts of purposes or shrunk to the point where they were no longer viable.

The Ansley family, itself struggling to keep its estate viable, had watched anxiously to know the fate of Spitalfrith Manor. Would it become a school? A public building? A socialist headquarters (the great wish of Lady Sophy, the youngest of the Ansleys' three children, who was dedicated to the cause of the Labour Party)? Or would it once more be a private house? And if the latter, who would come to live there? Until about two weeks ago, even Lord Ansley, the 8th Marquess Ansley and usually a fount of all knowledge through the House of Lords and his London clubs, had failed to produce an answer.

Two weeks ago, the news had come, but the rumours had multiplied. It had not gone unnoticed by Mr Peters, the Wychbourne butler, that, against all the rules of etiquette, Sir Gilbert and his family had not replied to the calling cards politely left by the Ansleys on their arrival. And yet they were coming to *luncheon*. This, to Nell's amusement though not surprise, was an outrage. How, Mr Peters had enquired grimly of his fellow upper servants, had this invitation been extended? Even he had not been informed before it was arranged.

'Lady Enid's doing, I'll be bound,' he had said darkly. 'And that Lady Saddler's a foreigner. French. Fancy not returning the call with her own cards. She doesn't know what's what.'

Nell had managed to keep a straight face. Such breaches of convention were not the social crime they would have been before the war, but they still existed. At Wychbourne Court, the Ansleys did their utmost to adapt to the new times. Their son Lord Richard helped his father run the estate with a breezy friendliness that made him generally popular in the village, his elder sister Lady Helen added the dash of London glamour as a Bright Young Thing, and Lady Sophy, while regarded as 'strange' by the village, was accepted as harmless. Since the General Strike had collapsed in May, she had been remarkably quiet on the subject of socialism, however, with only a few impassioned outbursts about the reduction of the miners' wages and unemployment.

Now with the contentious luncheon only three-quarters of an hour away, Nell took a dose of her own medicine. Stir your stumps and get cracking, she told herself. The duckling needed checking, the broad beans cooking, the quails' eggs preparing and artichoke bottoms stuffed. The head gardener, Mr Fairweather, had miraculously produced some late strawberries from the kitchen gardens and some raspberries were currently in the scullery for maggot removal.

Nell allowed herself a cautious pat on the back. All was well in her department, but Lady Ansley's doubts remained. As Lady

Ansley was usually the most charitable of people, Nell took those doubts seriously. When she had taken the day's menus to her for approval, Lady Ansley had asked if she would remain during luncheon in the servery, which overlooked the dining room. She only made such a request occasionally and this time she was very frank as to why.

'I'd like to know what you make of them, Nell,' she had said. 'It's wrong to prejudge people just from gossip, and Lady Enid speaks very highly of Sir Gilbert, although she has not met his new wife. A French model, I gather, who was a wartime heroine as a spy rebelling against the Germans in occupied Lille. I'm told she isn't popular with our local villagers so far, but perhaps that's as a result of the war. Perhaps it makes her wary of new faces.'

Nell was about to leave when Lady Ansley had added in a rush, 'Spitalfrith Manor has always seemed a strange place, as if it's not part of Wychbourne village at all. Some of the villagers say that Spitalfrith attracts bad luck, even evil, but surely that's just superstition? I do agree that the last owner, whom you won't remember, lived a sad life, as did the owner before him, but that wasn't their fault, nor that of Spitalfrith. Nevertheless, with all these rumours about Lady Saddler percolating, I can't help but be somewhat anxious.'

So this was Lady Saddler. Nell gazed at her in fascination through the servery hatch as her ladyship entered the dining room with Lord Ansley. In her earlier career at London's Carlton Hotel, Nell had seen and worked with people of all nations and was well used to stylish French fashions, but never had she seen a lady quite as strange as this. Sleek and sinuous, her fashionable silk day dress clung to her figure like a snakeskin – an apt comparison given the way Lady Saddler seemed to shimmy into the room. Her dark hair was drawn back tightly into a chignon. Her painted face was like a doll's – no, not a doll's, Nell decided; it was motionless, almost like a mask, the eyes heavily kohled and almost hooded, the mouth vividly painted. Not a gentle face and yet one that fascinated her. Nell could not take her eyes off her. She said very little, sat very still and yet managed to be the centre of attention.

Lady Saddler was in her early thirties, Nell guessed, but Sir Gilbert was much older, probably well into his fifties. He seemed somewhat out of his depth, as though wondering how to compete with his striking spouse, who was a stark contrast to this plump, seemingly affable man, who looked rather like Lewis Carroll's Father William. Sir Gilbert, Nell had heard, had a daughter, Petra, by his first marriage, but she was not present, as she lived in London.

First impressions of the new neighbours? No doubt about it, Nell thought. War heroine or not, Lady Saddler looked a very determined cuckoo in the Saddler nest. No mercy would be shown to fledglings here. Perhaps that was why Miss Petra Saddler preferred to stay in London.

Lady Ansley was struggling with the conversation, and with no response at all from Lady Saddler, it was left to Sir Gilbert to cope. 'Splendid place you have here,' he remarked in the middle of an awkward silence.

Lord Ansley's mouth twitched at this unconvincing comment. 'Thank you,' he replied gravely.

Lady Saddler did rouse herself at this point. '*Versailles est plus grand*,' she commented dismissively.

Let battle begin, Lady Enid, Nell thought, willing her on. *You can deal with that.*

Lady Enid did. She treated her guest to the expression that had quelled generations of shopkeepers and family alike. 'Versailles is a splendid building, but, alas, no longer a family home like Wychbourne.'

This broadside had no effect on Lady Saddler. She ignored it. Not a good omen, Nell thought, torn between dismay and an urge to applaud.

Oblivious to the atmosphere, Lord Ansley's sister, Lady Clarice, blundered eagerly into the danger zone. 'We have more ghosts at Wychbourne Court than Versailles. I believe Versailles only boasts poor Queen Marie Antoinette – beheaded, of course, but her ghost and those of her court still haunt Le Petit Trianon. Do allow me to take you on a tour of the Wychbourne phantoms. And indeed your own – I have reason to believe that at Spitalfrith—'

Nell froze. This was hardly the most tactful way to forge a friendly atmosphere. Lady Clarice's addiction to ghosts was tacitly tolerated by everyone at Wychbourne, but they were not an interest that everybody shared.

'My dear Clarice,' Lady Enid firmly restrained her daughter, 'no doubt Sir Gilbert and Lady Saddler would be most interested in our phantoms and indeed their own, but do permit them time to appreciate their new home before indulging in its spectral history.'

'Of course, Mama,' Lady Clarice murmured, downcast at this rebuff. Nell was fond of Lady Clarice. Now in her early fifties, she lived at Wychbourne Court as she had never married owing to the death of her fiancé in the Boer War. The ghosts of Wychbourne were her great passion, often to the exclusion of all else, and her thin, determined figure anxiously in search of the latest phantom was a familiar sight in the many corridors of Wychbourne Court. This was the first Nell had heard about ghosts at Spitalfrith, though.

'Are there any ghosts at Spitalfrith?' Sir Gilbert asked, manfully doing his duty as a guest. 'I haven't seen any myself. Have you, my dear?' he addressed his wife.

As Lady Saddler remained silent, he continued hastily, 'It's a pity ghosts can't be painted, eh, Lisette?' He managed a weak grin, but his wife did not grin in return, Nell noted.

Lady Saddler was indeed not a lady to cross, Nell decided, wondering what Robert, their chief footman who was waiting impassively to serve the duck, was making of all this. He wore his usual poker face, but no doubt the servants' hall would hear all about it later.

Lady Ansley clutched at this opening. 'I do hope that you will find a great deal else to paint in Spitalfrith and Wychbourne, Sir Gilbert.'

Full marks to Lady Ansley, Nell thought with relief. Back to safe ground.

Sir Gilbert beamed. 'The Clerries will.'

Nell blinked. No safe ground yet. The *what*?

'Who are they? My dear Gilbert, do tell us more,' Lady Enid said somewhat frostily.

'The Clerries – more formally the Artistes de Cler – owe their name to the great General Joseph Gustav Cler who was killed at the battle of Magenta between the Emperor Napoleon III and the Italians,' Sir Gilbert obliged enthusiastically. 'He was also an artist. The Clerries' founder, Monsieur Pierre Christophe, is a great admirer of his gifts; he bases his own artistic aim on presenting truth.'

'I trust that this is not one of those avant-garde movements?' Lady Enid responded icily. 'You are a prominent academician, Gilbert. Surely you cannot regard such movements as more than temporary interruptions to the true path of art.'

To Nell's amusement, Sir Gilbert turned as pink as a cooked prawn, but he did his best. 'I experiment with the principles of the Clerries, because—'

Lady Saddler's bored voice stopped him immediately. 'Truth. *La vérité?* There is no such thing as the truth in art.'

'All art is truth,' Lady Clarice offered eagerly. 'I remember Adelaide, the ghost of—'

Her mother waved this quickly aside. 'Gilbert, kindly explain,' she commanded. 'Do you count yourself one of these Artistes de Cler?'

'I do,' he answered anxiously. 'After the war ended, I visited Paris to find inspiration, recapture the vision that we artists had in the 1890s. It had since given way to so many art forms – cubism, fauvism, expressionism and now surrealism – that despite the life, the energy, the excitement of art today, I felt I had lost my way.'

This sounded to Nell like a well-rehearsed speech, but then he brightened up. 'And then I found it. At last I realized that by stripping away the dross to the skeleton one reaches the essential truth, whether it be of the body or a leaf or the imagination itself.' Sir Gilbert looked round, clearly pleased at this explanation.

Nell had a fleeting image of her kitchen reduced to its skeleton. What, she wondered, as she organized the arrival of the dessert dishes in the servery, was the essential truth of a trifle? Should one return to cream, custard and jelly or further still? Or was a trifle only skeletonized as it was being eaten? *Take this seriously*, she instructed herself. Was there more truth in a barren tree than a leafy one? Surely both were true? Or did one have to strip off the bark as well? On the whole, Nell decided, she'd stick to trifle, truthful or not.

Bemused, she saw the Ansleys' polite but blank faces, as Sir Gilbert might have done because he added hastily, 'Our friends who are visiting us for our festival in two weeks' time will explain the Artistes de Cler more clearly. And we are to hold an exhibition of their work next year at the Academy of Modern Art in London.'

'That,' contributed Lady Saddler smoothly, 'is not yet certain.'

She smiled, but it wasn't the kind of smile that warmed the cockles of one's heart. It was more the smile of a crocodile, Nell thought, then felt ashamed of herself for such a disparaging view of a war heroine. War changed people, it ruined lives. But what was all this about a festival?

Sir Gilbert's sudden burst of confidence seemed to drain away. 'As my dear wife says, it is not yet certain,' he said unhappily.

Nell shivered. There was something strange about his 'dear wife', apart from her appearance.

'You referred to a festival, Sir Gilbert. Might I ask what it is?' Lord Ansley asked quickly, signalling to the chief footman Robert to serve the dessert.

'Ah.' After a quick glance at his wife, Sir Gilbert was only too happy to tell them. 'In two weeks' time, on Saturday the twenty-first of August, we shall be holding the very first Festival de Cler in the grounds of Spitalfrith Manor. Monsieur Christophe himself will be doing us the honour of attending it, as will other fellow Clerries. He has naturally chosen Africa as its theme and we artistes will be exhibiting our work.'

Africa in Wychbourne? Nell struggled with that concept with one part of her mind, while the other watched the reception of her Coupe Melba. What did Sir Gilbert mean by 'naturally'? What on earth would the Wychbourne villagers make of this Africa theme and the artists themselves? She tried to suppress a mental image of a group of unclad skeletons tramping round the village.

'Will there be shamans present?' Lady Clarice asked with excitement.

Sir Gilbert looked blank. 'I cannot be sure of that,' he added less certainly, perhaps conscious of his wife's cold lack of support or perhaps, like Nell, unsure what shamans were. 'But Africa is certainly a cornerstone of the Clerries' art.'

'Why?' Lady Clarice asked eagerly. 'Is it because Josephine Baker is taking Paris by storm?'

Trust Lady Clarice to ask what all of them were wondering but no one dared say, Nell thought.

'Perhaps,' Sir Gilbert replied miserably. 'Look at Gauguin's work. Africa is untarnished by the complications of Western life. Nature in its rawest form, stripped of modern life's fripperies.'

From what Nell had seen in the newspapers, the word 'stripped' was all too applicable, given Josephine Baker's scanty costumes. The American singer had indeed taken Paris by storm with her singing and dancing. Fortunately, however, Nell could see no call for stripping down her cuisine to bare bones. Nor, on reflection, did she see much point in the Clerries' aims. Shouldn't every artistic work reflect the truth?

'Everyone in Wychbourne is invited to our festival,' Sir Gilbert continued. 'Including everyone here at the Court.' He smiled nervously at his hosts. 'High and low,' he added. 'From aristocrats to lowly servants.'

Lowly servants? Nell managed to hold back a snort of laughter at the thought of what Robert would undoubtedly relay to the servants' hall. Then she shivered again as she saw Lady Saddler's expression. She was staring at her husband with what was surely pure disdain. Just what was going on at Spitalfrith?

'Lowly servants, that's what he called us,' Robert declared indignantly later that day in the servants' hall. 'What tripe! Those days are over. That's his blinking truth and I felt like telling the old geezer so.'

Nell saw his point. Robert was a gentle giant of a man generally, and a patient one, so his annoyance was unusual. But he was right. Even in Wychbourne Court, the distinction, at least by name, between upper servants and lower was vanishing fast, although the same hierarchy remained, despite the fact that the interaction between the family and the servants was closer. The war had shown that everyone had a job to do, whatever their rank, because gas, bayonets and shells had made no distinctions.

The upper servants used to eat separately in the butler's room, but nowadays they frequently ate together in the servants' hall. Before the war, meals had been taken in silence by the lower servants. Now everyone had a right to their say, and today they were making full use of it. The subject was still modern art, it appeared, when Nell joined them for their supper.

'I saw a picture in a window in Sevenoaks last week,' Kitty

contributed. 'It was called "Lady with Grapes" but it was only a lot of bulges and squares. Not like a lady at all.'

'I've enough bulges of my own, thank you very much,' Mrs Fielding, the housekeeper, commented in a rare jovial mood. It was everyone's secret that she and Mr Peters were sweet on one another, even though it was not talked about publicly.

'The artist was just experimenting, I expect,' Nell contributed. 'We're all doing that nowadays in all sorts of ways. It makes life fun.'

'What are those artists going to be experimenting on at Spitalfrith, though?' Mrs Fielding returned to her usual snappiness.

'Living after the war,' Michel replied seriously. His father had died at Verdun and he had come to England with his mother at the age of fifteen.

'Or, like Robert says, experimenting in skeletons,' Kitty said brightly. 'Perhaps there are some at Spitalfrith Manor.'

'It's a creepy old place,' Mrs Fielding observed. 'I've asked her ladyship if I can go to this festival, though.'

'Perhaps Mr Peters would like to go, too,' Robert remarked innocently. 'Anyway, we can all go. That's what the old chap said,' he pointed out.

To Nell's surprise, Mr Briggs, Lord Ansley's valet, seemed to be listening. Mr Briggs must be about thirty and suffered from war damage, living in a war of his own. He only rarely paid any attention to what was going on around him. This time he dealt with it in his now familiar way.

He pushed his chair back, stood up and saluted. 'Corporal G/26420, *sir*,' he snapped out.

Then he sat down again. That was rare after such outbursts, so Jenny Smith went round to him, picking up his napkin and gently persuading him to continue eating his cake. Jenny had brought a gust of fresh air when she arrived at Wychbourne as lady's maid to Lady Ansley earlier that year from London. As she was as attractive and as bubbly as Mary Pickford in the Hollywood pictures, Lord Richard had rapidly had his eye on her – and she had equally rapidly removed it, although she still seemed on good terms with him.

'How can we all go to this festival at Spitalfrith?' Muriel, one of the scullery maids, piped up. 'We've work to do.'

'Lady Ansley says we can *all* have permission to go,' Mrs Fielding said importantly. 'Those of you who want to visit this festival can do so, provided their job's covered.'

Mrs Fielding in an obliging mood? Wonders would never cease, Nell thought. It must be because Mr Peters was present.

'What's this art festival about, though?' Jenny (as Nell realized she was now thinking of her) said.

'Lady Ansley told me,' Mrs Fielding announced with an air that conveyed she was in her ladyship's confidence, 'that artists will be talking about their work as well as showing it off.'

'What's the point of talking about it if we can see it?' Kitty asked politely.

'Because it won't mean anything to any of us.' Jenny laughed. 'It's going to be all shapes and sizes and bright colours.'

'Very narrow shapes and sizes if everything's a skeleton,' Nell contributed.

Kitty was still worried. 'But what's the point of our looking at it if it doesn't mean nothing? I saw a print of a nice picture of Knole Park with a field and sheep in it by Sir Gilbert in my auntie's house, and that meant something to me because I went there once.'

'That was painted when Sir Gilbert was younger, I expect,' Jenny explained. 'Now he wants to be avant-garde and move with the times to keep up with Picasso and Matisse.'

Nell glanced at her. Jenny was certainly proving a lady's maid with a difference. Not only had she succeeded in attracting Lord Richard's attention, but she was proving knowledgeable on modern art. Despite having worked with her for over six months now, Nell knew little about her, save that she had been employed through a London agency. Even in sleepy Wychbourne, the days when domestic servants were drawn from the local village were fast fading.

'It is *la vérité*,' Robert intoned solemnly. 'The skeleton of a body, of a leaf. Wonder if they ever draw kippers! They've got a lot of bones.'

'True enough,' Jenny agreed, as scullery maid Muriel giggled. 'But I don't think we'll find too many kippers being sketched in Paris, and that's where all the new kinds of art are being dreamed up. You ever been to Paris, Miss Drury?'

'Not yet,' Nell said cheerfully. 'That's where the Clerries are based, though.'

'Paris' brought back an uncomfortable, if happy, memory for her. Someday, she and Alex Melbray had agreed, they'd stroll down the Champs-Élysées and along the Seine riverbank together – a metaphor, she was acutely aware, for a closer relationship. Her doubts arose because she couldn't resolve the tug of war within her. Leave her job, as she would have to do as Alex was a detective chief inspector at Scotland Yard? Or give up Alex? If, of course, he hadn't given up on her first. 'But,' she hurried on, 'Paris is where Sir Gilbert met his new wife.'

'Poor old fellow. I'm sorry for him, I am,' Robert said in heartfelt tones.

'Sir Gilbert spent some years there after the war apparently,' Nell continued. 'She was a model, so perhaps she modelled for him.'

'Is she one of these Clerries, too?' Kitty asked.

'I don't think so. But that might just be my impression,' Nell added hastily, belatedly aware that Mr Briggs was now crooning to himself, one of his signs of distress.

'*Mademoiselle from Armentières, parlez-vous . . .*'

'It's all right, Mr Briggs. You're safe here,' Jenny said soothingly, as he continued with the same two lines over and over again.

Nell was worried. Mr Briggs's reaction to what was going on was unusual because, as a rule, he attended meals only in body, not in mind. Was it the talk of France that upset him?

Mr Briggs took no notice of Jenny or anyone else for a while. Then he abruptly stopped, stood up, saluted again and left the table.

'He hasn't finished his pudding yet.' Muriel looked worried. 'Is he all right?'

'I'll make sure he is,' Nell volunteered. 'He's probably just setting off on his usual nightly walk to listen to the nightingales.'

But tonight proved different. There was no sign of Mr Briggs outside the rear entrance to the servants' wing which opened on to the eastern side of the gardens, and so Nell went around to the tradesmen's entrance which led on to the kitchen yard.

No sign of Mr Briggs. She was about to go back inside when she saw him wheeling his bicycle through the yard – that was very strange at this time of night. Although he frequently went out at night, he usually walked. Concerned, Nell hurried towards him, but she was too late. He was on the bicycle, cycling away into the still of the night. Running around to the front of the house, she could see him cycling down the main drive towards the village and all she heard, wafted back by the breeze, were a few words spoken perhaps to her, perhaps to himself: 'The birds that sing . . . the singing birds . . .'

Nothing was wrong, she thought thankfully, as she returned to the servants' hall. Mr Briggs must simply be bicycling to the estate woodland where he would listen to the nightingales. Although it was unusual to hear him singing and for him to take a bicycle there, it must just have taken his fancy to do so. That was all.

TWO

'There's coconuts and all sorts of funny things being delivered to Spitalfrith Manor,' Kitty reported excitedly. 'That's what Mr Fairweather told me. The old gardener there wanted to pinch some pineapples from him.' Kitty's current boyfriend was now one of Wychbourne's assistant gardeners, and Kitty's interest in negotiating with Mr Fairweather by visiting the vegetable garden had markedly increased.

There were only two days to go now before the great day when the Artistes de Cler would reveal their paintings amid their African glory. In the words of Alice in Wonderland, curiouser and curiouser, Nell thought. Even Alice might have been taken aback at the Clerries, though, if their paintings followed the lines she had heard about.

'I hope he didn't part with any,' she said, alarmed. Pineapples and the pits in which Mr Fairweather wintered them were highly prized. The fruit would probably be cheaper to buy at market, but he clung to his old pits and tended them carefully. Result? Excellence.

Kitty giggled. ''Course not. You know what he's like.'

Nell did. It was as much as she could do to get him to part with *any* of his produce in the kitchen gardens. For Mr Fairweather, it had to be perfect before he would allow a single bean to leave his domain, but the trouble was that *nothing* was ever perfect to his eyes and nose.

'I heard there were monkeys going into the manor. *Live* ones, like you see at the pictures,' Kitty added.

'Perhaps Father Christmas will drop in, too,' retorted Nell. How did monkeys fit in with the Clerries? What would arrive next? Perhaps a gorilla or two might turn up. Or an elephant the size of the famous Jumbo. First things first, though. 'How about tackling the quince compote for tonight's pork?' she suggested meaningfully. 'Interested?'

The kitchen picked up speed and began to hum, like the new mains electricity installed at long last. Thankfully, the old generator was no more, save for emergencies, and the electric ranges were a delight, despite Nell's own devotion to her old coal stoves.

It was hardly surprising that the Spitalfrith festival was causing such a furore in the kitchen, as the whole village was humming with excitement, and even the Ansley family had become caught up in the drama.

'What the dickens is going on, Nell?' Lady Ansley had asked in exasperation only this morning when Nell had presented the day's menus to her. 'I feel I ought to offer more support to Sir Gilbert and Lady Saddler, and yet something keeps holding me back. My husband, for example,' she added ruefully. 'He hasn't taken to our new neighbours, I'm afraid, and I don't blame him. Nor have I.'

That hadn't surprised Nell. Lady Ansley had been a Gaiety Girl in the 1890s and had adapted to her new role as marchioness perfectly, so this had been a rare moment of outspokenness on such matters. But Nell shared her unease. There was certainly something odd about Spitalfrith. Its earlier drab reputation had suddenly transmuted into something darker over which this festival lay superficially like a layer of icing sugar. She was well aware, however, that Lord Ansley would be quietly judging the situation before committing Wychbourne Court to a situation they might regret.

'After all,' Lady Ansley had continued, 'we haven't had an official invitation to this art festival, merely that all-encompassing verbal mention at luncheon. If it weren't for Lady Enid's friendship with Sir Gilbert, I would quietly forget about it, but I fear we should all be present.'

'Of course,' Nell murmured, wondering what the dowager would make of the Clerries' view of art when she saw it. Africa and the Clerries were a big leap from Sir Gilbert's portrait of her thirty years ago as a Victorian lady at the height of her glory. Come to think of it, what was she, Nell, going to make of this new avant-garde movement? Was it a mere passing fad, she wondered, or were the Artistes de Cler here to stay? Would the new artists in Paris such as Picasso and the Dadaists recognize them?

With this in mind, she had taken the longer route back to the east wing, down the grand staircase to the Great Hall, in order to take another look at the dowager's portrait. The Victorian age had certainly passed, but it was still a magnificent painting. Lady Enid was majestically seated, clad in full evening dress and plentifully supplied with jewels including a tiara, her hand resting on a proud-looking dog at her side. Nell had tried to imagine the dowager whittled down to a bony structure, but that was definitely *lèse-majesté* and Lady Enid already seemed to be glaring down her from her portrait as if she could read her mind.

Back in the kitchen, the chatter about Saturday's festival continued until nearly lunchtime, when the coming deadline concentrated minds on the job. Once in the servants' hall, however, it broke out again.

'We're all working out how we can get there, Miss Drury,' Kitty told her excitedly, 'thanks to Mrs Fielding,' she added diplomatic-ally, obviously having noticed Mrs Fielding's ample chest ready to rise with indignation. 'We'll go in two groups, one at three o'clock, the other at half past five.'

The servants' hall could seat over forty if needed, although in practice they were rarely all there together, but today it was nearly full, with one or two of the garden staff present. They rarely came to the east wing, usually choosing to eat with Mr Ramsay, who was in charge of the stables and garages. Other servants came and went as their duties allowed. Mr Briggs often preferred to eat in Pug's Parlour, the old name for the butler's room and place where the upper servants traditionally dined. Today, though, he was quietly eating lunch in the servants' hall despite the hubbub.

'When will you be going to the festival, Mr Briggs?' Jenny Smith was obviously trying to draw him into the general excitement, but he merely stared at her blankly. Whoops! Danger signal, as Nell knew all too well.

'The art festival at Spitalfrith Manor,' Jenny prompted him.

Mr Briggs looked puzzled, then smiled at them all and slowly left the room. He hadn't given his usual cry of distress, and his departure caused no great concern, save to Nell, although Jenny looked taken aback, too. What, Nell wondered, had upset him about Jenny's statement? It had perhaps demanded too much of him, but no more than that.

The conversation at the table had now moved on, although Saturday's event was still its focus. Mrs Fielding appeared to be the most knowledgeable on the subject of Spitalfrith.

'I was told by Mr Peters who heard it from the telegram boy that guests are arriving at the manor today. *Guests*,' she emphasized heavily. 'A person has already arrived at Sevenoaks railway station enquiring about a taxicab. A most *strange* person. He was wearing a bright yellow suit.'

'*Yellow?*' repeated Kitty, open-mouthed.

'As the sun, so Mr Peters was informed. And worse!'

An intake of breath from her audience, as she continued, 'A bright yellow hat with a *feather.*'

There were too many trees in the countryside, Lance Merryman decided, removing a leaf from his delightful new yellow jacket. He'd had to pay the taxicab driver twice as much as he suspected the usual fare would have been, as several other cab chauffeurs had taken one look at his fashionable attire and decided they could not oblige – well, poor them! And here he was at Spitalfrith Manor in the middle of the countryside, quite unlike his native London or Paris where he now dwelt. Not, he hoped, for much longer. He tried to reassure himself that even Gilbert was not foolish enough to let anything (or rather *anyone*) mar the Artistes de Cler exhibition at the London Academy of Modern Art arranged for next year. London was the thing nowadays. Paris might host excellent designers such as Molyneux, but he, Lance Merryman, would rule London. His designs would take *Fashion Tomorrow Magazine* by storm – and *Vogue* would be hammering at his door.

Lance looked around him as the taxicab drove away and left him standing on the forecourt with his suitcase awaiting a footman to welcome him in. There seemed to be a great number of trees overhanging the forecourt. Very *rural*. Trees were all very well as a concept for the Artistes de Cler, and for the theme of Africa they were even better – 'diamonds positively glittering on the leaves, my darlings, and *lions* strolling among all those naked tree trunks' – but London was to be his El Dorado. There was just one snag to his plans: the spectre of the monstrous Lisette who had ruined his time in Paris by slandering his winter collection. Now that she had married poor Gilbert, she would doubtless continue her campaign against him, but after the London exhibition next year he could break away from the Artistes de Cler.

He noticed an elegant, statuesque figure appearing through the trees lining the forecourt. For a moment he had feared it was Lisette, but to his relief it was Miss Huntley-Doran, dear Thora, poetess and fiancée of the Clerries' so *very* noble founder, Pierre Christophe – to whom he must pay due deference, of course. Given that no footman appeared to be rushing from the house to carry his luggage, he was relieved that he was no longer isolated in this strange world of fields and woodland.

'Miss Huntley-Doran – Thora!' he cried out in welcome, mentally recladding her out of that most unfortunate purple jumper suit and into one of his own silken creations. 'Are we not fortunate to be here amid the beauty of the countryside?' The stately Thora was always reasonably friendly to him, unlike Pierre, who treated him as a court jester.

Thora looked anxious. 'Are we?' she asked. 'Does this really inspire you, Lance? I myself find Hampstead more artistically supportive. Have you read my "Elegy to a Fallen Hero", for example? I wrote it there, and it was when he first read it that Pierre asked me to join the Artistes de Cler.'

'Your poetic gifts are outstanding,' Lance murmured diplomatically. In his view, Pierre had only one goal where dear Thora was concerned – marrying into her wealthy family. 'Is dear Pierre here yet? No doubt—'

'He might be,' Thora interrupted, looking distinctly cross. 'Have you seen Lisette?'

He shuddered. 'Our dear hostess?' was all he could manage to reply. 'Not yet.' And then he realized what she was fearing: that the magnificent Pierre might be with that snakey lady. What *fun*, he thought. Of course, there had always been delicious gossip about Pierre and Lisette . . .

Pierre Christophe drew up outside Spitalfrith Manor and contemplated this grey, uninspiring-looking mansion, one hand lazily resting on the door of his brand-new 14/60 Lagonda while he did so. Well, the Lagonda was his for five days anyway. He couldn't afford to hire it for longer. No mere railway travel for him. Sleek and beguiling, the Lagonda represented the principles of the Artistes de Cler, and Thora would adore it – unfortunate though it was that it was such a temporary possession. But he was, after all, the founder of the Clerrian movement, and as art was a business, one could not ignore such sordid matters as money. There were times, he considered, when it was necessary to spend it without regard for bank accounts.

He had many concerns about this visit. The first was the need to impress Gilbert with the importance of the artistes' appearance at the exhibition next year, in view of the fact that although Gilbert was a member of the Artistes de Cler, his fondness for his old style of painting sometimes overrode his convictions about the worthiness of their cause. Some of his fellow artistes – in particular Lance Merryman – had no sense of occasion. Lance would undoubtedly arrive clad in his usual flamboyant attire, and Pierre shuddered at the thought of his Thora at the same house party as that brightly clad butterfly. Lance's private life was his own affair, but he should have some regard for those around him. Thora's family would not be impressed.

Pierre's second concern was Thora herself. Everything depended on his new fiancée – his new *rich* fiancée – who now truly believed in the artistes' principles. As she was not an artist but a poetess, it had taken much patient explanation on his part to show her just how well her poems suited the Clerrian way of thinking. Nothing must go wrong with this festival on Saturday, nor with the plans for next year's Academy of Modern Art exhibition in London's Kensington. His career depended on it.

Which brought him to his third and major concern as he sprang down from the Lagonda. The presence of Lisette Rennard, his former mistress and model, now Lady Saddler. If only he had known earlier that Gilbert had married her two months ago, he wouldn't have persuaded Thora to join them this weekend. He had known that Gilbert had used Lisette as a model in Paris, but for him to marry her so suddenly after he, Pierre, had shed her from both her roles in his life had been a shock. And here she would be the hostess at Spitalfrith Manor. He had hoped that a sense of propriety would keep her away from the Artistes de Cler now that his betrothal to Thora had been announced, but that was doomed. Lisette would be here with her dark eyes and dark, lustrous hair that flowed over her slender shoulders – when it wasn't dragged back into an elegant chignon to display the wonderful contours of her face. The angular body, the perfect model, the perfect mistress. But *not* the perfect woman to have around when one's future wife, with her old-fashioned morals, was at one's side.

Surely even Lisette, Pierre comforted himself, would not be a danger to the exhibition next year. Those of his fellow Artistes de Cler who were present this weekend – Thora, Lance, Vinny Finch, Gert Radley and Gilbert himself – would be eagerly discussing it. Even Lisette could not stop it now.

'Pierre, *mon cher! Bonjour!*' Pierre saw Gilbert waddling towards him, arms outstretched. 'Welcome to Spitalfrith.'

There was no sign of Lisette thankfully, but she would be there, waiting, casting her dark shadow. Pierre braced himself.

The whole village seemed obsessed with this festival, Nell fumed, having remonstrated with the butcher for bringing beef shin instead of flank. Normally the most punctilious of men, Mr Podland had been so abashed that he seemed about to fall on his sword like the king's chef in France whose fish didn't arrive in time.

'Sorry, Miss Drury, it's that big delivery to Spitalfrith – took my mind right off what I was doing,' he apologized. 'And I don't have no sausages. Three hundred is what they wanted. Made with chitterlings, which I ain't never heard of. What they'll get is good straight pork. And shrimps, they said. It's August, I told 'em. No shrimps. Anyways, I'm a butcher, not a fishmonger. I'll do them some nice ham puffs. Sir Gilbert said they'll do, but now I've the job of making them.'

Nell did her best to sound compassionate while running through her mind what she'd say to Mrs Squires who had ordered sausages for the servants' lunch. There was, however, no sign of Mrs Squires when she enquired on her return to the kitchen.

'Gone to the manor. She's helping Mrs Hayward,' Kitty sang out to her. 'Mrs Fielding says we all should.'

Nell groaned. It was only Thursday and the festival wasn't until Saturday. Meanwhile, there was the small matter of the servants' tea and supper to cope with (normally Mrs Squires' responsibility) even as she called out '*Pommes dauphine*' for the family dinner.

'I will do this,' Michel shouted back, rushing over to the stoves and tripping over the meat trays that Kitty had left on the floor beside her.

Nell closed her eyes and counted to ten. 'This is a kitchen, not a circus,' she yelled as Michel clambered to his feet, only to back into Muriel carrying and then dropping a tray full of china from the scullery.

It was at this moment that Lady Clarice suddenly appeared, a situation all but unknown at Wychbourne Court. There was an unspoken agreement that the family did not appear in the east wing without due warning. None had been given, and Lady Clarice was flushed and clearly eager to talk.

'Miss Drury, can you spare just a moment for some exciting news?' she asked, but didn't wait for her reply before rushing on. 'I have been doing some research into Spitalfrith Manor, and I have made the most thrilling discovery.'

Flaming fishbones, what next? Nell managed to fix a smile on her face, as, leaving chaos behind her, she escorted Lady Clarice out of the kitchen and into the Cooking Pot, otherwise known as her Chef's Room retreat.

'I know you'll be so pleased,' Lady Clarice continued, as Nell seated her at the small table, which, as always, was covered with pads of writing paper and books of recipes.

This sounded ominous. Nell waited in trepidation.

'Spitalfrith does have a ghost – and, oh, Miss Drury, it is the ghost of a soldier. It must surely be my beloved *Jasper*. He lived there for several years before he departed for that terrible war with the Boers. After his death, his parents left Spitalfrith, but now I'm sure that Jasper haunts it. He will be awaiting me there on Saturday, and I believe it may not be in the house – though I shall investigate there also – but in the dell where he courted me.' She blushed.

Nell summoned up her courage to prepare her for disappointment. 'There will be a lot of people around, Lady Clarice; that might deter him. And we shall only be there in daylight hours and outside the house, so don't be too disappointed if he doesn't appear.'

Lady Clarice smiled. 'Jasper will find a way.'

When she returned to the kitchen, Nell's fears were justified. During her absence, the kitchen had not been ahum with work or even clearing up the debris. On the contrary, it appeared to be at a standstill as Jenny Smith held forth on a subject on which she was knowledgeable and, it seemed, up to date: Lord Richard's love life.

'About twenty-one or two, I'd say,' Jenny informed her interested audience. 'Not tall – not pretty, but looks as though she has a mind of her own. The sort you'd look at twice – or several times if you were Lord Richard.'

That brought a laugh, but awareness of Nell's presence rapidly brought order to her staff. Jenny laughed. 'Sorry, Nell. But with all this going on about Spitalfrith, it's inevitable that Lord Richard will be dashing after somebody to do with the festival tomorrow.'

'And this damsel is?' Nell enquired, casting an eye on Kitty and the progress of the peaches *au vin blanc* for dinner.

'Sir Gilbert's daughter, Petra. Lord Richard had met her – or seen her, anyway – at Sevenoaks railway station this morning and driven her to Spitalfrith.'

Poor girl, Nell thought. 'Did she look as though she could stand up to her stepmother? She'll need to.'

'Short answer: yes,' Jenny replied. 'Whether she'll win or not is less certain.'

'No, Father,' Petra Saddler said firmly, 'I will not pose for the Clerries.'

She had come all the way from London at her father's request, but this was the last straw. The very idea of posing at Saturday's Festival de Cler, with the whole village sniggering, was *not* her cup of tea, and she was well aware that this suggestion came from the Snake who knew how much she'd hate it. (The Snake was her private name for her stepmother – Madame Lisette Rennard, as she had been before poor Papa stupidly married her.) Petra had done her best to be polite to the Clerries when she visited her father in Paris and met his new friends, but were they really *friends*? In her view, they had taken her father away from his true calling in art. Couldn't he see they were in a blind alley leading nowhere? The Clerries had lured him into feeling he had to be avant-garde in his work, rather than remain with his true calling alongside artists like Sir William Orpen and the late John Singer Sargent.

Her father looked perplexed. 'I can't think why you are so reluctant. It is an honour.'

'Being gawped at by a crowd of strangers while I freeze in a flimsy Greek costume is not an honour. Especially if it's to be shown in next year's exhibition—'

'But if the Clerries paint the true you—'

'You don't know the true me,' Petra said in exasperation. 'None of these people know or want to know the true me. *I* don't know the true me, and as for Saturday's festival and then the exhibition next year—'

'Ah. My dear, I am having second thoughts about that,' he began even more nervously. 'Your stepmama does feel that . . .'

'Once and for all, she may legally be my stepmother, but I do not regard her as such, Papa.'

'If you could just get to know her a little better . . .'

Know her better? Petra shivered. How about getting friendly with a snake? And now it seemed Father was having second thoughts about the Academy of Modern Art exhibition, probably because the Snake was not one of the Clerries herself; she only modelled for them. True, the exhibition mattered not a jot to Petra, but it did to these weird guests staying with them. And it would do Father no good either if it was cancelled now, after all the hullabaloo. He was so far in with his own work for the Clerries that withdrawing would be worse than going ahead with it.

This weekend was going to be worse than she had feared. As far as she could judge, the only sane one among the five guests was Vinny Finch, a tall, quiet man who winked at her when the Clerries were greeting the last crazy arrival. That had been Gert Radley, who had marched up the drive in sturdy shoes, heavy walking skirt and a haversack on her back.

'Top of the afternoon,' Miss Radley had sung out to them, vigorously shaking their hands as she and Papa greeted her. (No sign of the Snake.) Miss Radley looked the oldest of the Clerries, save for Papa – perhaps about fifty – and was definitely weird, with cropped grey hair and an old felt hat jammed on anyhow. At least she was human, Petra decided. She must be the artist whose paintings were delivered an hour or two ago courtesy of carriers Carter Paterson.

Petra was already feeling trapped at Spitalfrith. Her life was in London, not here. She was twenty-two years old, and on her last birthday she had come into the trust fund that her mother had set up for her. After the Snake's arrival two months ago, she had moved into her own home in Chelsea and started to live, by which she meant she was now at the Royal Academy of Dramatic Art. That meant, of course, leaving Papa here alone with the Snake, but she resolved to keep as close an eye on him as she could. Especially this weekend.

'The tents are arriving tomorrow morning,' her father had explained as soon as she arrived, 'and we will have the afternoon to set everything up, with Saturday morning left for last-minute crises.' He had paused. 'You will behave, won't you, Petra?'

She sighed. 'For you, Pa, yes.' Crises? The Snake would do her best to create those, leaving Petra to behave beautifully towards the Clerry guests. In addition to Mr Finch and Miss Radley, there was the gushing Pierre Christophe so eager to impress, the maniacal Lance Merryman dancing around like a grasshopper, and the dreamy Thora Huntley-Doran – all loopy in Petra's opinion. She would do anything for her father – except be nice to the Snake. Already she felt like Cinderella stuck in the kitchen while her stepmother reigned supreme, and it was only Thursday. Father seemed blind to any fault in the Snake. He was besotted with the woman. The Snake had had the nerve to suggest that since Petra wasn't an artist, she might like to wash up the crockery, as their housekeeper and one maid had enough to do. Petra had pointed out that since Lisette wasn't an artist either, she could help.

And here came the Snake now, gliding along ready to swallow her prey whole. Wouldn't it be nice if some magician could snap his fingers and make her disappear for good?

'So here we are, Gert. Will it work, this festival on Saturday? It's one thing meeting in Paris in a studio when one can leave when one wishes,' Vinny Finch remarked, looking round the bleak drawing room of Spitalfrith Manor, 'but here we are with Gilbert married to Lisette and ourselves captive until Monday. Happy about it?'

True, Sir Gilbert and Lisette had only been living here for a week or two, but its sombre if fashionable décor of spindly furniture and almost barren walls, save for the occasional print or painting – not one of Gilbert's superb works, Gert noticed – spoke of effect and not welcome.

'No,' she grunted. 'I'll make sure she doesn't get anywhere near my work again.'

For Gert, there was only one drawback to the Clerries: Lisette Rennard, now Saddler. Perhaps it had been her own mistake to choose Lisette as a model; she'd wanted one to capture the headiness of the newly named Art Deco's drive forward by posing for a huge poster for the Paris Exposition Internationale des Arts Décoratifs held last year. The poster was to represent the Eden of the future. But what emerged through her brushes was not Eve, but the Snake element. Lisette had seen it in her studio – and destroyed the whole painting before it could reach anyone else's eyes. And then Pierre Christophe had stolen the theme.

Vinny was a good man though, bless him, Gert thought. He was a member of the Clerries but preferred to live in England much of the time, paying regular visits to the group. She was the other way around: based in Paris but regularly visiting England. They were both true believers in the Clerries' aims, however. Somehow, even though not in Paris all the time, Vinny had managed to weld the Clerries together, something that Pierre Christophe had never succeeded in doing. Vinny thought about things. You could see that from his paintings. Set in war or peace, portrait or landscape, there was a haunting sadness about his work with which she could sympathize, even though she was determined to look forward with her own work. These were the 1920s, after all.

'Your Eden painting,' Vinny commented. 'I heard about that disaster.'

'Best work I ever did. Poor old Gilbert.'

'You may say you march forward, Gert, but your war isn't over. It rages on inside.'

She considered this. 'I was a war artist, like Gilbert. Even though you march forward, you don't forget what war was like. Where did you spend it, Vinny?'

'Intelligence – Montreuil mostly. Whether we were in the trenches or not, Gert, the war touched us all in different ways. Lisette was a heroine, Pierre told me he was at Verdun, Lance was a medical orderly, and Thora was a VAD in the last months of the war.'

'And here we are marching forward under Lisette's roof. Life's a funny old thing, isn't it?'

There was Mr Briggs on his bicycle again, Nell registered through the window of the grocery shop in the village. The sight knocked all thoughts of *Poulet à la Provençal* out of her head. It was gone half past five, so where could he be going? It must be his day off; Lord Ansley would be changing for dinner shortly, and Mr Briggs would normally be at his side. Instead, he had just come through the Wychbourne gates and was taking the road to Sevenoaks.

'Does he often do that?' she asked Mr Turnbill, the grocer who had served the village for forty years and consequently had become one of several founts of all knowledge where the village and its residents were concerned. Needless to say, he too was busy with orders for Spitalfrith Manor.

Mr Turnbill paused for thought, however, abandoning his task of shovelling Peek Frean Garibaldi biscuits into a large paper bag. Busy or not, he always did pause before pronouncing on Wychbourne gossip, although Nell suspected that was just for effect, as he was always only too eager to impart his wisdom or otherwise. 'Once every week or two,' he said, 'but this past week I reckon he's gone every day, just for an hour or so, and then I see him coming back. Proper dunty he is, poor chap – all muddled up in his head.'

The Sevenoaks road led past Spitalfrith, but why, Nell wondered, would Mr Briggs be going there? 'Do you know where he goes?'

'See his friend, he told me. He's upset.'

Friend? Most of the staff at Wychbourne had friends outside the Court, so why was she so surprised that Mr Briggs had one? Because, Nell supposed, she had thought of his life as a solitary one centred only on Wychbourne.

'Where does the friend live?' she asked curiously. She had a feeling she knew the answer – and she was right.

'Spitalfrith. He's matey with Freddie Carter, son of Joe Carter, the gardener along there.'

Nell remembered Joe. She had seen him quite frequently in the village when the manor was empty and recalled that when she had first arrived at Wychbourne someone had mentioned he had a son. She wasn't aware of seeing him in the village, though, which was odd.

'Does Freddie work at the manor, too?' she asked.

Mr Turnbill shrugged. 'Does what he can, does Freddie. Lost a leg late in the war and a bit more besides, so he can't do much to help Joe – only bits and pieces. Still living in France mentally, if you know what I mean. Joe set up a workshop for him, so Freddie does some metalwork for Joe, and then there's his wooden puppets. He sells them too, if you call that a job.'

Nell most certainly did, having seen some of the puppets on sale at the Gardening Club show and been much impressed.

'Freddie keeps himself to himself,' Mr Turnbill continued. 'It's his father who brings his carvings down here for sale. Never see Freddie in the village, not even at church.'

That must be why he and Mr Briggs were friends, Nell realized. Mr Briggs was still living mentally in France too. It occurred to her that, so used was Wychbourne Court to the old ways of living, that as one of the upper servants he was never referred to by his Christian name. What was it? Charles? That rang a bell. She comforted herself with the thought that she never addressed Mrs Fielding as Florence – indeed, she dreaded to think what the reaction would be if she did.

'I'll look out for Freddie at the festival on Saturday,' she said. 'Are you going, Mr Turnbill?'

'I reckon the whole village is going, the way everyone's talking. Nothing but chatter about the lorries arriving, steam-wagons, those ones with combustion engines and good old horse and carts. Every blooming busybody round here seems to have popped along to Spitalfrith to watch the fun. Mind you, no one knows what's going on there, but we'll find out, won't we?'

Why leave it till Saturday to see what was happening? Nell thought as she left the shop. She could stroll along to Spitalfrith as soon as dinner was served at Wychbourne and perhaps see Mr Briggs there. She'd planned to have a walk anyway. She could take the footpath towards the river and back to Wychbourne before darkness fell. Just the ticket, she decided, remembering with a lurch of her stomach the time that she had sat by the Wychbourne pond with Alex Melbray, now part of her life.

Was it love or companionable friendship that they shared? The testing time would have to be faced, because at present she knew she was deliberately pushing the problem away; she'd let it cook in a paper bag like those once-fashionable recipes by a grandson of the great chef Alexis Soyer. Much more comfortable, she tried to convince herself.

In the early-evening sun the overhanging trees on the Sevenoaks road provided pleasant shade, and the roadside banks boasted colourful displays of rose bay willow herb. Enjoying the walk, Nell reached the red-brick wall boundary of Spitalfrith Manor sooner than she had expected. It was only then that she remembered that the estate had a rear entrance reached by a track she had just passed, and that the gardener's cottage was not far from the gate. If Mr Turnbill was right, it was possible that Mr Briggs might still be there.

Once through the gate and into the manor park, she could see woodland ahead, greenhouses and kitchen gardens to her right, and to her left was the gardener's cottage, set within his own garden. The visible part of the garden in front of the house seemed to be a colourful mix of flowers and vegetables, and there were also two sheds, one on this side of the house and one on the far side. One of them must be Freddie's workshop, she presumed. There might be a garden behind the cottage too, between the house and the boundary wall, but it was cut off from her sight by fencing and bushes.

As she drew nearer, it was clear that Mr Briggs must indeed be here as she could see his bicycle propped up against a fence. There was no sign of him or of anyone else, however. No one was in the shed nearest to her. She hesitated. Should she go on searching for him or not? It was none of her business what Mr Briggs did in his spare time. The question was answered for her as Joe Carter appeared from the shed on the far side of the garden.

'What you want?' he asked grumpily as she approached him.

She recognized him immediately as the wiry old man – he must be over sixty – whom she had seen in the Coach and Horses from time to time. His keen eyes were busy summing her up.

'I was looking for Mr Briggs. I was worried about him,' Nell said. There had been no sign of his return to Wychbourne Court before she left.

'You're that cook at the Court, miss.' When she nodded, he added, 'Charlie spoke of you.'

'He *spoke* of me?' she asked, surprised. 'He very rarely says anything but his rank and number at Wychbourne.'

'Not here neither. Nor my Freddie. It's the war, miss. They understand each other. You can go through that gate down there. They won't mind.' He pointed down the passageway between the cottage and this workshop. 'Go in silence, miss. Come back singing.'

An odd thing to say, she thought. Pleasant, though. She walked through to the gate, even though she hadn't the foggiest idea what he meant by it. Nevertheless, she was encouraged by his permission to proceed. There was indeed silence, no sound of voices, let alone singing, as she gently pulled up the latch on the gate and went inside.

At first, she saw nothing but vibrant and colourful flowers and bushes ahead under a huge covered colonnade with wooden pillars, bushes and climbing plants. These mingled with the flowers and bushes so completely that the whole colonnade seemed an extension of the rest of the garden around it. The only sound was the trickle of water from a miniature waterfall into a stream running between bushes. A narrow, paved path separated two magnificent borders of flowers and greenery among which she could see birds. Mr Briggs was kneeling down by a group of brilliant dahlias with a tall, fair-haired young man at his side – that must be Freddie, she realized. Both men had their backs to her and hadn't yet noticed her presence.

Nell blinked. *Well, stuff my figs and batter my fish*, she whispered in shock. There was something unusual about those bushes *and* about those birds. They were stationary, for one thing, and as she looked at them more closely, she realized that not all these bushes and flowers around her were live, growing plants. Some were, but tucked in among them were creations of carved wood with painted leaves. She had hardly taken that in when she realized that the more she looked around her, the more birds she could see. The bushes near to her sheltered blackbirds and thrushes. She spotted a robin nearby with a bush to itself, and there was a blue tit, a thrush, yellow hammers, finches and many others. All silent – and all carved of painted wood.

Nell stood dumbfounded, entranced by the beauty around her. Mr Briggs and Freddie were on the move now, working their way further along the colonnade. First the birds in one bush began to sing, then another, then a nightingale. Closing her eyes, she was surrounded by song. 'Come back singing,' Joe Carter had told her, and already it felt as though she were being swept into a world solely of song. When one bush fell silent, another began, joining the ongoing chorus in an endless melody.

When it eventually stopped, Mr Briggs was ambling towards her, smiling.

'Freddie. Singing birds,' he said in a rare attempt to communicate. Perhaps it was only in this garden that he *could* speak of anything other than his name, rank and number, Nell thought.

Mr Briggs turned and nodded at Freddie, as if assuring him that she presented no threat, and Freddie came stiffly to join them, his walking stick taking the strain. He looked at her anxiously, though.

'What do you think of it, miss?' he asked shyly.

'It's a garden of peace,' Nell replied. Peace was everywhere in this enchanted place, created by the birdsong, the birds themselves, the flowers and the bushes. This was a garden that had been created out of love, she realized; it was somebody's Eden. Freddie's, which he allowed Mr Briggs to share?

She longed to ask more but knew there was no point. It was not a time to seek answers. She had been privileged in entering this secret place, but she was not part of it and she must leave. Mr Briggs and Freddie were already returning to tending their birds. As she made her way through the gateway out into the real world again, Joe came to meet her.

'Heard them, did you, the singing birds?' he grunted.

'I did. The birds are automata, aren't they? Did your son make them? He's very gifted,' Nell managed to say, still half living in the sound of that birdsong. They were inadequate words for what she had heard, but Joe must have been satisfied because he continued, 'Twas Mr Danson who taught him. Him as owned the manor afore this Sir Gilbert. Trained by the Bontem family over in France afore the war. Tried to teach his son, the young Mr Danson, to carve, but he weren't no good at it, so he began teaching my Freddie when he was just a lad.'

Nell hesitated, then emboldened, asked, 'Was there a reason for Freddie to create the garden so lovingly?'

'Maybe.'

'It's his secret then. His and Mr Briggs's?'

Joe stared at her. 'His. Charlie Briggs helps out. War does things to you. It did to my Freddie.'

'The loss of his leg?'

'That and worse. Freddie met this girl. French, she was – a singer. And they was in love. You come over to England when this war's over, he told her, and I'll make you a garden of singing birds.'

'And he did. What happened?'

'Marie-Hélène never came.'

'Did she marry someone else?'

'No, miss. She died.'

THREE

S he hadn't finished the mousse for today's luncheon yet, Nell realized, and here she was pondering about that peaceful garden of singing automata. How would that fit side by side with what promised to be a frenzied day tomorrow in which avant-garde artists would be endeavouring to explain their probably inexplicable work to a mass of noisy and excited visitors?

She had returned to Wychbourne Court last night with the song of the birds still ringing in her head, mingled with the tweets and the goodnight calls of living ones. It had been a lonely walk, too. The overhanging trees and bushes along the track back to the road seemed almost threatening, as though they were watching her every move. Poppycock, she had told herself briskly. Perhaps the rustling she heard had not been the breeze but one of those monkeys that Spitalfrith had imported, or perhaps one of Lady Clarice's ghosts had escaped from under her careful guardianship. Why was Spitalfrith, with all its mysteries, still on her mind, though?

Get your skates on, Nell ordered herself. To work. Forget monkeys, forget ghosts and concentrate on mousses. And just where were the cucumbers she had ordered – sorry, requested – from Mr Fairweather? No sign of them. Think feasting not festivals.

And then Mr Peters appeared, a rare occurrence as usually a footman would deliver his orders. 'Two less for luncheon,' he announced. 'Lady Helen is staying in London, and Mr Beringer won't be coming either.'

Of course not, Nell thought with resignation. Rex Beringer was a frequent visitor owing to his unrequited love for Lady Helen. 'O whistle and I'll come to you' was his form of courtship, unfortunately. Why couldn't he realize that Lady Sophy, with whom he argued so happily over the merits and demerits of socialism, was a far more suitable partner for him? And why don't you pay attention to *mousses* instead of righting the wrongs of the world, Nell Drury? She took her own advice. After all, she'd done her best to steer Mr Beringer tactfully in the right direction and had been hopeful of some success until this news arrived.

And now there was Mr Briggs to worry about. She had seen a side of him last evening that had never been obvious at Wychbourne, and he had been as withdrawn at breakfast this morning as though yesterday had never been.

'What about you, Mr Briggs?' she had asked, seizing the moment when everybody seemed engrossed in discussing monkeys and whether there would be enough sandwiches and sausage rolls available. 'Are you going to the festival?'

He had not replied, although he did register that he had heard her. He had smiled. She must keep the story of the singing birds to herself, she decided. They were Mr Briggs's secret and a world apart from festivals and monkeys.

There would be another thirty-two hours of this torment to endure, Petra Saddler estimated, not counting the merciful hours of sleep. It was only luncheon time on Friday and the Clerries would not be leaving Spitalfrith until Monday morning. That meant she had to stay here until then in order to protect her father. If only the Snake would leave on Monday, too. As it was, she would undoubtedly be planning how to ruin tomorrow's festival as well as her usual interfering with household matters. Her insistence on French cuisine had collided headlong with Mrs Hayward. She was not a good housekeeper, but she was the only one they had, and she had informed Petra grimly that her treasured book of ancient recipes culled from her grandmother was all that was required. These recipes included useful tips as to what to do if one fell ill with cholera, but they fell short of entertaining a group used to international cuisine, and the prospects of providing refreshments for tomorrow's festival didn't look bright either.

Her father seemed unusually on edge too, which didn't help. 'We shall have an excellent time tomorrow,' he dropped weakly into the silence at the luncheon table. 'And this afternoon we shall enjoy setting up the tents outside.' Greeted with silence, he added forlornly, 'Shall we adjoin to the drawing room for coffee?'

'We shall remain here. Send for another decanter of burgundy, Gilbert,' the Snake's bored hiss of a voice demanded.

Petra braced herself to intervene, knowing full well, as did her father, that now that dessert had been served, there would be no one to answer a call for wine. Hayward, the housekeeper's husband, performed many jobs of which being wine waiter and butler were merely two. He would be nowhere to be found. Should she rush out and find the beastly burgundy herself? Just as she decided on this extreme measure, Vinny Finch came to her rescue, ignoring etiquette.

'I suggest we should indeed retire to the drawing room for coffee as you propose, Gilbert,' he said smoothly. 'There is much to do this afternoon, but this evening we might perhaps take a glass of the rather fine cognac I spotted yesterday. It would round off the day superbly.'

Sir Gilbert brightened at the immediate scramble to leave. There was enough tension in this room to set off a hot-air balloon, Petra thought, and a change of seating might help. Taken individually, the Clerries were crazy but endurable. Taken together at this table, with the Snake's piercing disdain, they were another matter.

'Thank you,' she whispered to Vinny.

'The Cat that walks by herself, would you say?' he murmured.

'I wish she did,' she answered fervently. 'It's her walking with us that I object to.' Petra had met many of the Clerries on her visits to Paris, but only Vinny and Gert bore any resemblance to human beings.

Once they were in the drawing room, Petra summoned up all her courage. Even though she was clad in her best afternoon frock, its scalloped bodice and pleated skirt made her feel a frump compared with the Snake who was lying lazily and elegantly on the sofa – even if that slim-fitting dress made her look like a corkscrew. Nevertheless, it was up to her, Petra, to ensure this party worked. After all, at least some of the guests were also looking ill at ease. Lance Merryman was squeezed into the tiny space left on the sofa, his flamboyant blue silk smoking jacket looking even more ridiculous. They were a strange mixture: Gert Radley was daringly wearing trousers, Thora looked like a cross lamppost in that knitted jumper suit with arms stuck out along the chair arms, and Pierre Christophe appeared like a Greek hero knocked off his perch. Vinny, thankfully, looked normal.

It was Petra's turn to rescue the situation from silence this time.

'Will you all be displaying tomorrow some of the canvases you plan to show at the Academy of Modern Art exhibition next year?' she enquired. Too late, she realized her mistake, mentally adding a 'sorry, Father' as she saw the Snake's eyes flickering. She was crouched, ready to pounce.

The Clerries, however, fell on this subject with relief. 'Perhaps,' Monsieur Christophe declared, gazing rapturously at his fiancée, 'but how can we tell what *la verité*, truth, might reveal in the next few months? Truth is *la vie* and life moves forward, even though the past is then seen with more clarity.'

And just what did that mumbo jumbo add up to? Petra managed to hold back a giggle, murmuring in response that she quite understood. If only she did!

Miss Radley, or Gert as she had firmly insisted Petra call her, seemed in full support, though, because she snorted. 'We all have our own interpretation of the truth, wouldn't you agree, Lisette?'

Seeing Gert's inimical glance at the Snake, Petra couldn't fail to pick up the heavy sarcasm. What, she wondered, was *that* all about?

The Snake merely stared at Gert, and it was the mercurial Lance Merryman who bounced back into the conversation. 'Next year's exhibition will be perfection, my dears. I shall present "Spring Greets Summer" designs for *Chic* magazine, a theme inspired by you, dear Lisette. Each will cling to the truth of form.'

Petra liked Lance, despite his outrageous garb and ideas, and suspected that his Clerrian principles, which meant as much to her as they would have done to Peter Pan, were merely a means to an end for him.

The Snake inclined her graceful neck, but ominously her expression did not change, which alarmed Petra. It meant the Snake's prey was still in her sights.

Vinny took the stage next. 'My work with the Artistes de Cler,' he announced, 'reveals the future with overtones of the past. The truth can be recognized in many forms, and my work for the exhibition next year will convey that.'

He spoke so solemnly that Petra was almost convinced, but a wink from Vinny changed her mind. The Snake must have something up her skinny sleeve, though. To Petra's alarm, she saw the mask on that witchlike face begin to move and the dark eyes travelling round her guests.

'*Pardonnez-moi*,' she began.

Petra was instantly alarmed. The tremulous note inserted into the Snake's voice was a warning signal.

'I regret,' the Snake continued, 'that this exhibition in the academy – as I have explained to Gilbert – will not take place.'

Petra froze. So that was why her father was looking so much on edge. He was ashen-faced as he said to his wife, 'My dear, as *I* have already explained, I cannot stop the exhibition.'

'But I can,' the Snake purred softly. 'The theme of this exhibition was to have been war. Yes?'

Silence. Petra could hear her heart beating.

'*Non.* How can you paint it when none of you know what war is about? You have not lived in an occupied territory, where we had no food, where we feared always starvation and death, the knock on the door, the shelling. We were powerless, with the enemy in control. None of you paint the truth. You, Pierre, were stationed in an office far behind the lines at Verdun. You, Vinny, were also safe in an office, not even fighting in the trenches. You,

Lance, were rejected for the army and worked in a hospital also far behind the lines. You, Gert, were safe as a war artist. You, Gilbert, were too old to fight. How can any of you know the truth of war? You have all used me as a model for your work, but I do not give my consent for it to be exhibited.'

Petra was aghast. Poor, poor Father. And the guests. All at the mercy of this frightful woman. She would ruin their careers if she stopped next year's exhibition. The Snake might be a war heroine for her work in occupied Lille, but that was past. It was now that counted. Petra waited for the outburst of fury, but none came. Vinny appeared to be listening politely, Lance Merryman looked too frozen to say anything, Gert Radley looked apoplectic with rage and Thora was clearly out of her depth. Only Pierre made a valiant attempt at a comeback.

'*Mais non*. You cannot do this, Lisette. You understood very well that the portraits were to be publicly shown.'

'I did not,' the Snake said coolly.

Petra bit back her immediate reply – that would play into the Snake's hands – and tried a safer tack. 'There are many sad war stories, Madame Lisette,' she said, 'and yours is one of them. You acted bravely then despite the great risks, and that is what the Clerries want to remember in their work. They are recording the truth of war, just as your gardener's son has done with his garden of bird automata.'

'Very true, my love,' Sir Gilbert said eagerly.

Petra could see the Snake's eyes glittering. Whatever she had said had touched the Snake on the raw. Whatever she was planning, she couldn't be stopped now.

'There will be no exhibition next year,' the Snake repeated calmly. 'I have already informed the academy that I give no permission for my image to be shown in any guise.'

'But we will prove to the academy that you were a paid model with no rights as to what we do with our paintings,' Pierre said grimly.

'And then I shall tell them my story of hunger and despair, of the fear I had, of the dangers I went through while recording all those troop train movements and sending them to you here, safe in England, so that you had the necessary intelligence to combat the Germans' advance. Think of that, think of me, a young girl, singing to the enemy in cafés, picking up valuable information as the drunk officers boasted of their prowess. I will tell the academy that I was forced to work for you to earn a pittance on which to live after the war, tell them that I had no wish to take off my clothes as you Artistes de Cler demanded, that you all took cruel advantage of my body *in many* ways, especially you, Pierre. And so,' she added calmly, 'will the newspaper editors. I shall explain to them that the work of the Artistes de Cler is not the truth. You could force me to strip my body to the very bones, but you will not find the truth of war there or the truth of anything save your own lust,' she finished.

Petra looked in horror at the stunned faces, which included her father's. And what was her gibe about Monsieur Christophe about?

He was the first to recover, though. 'Lisette, you do not realize what you say. We took no such advantage, nor forced you into posing against your will. To say such things here is not right. *Ma chère*' – he turned to Thora, taking her hand to kiss – 'this is truly nonsense.' He smiled at her, and the thunderous look on her face subsided.

Lance's face was a picture of misery. 'Lisette, darling,' he choked, 'do reconsider. After all, my fashions – they simply must be seen at the exhibition, and you can hardly claim that *I* took unfair advantage of your body.'

Gert looked ready to explode, and Petra braced herself. She had to intervene for her father's sake. 'The Academy of Modern Art exhibition is next year, Madame Lisette. But we are still holding our festival tomorrow, where everyone will show their work. After that, madame, you might wish to reconsider your decision. Isn't that a sensible plan?' she threw out in a last-ditch hope.

'*Oui*,' Pierre Christophe replied instantly with nods from Lance, Vinny and Gert.

Petra relaxed a little, even though there was silence from the Snake and her father still looked stricken.

'I am not yet decided about tomorrow,' the Snake said at last. A long pause, but then, 'I will agree. Wychbourne will see the real truth of the squire's wife.'

There was a general sigh of relief, but Petra did not join it. What on earth had the Snake in mind? There would be trouble, she was sure of that.

*   *   *

That's jazz, Nell realized in amazement. It's Louis Armstrong. 'Everybody Loves My Baby'. Not what she had expected from an art festival, but why not in today's world? She could hear it quite clearly as she walked along the Sevenoaks road, late on Saturday afternoon. By this time, the show should be in full swing – very appropriate for jazz. She'd decided on coming here later rather than earlier, partly as Lady Ansley had asked for a late buffet dinner and partly as it would leave her freer as to when she left.

Nell's spirits rose – she was going to enjoy this evening. Her earlier doubts had vanished. After all, what could go wrong on a Saturday evening spent with interesting people?

As if to prove her point, walking towards her were two lovebirds. Mrs Fielding and Mr Peters were coming away from Spitalfrith and amazingly they were walking hand in hand. They didn't even bother to drop their hands hastily when they saw her. Nell decided she had been right. It was going to be an enjoyable visit.

'Well,' Mrs Fielding greeted her, still clutching her beloved's hand. 'It's not what we expected at all. You're in for a surprise!' She actually laughed, to Nell's amazement.

Mr Peters chuckled, too. 'It's a doozy all right.'

'Just you wait, Miss Drury. Shocking it is. *Shocking*,' Mrs Fielding added.

She didn't look too shocked, though, Nell thought. Rather the opposite. She caught a wink from Mr Peters that confirmed it.

Mrs Fielding had another shot. 'Lord Richard certainly has his eye on Miss Saddler, though she's not in his class, of course.'

Nell was curious to see this new ladylove in his life. She'd keep her eyes open for them both – if her eyes weren't too busy looking out for Lady Saddler. When she reached the manor gates, they were wide open, and as no one seemed to be on official welcoming duty, Nell walked straight in. Instant disappointment. No African dancers could be seen, no jazz musicians, no up-and-coming Monets or Matisses wandering around the grass this side of the manor house – only a lot of motor cars on the forecourt. The festival must be confined to the rear of the house; she could hear a low hum of sounds coming from there.

As she walked around the corner of the manor house, there it was! Africa! Jungle loomed in the background, and there was what seemed to be a strip of sandy desert through it. Amazing! The rest of the open garden space was given over to large tents and people swarming everywhere. The jazz band was playing somewhere, though she couldn't see it. She *could* see ice cream and food stalls, though.

There's only one thing to do with a scrum like this, Nell told herself briskly. Just plunge in.

Taking a deep breath, she headed for the nearest tent. This held the work of Monsieur Pierre Christophe, so the vibrant red lettering over the tent proclaimed, founder of the Artistes de Cler – and there he was in person. What better place to begin her tour? She'd seen many men like Monsieur Christophe during her years at the Carlton: tall, imposing, classical Grecian features, and an air of being automatically in command.

He was deep in conversation as she entered, which gave her an opportunity to study the strange pictures on show, some black-and-white silhouettes of soldiers, some clearly of Lady Saddler, though not dressed as Nell had last seen her. In fact, not dressed at all in many of them. Nell had read somewhere that in animal skeletons the eyes of a hunting animal are close together, and she noted that on Lady Saddler's mask of a face they were indeed close. What prey was she hunting today? she wondered. There were other paintings, too, in which Lady Saddler did not appear, but the one that caught Nell's attention most did show her all too markedly. In an Eden of trees and blossom, her sinewy shape reared up like a serpent on one side, its eyes fixed on victims.

'Madame.' Monsieur Christophe came over to her. 'My work interests you?'

'It does,' Nell said. 'This one in particular.'

He smiled graciously at her. 'Always in life there is a serpent, yes?'

'Did you paint it during the war?'

'No. After the war, but war is still with us, is it not? The serpent is everywhere around us.'

She supposed it was, but he already had his smile ready for another viewer and moved on. She took another look at the serpent – yes, it was undoubtedly Lady Saddler.

Mr Lance Merryman's tent was completely different. The ladies illustrated – for magazines he explained to her – were just as skinny as skeletons, but these were clad in interesting dresses of the day rather than as objects in a quest by the artist to put over his own philosophy. When she asked him how his designs conformed to the Artistes de Cler's principles, he explained deftly that ladies – and, indeed, gentlemen also – chose their apparel not to hide but to reveal the truth of their aspirations.

Nell decided she would have to think that over. 'Does that apply to me?' she enquired.

'Of course, madame. You are charmingly clad in this rose-pink dress, an aspiration for the future and an indication that your heart is already spoken for.'

A lucky guess? she wondered, taken aback. 'Was Lady Saddler one of your models?' she asked curiously. 'Do her clothes reflect her future?'

Mr Merryman's smile vanished and he gave an unconvincing laugh. 'Perhaps. Today she wears black. Like many ladies, she dresses to kill.'

A lady who was not popular with her guests, then, Nell thought as she moved on to Mr Vincent Finch's tent. His work was interesting. Some canvases were of happy, merrymaking dancers – slim, almost beanlike, figures in a kaleidoscope of colour superimposed on a grey fog of clouds. Others were more sombre. One in particular struck her. A colourful harlequin stood poised, watching what was going on in the gloom around him: a large pool of water in the muddy scene, a withered rose, a small, slender shape in the background presumably his Columbine, a hill and what looked like a riderless horse making its way across a sea of mud through stumps of barren trees. It was sombre indeed.

'And no birds sing,' she commented to the artist.

'Why do you say that?' he asked.

She had to rack her memory. 'It's from a poem by Keats,' she remembered.

He smiled. 'Consider that the artist might see more than the poet. Perhaps Harlequin's war-weary eyes are looking at ghosts. Perhaps we all need a hill in life to survey the still and silent waters beneath when we suffer from the *Belle Dame sans Merci* called fate. There no birds sing. And yet birds went on singing while men waited for battle in the trenches.'

'Isn't Harlequin longing for his Columbine, though?' Nell asked, puzzled.

'Who knows? I'm only the artist. Perhaps he is desperate to dance in a new world, but can't shake off the old. That's truth as the Artistes de Cler see it.'

By the time she reached Miss Radley's tent, Nell had decided that there was no point in trying to work out what Clerrian art was all about. Even the artists didn't seem very clear about it, some coming straight to the point, some experimenting in lines and shapes. Instead, she would just decide whether whatever she was looking at was a good painting. And Gert Radley's were good paintings – although Nell guessed that not all her subjects would be happy with the results. Again, Lady Saddler featured in one or two, though here she was clad in exotic reds and purples.

'I believe that clothes are part of a man's true self – and a woman's,' Miss Radley said gruffly.

'What about the Emperor's New Clothes?' Nell asked irrepressibly. 'His courtiers only saw the truth when they vanished.'

Miss Radley laughed. 'Ah, there you have me. Still, let's consider that challenge. The Emperor chose the clothes, and that must surely reveal the man's true self. I understand you're the chef at Wychbourne Court, Miss Drury, so tell me this. Must one of your dishes be judged as the truth from the taste of each of the ingredients you have chosen or by the whole of it? Judge my work from its whole, too, if you please.' She hesitated. 'Miss Drury, I've heard of your prowess in solving the Gaiety Theatre murder.'

'The police reached the solution,' Nell said ruefully. 'I just helped.'

'Now there's a subject for a Clerry.' Miss Radley spoke with relish. 'Are the police the truth and those they arrest falsehood, or are they all true to themselves, good or bad? Is it truth or morality that matters?'

Nell meditated on that as she left. The difference between Clerrian art and her own job, she decided, was that the former left room for discussion but her own ponderings had limits. Her creations had to be on the table at a certain time and moreover their ingredients had to agree with one another. This did not seem to apply to the Clerries. Each had his or her own version of truth.

'Miss Drury, have you met Miss Saddler?' Lord Richard

interrupted her meditation on Clerrian art. Before her was a young woman in her early twenties. So this was Sir Gilbert's daughter, Petra. Not Lord Richard's usual style. Miss Saddler, like Jenny Smith, looked as though she had a mind of her own.

'You must see the jungle,' Miss Saddler declared, straight-faced, when formalities were concluded.

'Intrepid to the last, I'll don my boots now,' Nell responded.

'Don't miss Josephine Baker,' Lord Richard instructed her gravely.

'Has she popped over from Paris for the day?' For a moment, Nell was fooled, then rallied. An American dancer and singer whose skimpy costumes were the talk of the town and sometimes non-existent was hardly likely to have picked out Spitalfrith Manor for a performance.

'I wish she had,' Miss Saddler said fervently. 'Our own Josephine Baker, however, is my father's new wife. Do take your seat for the next performance, Miss Drury. Just follow the path into the jungle and listen for the growls.'

From the look on her face, Nell suspected that she had been right and that all was not well between Miss Saddler and her stepmother. All those serpents in the paintings suggested that the impression Nell had had at the Wychbourne Court luncheon was correct. Now her ladyship was giving stage performances in the jungle. What on earth was going on there? Perhaps even Kitty's story of monkeys was true. With artificial peacocks and parrots ornamenting the trees, a real monkey or two would be welcome. Perhaps the odd lion and tiger, too.

The path Nell followed led to a clearing set out with seats and an improvised stage. Nothing was happening as she arrived; the band was taking a rest – or time for a smoke, judging by the way they were lolling around by the trees. And, yes, she could see two monkeys. One was peering down from a tree surrounded by what appeared to be a hastily erected wire cage and the other appeared to be picking nits off his companion's back. At least they wouldn't be leaping down from trees on her way home. No creepy experiences tonight.

As she found herself a seat together with a hundred or so other people, the band struck up with 'Bye Bye Blues', but there was still no sign of 'Josephine Baker'. She didn't have to wait long, though, for Lady Saddler to appear on the stage. Not that she was instantly recognizable. Her hair was hidden in a tall beaded headdress, and what there was of the rest of the costume was flimsier than the briefest bathing dress Nell had ever seen. The feet at the end of her long legs were encased in high-heeled shoes, and she certainly seemed to be aiming at shocking the world.

After a short, frenetic dance, the music stopped as she spoke in a husky, almost hypnotic voice. 'I sang for the enemy during the war, though I despised them; I learned their secrets to pass on to British intelligence, so that I can now sing for you in peace.' And then as the band struck up again, she began to sing in the same hypnotic voice. 'It had to be you . . .'

Nell shivered, wondering whether Lord and Lady Ansley had sat through this extraordinary show. True, Lady Ansley had been one of the Gaiety Girls in the 1890s, but the essence of their attraction had been a roguish glimpse of an ankle from time to time. Lady Saddler had put on this weird performance for one reason only, Nell decided. Her ladyship was intent on cocking a snook at someone or something.

How's that for Clerrian art? she thought, watching in fascination as Lady Saddler proceeded to flaunt the skimpy costume she was wearing. This was a woman who thought she could get away with anything, no matter how much she offended convention, believing she was above judgement.

Dusk was falling now, but there were quite a number of visitors still walking around or chatting on the terrace with drinks, even though the festival had officially ended at nine o'clock. No one seemed in a rush to leave, though, and Nell was curious to see how the evening would develop, given what she had seen and been told. There was clearly no love lost between the Clerries, as Miss Radley termed them, and their hostess.

As she approached the terrace, she could see Mr Peters and Mrs Fielding who must have returned for a second visit. They were clearly enjoying their time together away from Wychbourne and were daringly drinking cocktails on the terrace, looking very pleased with themselves. Then Miss Saddler waved vigorously to her from the table she was sharing with Lord Richard. No sign of Lord and Lady Ansley, though; Nell suspected they had left earlier than planned.

'What did you think of the jungle show?' Lord Richard asked her.

'Very – er – primitive,' Nell said with a straight face.

'I saw Briggs earlier on. I wonder what he made of it,' he said idly.

Mr Briggs? Nell had assumed he would be with the Carters. 'Was he at the show?' she asked.

'He'd been wandering around it. Seemed quite happy, so I left him to it,' Lord Richard said, 'but Peters hasn't seen him back at the Court and there's no sign of him now. It's nine fifteen and he didn't turn up for duty.'

'I'll have a look for him,' Nell said uneasily. 'He might be with the gardener and his son.'

She set off, her unease growing. Now that it was getting dark in earnest and the remaining visitors were few, the woodland and the shady paths to the far side of the grounds were no longer as enticing as they had seemed earlier. In fact, there was a creepiness about them as though night was announcing that all was not well at Spitalfrith. Nonsense, she thought as she hurried on her way to Freddie Carter's singing garden, anxious to complete her mission. Thankfully, she'd had the sense to bring a pocket torch with her.

Along the last part of the wooded pathway to the cottage, she was startled to see someone rushing towards her, obviously in great distress and stumbling over the rough path. To her horror, she realized it was Lady Clarice.

'What's wrong?' Nell cried as Lady Clarice clutched at her in relief, breathing heavily.

'He's here,' she cried, half sobbing, half excited, but – to Nell's relief – not frightened.

'*Who's* here?'

'Jasper!' Lady Clarice gasped.

Hold on, Nell told herself. The real Jasper had died almost thirty years ago, and surely it couldn't have been a ghost, however much Lady Clarice had hoped for one. 'You saw someone who reminded you of him?' she asked gently.

Lady Clarice shook her head impatiently. 'It was Jasper himself. His *ghost*. He came to me.'

Nell was even more concerned. Although imagination was a powerful thing, something must have happened, she reasoned, with visions of ghostly hands embracing poor Lady Clarice. There was a fallen tree trunk nearby, and Nell led her to it and then sat with her. 'Has he visited you at Wychbourne Court, too?'

'No. He loved Spitalfrith, you see. As I told you, we courted here.'

'Did he come right up to you tonight?'

'No, but I heard him whisper to me in the bushes near our special dell in the wood. There was no doubt, Nell. There was a presence there and he whispered to me. "Clarice, Clarice," he was whispering, just as he used to. I waited, but he came no further. It was him, though, Nell. I know. Only he could pronounce my name just the way he did.'

Nell escorted her back to the terrace, with Lady Clarice still reminiscing about Jasper and their courting days. Fortunately, Lord Richard was still there and he immediately took care of his aunt. He of all the family dealt with her crises best, gently teasing without mocking her, and consoling with genuine understanding.

Having handed her charge over, but somewhat shaken, Nell set out again for the Carters' cottage. She knew it was stupid to worry about Mr Briggs. After all, he knew perfectly well how to get home to Wychbourne Court. He must still be with Freddie. Yet for some reason she was anxious.

She grew even more concerned when she reached the Carters' home. There were no lights to be seen in the cottage. It was gone half past nine, so were they already in bed? With the help of the pocket torch, she picked her way round to the rear gate and was about to open it when her ears were pierced by a howl coming from inside the garden; one howl followed another, and she had to force herself to open the gate to find out what horrors might lie within.

There, in the remaining light, she saw Mr Briggs. He was standing in the centre of the colonnade, head thrown back, sobbing and howling with grief.

What on earth was causing this? What could be wrong? She rushed forward to comfort him, almost tripping over on the pathway. Recovering, she looked around her and saw with growing disbelief and shock the reason for his distress.

Everything in this colonnade of beauty had been destroyed. There were no more singing birds, no more lovingly carved bushes and flowers. They had been smashed to pieces, the wreckage lying all around. She could see only one lone wooden bird lying there intact, as if to mock helpless onlookers.

Another cry of anguish, and this time she realized it was hers, as she picked her way through the strewn wreckage to reach Mr Briggs. He took no notice of her even when she put her arm around him and tried to lead him away. He would not budge. In tears herself, she knew she must get help quickly, and assuring him that she would be back directly, she stumbled her way back along the path to the manor house in the flickering torchlight. The sound of his howls was still ringing in her ears.

FOUR

All the cocoa in the world wouldn't have worked its usual magic and brought peaceful sleep. The nightmare of what she had witnessed refused to leave; her memories of those howls and of a garden smashed to smithereens remained. Nell had raced back to the manor to call for help as all her entreaties to Mr Briggs to leave the garden had failed. Thankfully, Lord Richard was still there with Lady Clarice and Miss Saddler when she arrived. The last she had seen of Mr Briggs was his upright, silent figure sitting beside Lord Richard in his beloved Lea-Francis, with Lady Clarice behind them, as the motor car passed her on its way back to Wychbourne Court. Mr Briggs's grasp on modern life was frail enough without this horror, and she would do all she could to help.

There had been so many people still on the terrace last night that the news must quickly have spread, because the servants' breakfast presented far from its usual calm. True, everyone there would have visited the festival, which would have made for lively enough conversation in itself, but its unhappy sequel would be an extra talking point. Ominously, Mr Briggs was absent. After twenty minutes he was still missing, and Nell's heart sank. She would have to consult Mr Peters immediately in the circumstances, so, murmuring excuses, she set off in search of him. She tracked him down to his office in the Great Hall which he used during the daytime to be at hand for Lord Ansley, whose estate office adjoined it.

Mr Peters was as anxious as she was. 'Mr Briggs—' she began, but he interrupted.

'He's not in his room, Miss Drury. I've just checked.' Even as he spoke, his telephone rang and he looked increasingly alarmed as he listened.

'It's his lordship,' he said, hanging up the receiver. 'He's asked to see both of us in his study immediately. Mr Briggs did not appear in his lordship's dressing room, nor is he answering the house telephone.'

This was getting worse, Nell thought, one terrifying guess after another flashing through her mind. Had he returned to Spitalfrith? Gone wandering? Gone to see Freddie? Mr Briggs had only been missing once before in the whole time she had been at Wychbourne; he had been found marching down the Tonbridge road, perhaps under the illusion that he was returning to France.

'Any sign of Briggs yet?' Lord Ansley was standing at his first-floor study door waiting for them. Normally, he was calm in emergencies, but his concern was obvious now.

'No, my lord,' Mr Peters replied. 'When I checked his room, his bed was neatly made.'

'Richard tells me he saw Mr Briggs to his room last night, and explained why,' Lord Ansley said, ushering them into the study and closing the door. 'If he was as upset as my son described, it's possible that, once left alone, he went straight back to Spitalfrith,' he said hopefully.

Nell clutched at this straw. Of course, that's what could have happened. 'He could be with Freddie and Joe Carter,' she suggested. 'But neither of them seemed to be in their cottage last night. Not when I arrived anyway, and that must have been about half past nine or a little later.'

'Richard said something about a smashed garden,' Lord Ansley said. 'What's that about?'

'It's the garden behind the Carters' cottage. Mr Briggs worked there with Freddie,' Nell tried to explain. 'There's a colonnade in the garden full of singing bird automata in carved flowers and bushes that are – or were – mixed in with real flowers. When I found Mr Briggs there yesterday, they had all been destroyed and he was howling with grief.'

She knew it had been a stumbling description on her part, but how could a few words properly convey either the glorious sound she had heard there on Thursday night or the impact of the disaster that had followed?

Lord Ansley had listened intently, though. 'Why should Briggs be quite so distraught if it's Freddie Carter's garden?' he demanded, almost as though he were prosecuting counsel. She could see he was very, very worried. 'Could there be some other reason for his being upset?' Lord Ansley continued. 'Is there any chance that Freddie or his father could have smashed those automata up themselves, and Briggs was angry when he discovered them?'

'I can't see why they would,' Nell replied. Then forced herself to add, 'It might be a worse situation.'

Lord Ansley picked up on this instantly. 'You mean that *Briggs* might have smashed them and then repented?'

Reason came to the fore. 'No,' Nell said steadily. 'Why would either he or the Carters have done such a thing? Mr Briggs would never hurt either people or beautiful objects.' She remembered with affection the many occasions he had spent painstakingly trying to free trapped bees or insects. 'He saves lives; he doesn't destroy them.'

Lord Ansley was silent for a moment. 'Did you know Briggs was mentioned in despatches? He went out into no man's land under fire at the Somme and brought back a badly wounded man. My son Noel told me about Briggs the last time I saw him. They were in the same battalion.' Lord Ansley stopped abruptly.

He only very rarely spoke of his second son, Noel, who died at Passchendaele. To do so now, Nell thought, again revealed his deep concern for Mr Briggs.

'I'll telephone Sir Gilbert,' he continued, 'then go to Spitalfrith to see if I can find Briggs.'

'May I come with you?' Nell asked immediately.

Lord Ansley nodded. 'I'd be glad if you would, Nell. Richard

would come, but Mr Briggs might be more comfortable in your
company.'

'I'll bring some flead cakes,' Nell said, rapidly running through
the day's menus and work schedule in her mind. Seeing that Lord
Ansley looked puzzled, she added, 'He's very fond of them and
we baked some yesterday.'

'Then bring some for all three of us. It might help Briggs relax.'
He paused. 'May I beg a favour, Nell? Arriving at Spitalfrith in
our Rolls-Royce would be too formal. We don't want Briggs to
feel our visit is anything out of the ordinary. We need everything
to seem as normal as possible.'

Nell took his point immediately. 'We'll take my Ford. He's used
to riding in that.'

By the time she had fled back to the kitchen to give a speedy
change of orders, then to the yard to drive the Ford round to the
front door, Lord Ansley was already anxiously waiting for her.

'I'm even more worried, Nell,' he said as he jumped up into
the Ford. 'No one answered the telephone at Spitalfrith.' He was
wearing his old summer blazer and that too would help make
Briggs feel that nothing was amiss.

'That's strange,' she remarked. Everyone in Wychbourne
knew about the wayward housekeeper. Mrs Hayward's reputation
was even worse than Mrs Fielding's. Even so, the telephone
should have been answered by somebody, even if Petra had had
to step in.

'Very,' Lord Ansley agreed, 'but it's an odd collection of guests
there at present, judging by yesterday's festival. Richard seems on
good terms with Miss Saddler, so he's heard all about them. I'm
afraid he also heard that there was a minor incident there yesterday
morning in which my sister was involved. Apparently, she was
intent on exploring the manor for ghosts and on talking to the
staff, which upset Lady Saddler, who was most indignant. Miss
Saddler apparently crossed swords with her stepmother on behalf
of Lady Clarice and informed her that she would take my sister
round the house herself, thus annoying Lady Saddler even more,
I fear. Later, so Richard said, my sister roamed the gardens and
the festival completely by herself for some strange reason. I tell
you this in confidence, Nell, as I know you keep a careful eye on
my sister's eccentricities.'

Should she speak? she wondered. No, she decided. Jasper's ghost and what Lady Clarice had told her should remain a secret between them, even though it was quite likely that Lady Clarice had recounted the story of her lost love both to Lord Richard and to Miss Saddler.

'There were more strange things about yesterday,' she commented as she drove the Ford through the village. 'The festival should have been fun, but somehow it wasn't.'

'My wife agrees. She told me it felt like a dress rehearsal without conductor or music.'

'And an unrehearsed tragic ending,' Nell said soberly. 'There were hundreds of people flocking through the gates, and any one of them might have smashed those birds. The damage could have been caused at any time before I arrived at about half past nine.'

'Sir Gilbert should perhaps investigate.' He glanced at her. 'Our first priority is Briggs, though. Assuming we find him here, could you drive him home? I'll walk back after seeing Sir Gilbert.'

'I'll park at the rear garden gate, then,' Nell agreed. 'That's—'

She broke off, taken by surprise as she noticed that the track bordering the estate wall was already in use for parking. She could see at least four other motor cars parked there – and she noticed with alarm that they were distinctive ones.

'They're police motor cars,' Lord Ansley said sharply, 'and, what's more, I think one is a mortuary van. What the deuce is up? This can't just be about the garden damage. Leave the Ford here anyway, Nell. We'll find out what's happening.'

He was down from the passenger seat in a trice and striding up the track, with Nell hard on his heels, until they were stopped at the gate by their new village bobby, the enthusiastic Robin Gurney. He was a gawky young man, aged only about twenty, and, Nell knew, very serious about his work. Now he just looked plain terrified.

'No one is to enter, your lordship,' he began nervously.

'I am not no one,' Lord Ansley replied grimly. 'What's happening here, Constable?'

'There's a body been found, your lordship.'

Nell caught her breath. Not Mr Briggs. Oh, please not Mr Briggs.

'Whose?' Lord Ansley demanded.

'I can't say, your lordship,' he said miserably.

'Then we shall find out.' Lord Ansley marched past him, ushering Nell through with him. She was clutching her bag of flead cakes, increasingly scared of what might lie ahead.

As they approached the cottage, she could see a crowd of perhaps a dozen people, including a uniformed policeman, grouped by its front door. There was no sign of Sir Gilbert, but Nell recognized one or two faces from yesterday's festival. More ominously, there were more police on the far side of the garden, standing by the workshop, and Lord Ansley made straight for them. Nell could see why. Two of them were obviously plain-clothed policemen, one of whom looked like Inspector Farrell from the Sevenoaks Police Station, a short, stout man with a bristling beard (and manner). Nell froze with fear. His presence suggested that this was no ordinary death. *Please not Mr Briggs.* But if it wasn't, why was he missing? Was he just being questioned? And where were Joe and Freddie Carter? The cottage was clearly not the dark and deserted place it had been yesterday evening.

Lord Ansley wasted no time and strode straight up to Inspector Farrell, who regarded him stony-faced. 'Can you tell me what's happening here, Inspector? Is my valet Briggs involved? And Sir Gilbert – where is he?'

'Not here, my lord. Not in the circumstances.'

'*What* circumstances?'

'His wife, sir. Lady Saddler. She's been found dead, sir. In the garden through that gate.' He pointed along the passageway to the rear garden entrance.

Lady Saddler? That shock was bad enough, but why, Nell wondered, hardly believing what she was hearing, were there so many police here? What would she have been doing in this garden of all places – and with all those damaged birds?

Lord Ansley looked equally taken aback. 'Dead? *Here?*'

'Yes, sir. My men are moving the body now.'

The gate opened and two policemen carried a stretcher through. To Nell's horror, the covering had slipped slightly and Lady Saddler's body was all too visible for a moment before it was quickly replaced; the face had been staring out, the neck shockingly bruised and tongue protruding through blue lips. Dead?

Worse than that surely, Nell thought. This had to be murder, and the dire implications of that stunned her.

Lord Ansley, too, it seemed, for he looked equally horrified, before he recovered enough to say to the inspector soberly, 'This is a terrible matter. I presume you fear it's murder, and, if so, I take it you will be calling in Scotland Yard, given that Sir Gilbert is a newcomer to Spitalfrith?'

'There's no need for that, your lordship. We have our man.' Inspector Farrell looked embarrassed, and Nell had a terrible premonition. *No.* Not that, surely. It must be Freddie or Joe. 'Mr Charles Briggs, your lordship,' the inspector continued. 'Your valet.'

So it was the worst. How could this possibly have happened? Then Nell remembered the smashed garden and the birds that would sing no more. Could it be – no, even if the carnage had been Lady Saddler's doing, she would not have returned here, especially at night. Or could the body have been here all the time while Nell had been trying to persuade Mr Briggs to leave?

'You've *arrested* him?' Lord Ansley's face was black with fury. 'You didn't think to telephone me first?'

'There was no time, your lordship. We've had a word with the chief constable. Briggs is guilty, all right. He said as much. He's in the cottage now with my sergeant.'

Nell reeled with horror. Mr Briggs had confessed? This grew worse and worse.

'You will take me to see him *now*, Inspector. Mr Briggs is war-damaged and needs immediate defence.' Lord Ansley turned to Nell. 'Miss Drury, it might be necessary for you to make some telephone calls.'

Nell knew there was only one such call Lord Ansley had in mind. She must telephone Chief Inspector Alex Melbray.

When she reached her Ford, Nell drew breath before driving back to Wychbourne, still dazed from the shock. Then she schooled herself. Only two days ago that garden had been a place of enchantment, but now it lay desolate and in ruins, and Lady Saddler had been found there, murdered. The priority was the desperate need to help Mr Briggs. Being a Sunday, Alex Melbray might not be on duty, but she would try his private telephone number.

She had to think carefully, however. Alex was not going to respond positively to an impassioned plea alone even if it came from Lord Ansley, let alone from her. No impassioned plea, then. Reason instead. Given that Scotland Yard had to be asked formally by the Kent Police – and not by Nell Drury – to step in, Alex's first question would be: what evidence do you have that Mr Briggs's arrest is wrong? Answer: she had none. How could she?

Think logically, she told herself. First of all, what could Lady Saddler have been doing during the night or early morning in a garden of what were once singing birds? Answer, assuming this was not a prior arrangement with the Carters – or Mr Briggs: there was no obvious reason. Second, could Mr Briggs have any motive for wanting to kill her? Surely only if he believed that she had caused the damage to Freddie's bird garden, but why would she have done that? Lady Saddler had certainly looked a malicious woman, but why choose that garden to destroy?

Third, and perhaps the most likely avenue to persuade Alex that there was need for his presence, there was motive. It would be Freddie or possibly his father who would be the most upset about their ruined garden – the Carters, *not* Mr Briggs, however much of a helping hand he had given Freddie with the automata. Where had Freddie and his father been last night and had they returned to the cottage yet? There were obviously people inside it now, but who were they?

Weighing up the pros and cons, Nell hovered before driving away. The gate into Spitalfrith was currently unguarded. Didn't she need to know just a little more before she rang Alex? Yes, she did – and just a few minutes wouldn't make any difference.

Noting that some of the motor cars had now left, she hurried back to the cottage. Most of the crowd had disappeared, and the police had either left or were inside the cottage, so there was a chance that she could escape notice from authority if she could reach that garden. To her annoyance, its gate was now guarded by the redoubtable Constable Gurney. Onwards, she instructed herself. Assuring him that she had the inspector's permission, she walked boldly through, stopping only to address him with as authoritative a voice as she could manage.

'Where was the body found exactly? Do you know? His lordship asked me to check that.'

She bestowed on him the same look that she awarded Mr Fairweather when seeking produce out of his warming sheds – in other words, an air of bowing to his superior knowledge. Sure enough, it worked.

'Here, miss,' Constable Gurney informed her with some pride, pointing to the colonnade. 'I was here first, see, before the inspector sent me to the park gate. I found her.' There was a note of satisfaction in his voice. 'Sir Gilbert's daughter telephoned at half past seven. Says his wife was missing, and could I keep a watch out. So I came looking for her, checking the grounds first, for all they said they'd done that. So I thought them Carters might have seen her, being early risers. No one opened my knock on the door, but the gate was open and there she was. Dead, all doubled up. And that Briggs chap standing by her.'

He gave a quick glance round, presumably in case any of his superiors were still lurking around, then led her along a path strewn with foliage, wilting flowers and damaged carvings until they reached the central point of the colonnade. Here four paths met and a statue of Eros pointed his arrow down where the body must have lain.

Nell could imagine the body lying here all too well, but it had not been here last night. When she came into the garden to persuade Mr Briggs to leave, she would have seen it.

'Was she strangled with a scarf or rope or manually?' she managed to ask, fighting to keep away the images that this presented.

'Piece of rope. Doctor says he reckons she was done in between about eleven last night and four this morning, only he'll have to confirm that later,' Constable Gurney said with an air of importance. 'I had to go to the manor house to telephone Sevenoaks, and when I gets back to wait, the Carters are there talking to the Briggs fellow. "Here, what's all this?" I said. "You get inside that house and wait, while I stays with the body." The rope what strangled her was still on her, miss.' He indicated the rear of one of the garden borders. 'Jumped on from behind, so they reckon,' he added. 'Strong man, that Mr Briggs.'

'He's not been found guilty yet,' Nell said firmly.

'He said he did it.' PC Gurney was indignant. 'I know he did.'

'What were his actual words?' Nell demanded. This confirmed, to her dismay, what the inspector had said, but she still couldn't believe it. There had to be some mistake.

'Just what I told you. He did it.'

She wouldn't get any further on that, she realized, unbelievable though she still found it. Take the situation ingredient by ingredient. 'Did he say what had she done to deserve it?'

'She must have bashed up this place, of course.' He waved an arm at the desolate scene around them. 'That's why that Briggs fellow killed her.'

'And he told you that?'

'Not in so many words, but it stands to reason, don't it?'

Return to the beginning, Nell thought grimly as she made her way back to her motor car. Why would Mr Briggs have been so concerned over Freddie's garden being smashed up and why the giddy gillyflowers would he assume Lady Saddler was to blame, unless he'd seen her do it? This story had gaps as big as an apple pie without its pastry. She had seen for herself Mr Briggs's distress at the destruction of the garden, but there was no body lying by Eros then. Lord Richard had taken him home to Wychbourne Court, so why had he returned here and when?

Patiently, she ran this through her mind once more. Had Lady Saddler returned here after wrecking the place earlier? Why would she? And that, Nell realized with relief, was the evidence she needed. In effect, Lady Saddler *was* the evidence. For some reason Mr Briggs had come back to the garden later, and for some reason Lady Saddler had also done so, but surely there could have been no fixed arrangement for them to meet? To meet by coincidence, however, was too great a flight of fancy.

There might be one possible explanation: suppose Lady Saddler hadn't been killed in this garden but her murderer had wanted to cast the blame on Mr Briggs or Freddie?

Hopeful at last, she took this a stage further. The killer had either lured Lady Saddler here or killed her elsewhere. The garden gate was unlikely to have been locked, but if it was, could he have brought the body in over the wall? No, it would have left a trail. Had Joe Carter or his son been intent on killing her among the carnage she had caused, gone away to give them some sort of alibi and then come back early in the morning? No, that seemed too planned; anyway, why on earth would Lady

Saddler heed a suggestion from her gardener that she come to his garden late in the evening or at the crack of dawn? It didn't make sense.

Back to the beginning: if the murderer killed her somewhere else in the grounds and decided for some reason to leave the body here, how would he physically drag it? Bodies are heavy. A cart? And why to this place, where it was just as certain to be discovered as anywhere else in the grounds? Nell decided she could take it no further. She had evidence of a sort – even if it was more a list of possible alternatives. Possibilities, though, that were far removed from Mr Briggs being a murderer.

What, Petra desperately wondered, did one do when, although paralysed by shock oneself, one had a duty to take command of the situation, especially when the person suffering most was her father? Mrs Hayward had been surprisingly helpful with an old recipe for a cup of milk and rum, then telephoned for the nearest doctor. The milky drink had indeed helped to calm her father and he was now resting in his room, though she doubted if he was asleep. As for herself, she hadn't yet come to terms with the fact that the Snake had been murdered, telling herself she must concentrate on looking after her father.

As far as the guests were concerned, Petra didn't care what they did, provided they didn't further upset Papa. Two had gone to church and the others were trying to keep busy by taking down their paintings from the tents and packing them up. One or two were adamant that they would be leaving for Gilbert's sake as speedily as possible, and the others equally adamant that they would be *remaining* for Gilbert's sake. It was immaterial anyway, as the police inspector had asked her to keep all the guests here, but what was the etiquette for entertaining guests when the official hostess has been murdered?

The solution was near at hand. Lord Richard was in the morning room, eager to help. He looked almost a stranger; instead of his usual sports jacket and flannels, he was formally clad. Whether this was for church or because this was a house of mourning, she didn't know, but he could have been wearing Oxford bags for all she cared; she was just delighted to see him.

'For Pete's sake, Petra,' he said when she blurted out her

problem, 'that's easily solved. You can't have all those Clerries here in the circumstances. Send them all up to Wychbourne Court.'

He was clasping her hands in his, and his offer seemed manna from heaven. Nevertheless, she pulled herself together. 'I can't do that,' she said, appalled. 'It's jolly good of you, but I'd have to ask your parents' permission.'

'Don't worry about a thing. I'll just have a word with them. How's Sir Gilbert?'

'In a bad way,' she replied simply. 'But he may pull through once the shock is over. One never knows with Pa. He seemed devoted to her, but I sometimes wondered how deep it went and whether it was like Clerrian art – something he was drawn to, but then realized too late it wasn't for him.'

'I gathered from the festival yesterday, though, that he seemed to share his wife's views on next year's exhibition.'

'No. That was only Madame Lisette's idea, not his. You know I wasn't on good terms with her, so don't ask me whether I'm knocked sideways by her death – because I'm not. Or won't be, once I'm over the shock.'

The grip on her hands grew tighter, but then he released her, looking awkward. He wore a look of 'This is not the place' about him, and Petra had an insane desire to giggle. Perhaps that was shock, too. She tried to make him understand.

'No one really *liked* Madame Lisette, Richard, except for poor old Pa. Murder is a terrible thing, though, so everyone's just silent on the subject, which is creepy. Thora spouted some poetry about life and death, but her fiancé isn't saying a thing. I gathered – not from my father, of course – that Madame Lisette was both Pierre's model and his mistress, which makes this situation doubly difficult for him, especially as Thora's now suspicious, to say the least, about the mistress part, thanks to Madame Lisette's heavy hints.'

'A bad show,' Richard agreed. 'What about the other guests' reactions?'

'Gert Radley was straightforward. I like her,' Petra replied. 'She came up to me and said, "We both know what we felt about Lisette. Neither of us wanted this to happen, though." Lance Merryman twittered his sympathy, but I think he was relieved she's no longer around. Vinny Finch was the most understanding as to how I feel.

Everyone must be wondering what will happen about the exhibition next year, though. Perhaps Father will go ahead with it now, once he's recovered from this nightmare.'

'That might depend on how the nightmare ends,' Richard said soberly.

Petra did not reply, but she understood all too well what he was implying: that if this Briggs man turned out to be innocent, the real killer might be among the Clerries here at Spitalfrith.

A trunk call always took such an interminable time to go through, Nell fumed, and it took longer if it was a daunting one, such as telephoning Alex Melbray. At last she heard the welcome sound of the operator ringing back with Scotland Yard on the line – welcome, save that it was only to tell her that Chief Inspector Melbray was not on duty today. The call to Alex's private number took even longer before she heard his voice. She imagined him sitting in his London flat staring down at the small garden he loved.

'Nell?' Alex sounded delighted to hear from her, but whether he would remain delighted was another matter. 'Picnic?' he asked hopefully. 'Or another corpse?' he joked.

Nell braced herself. 'The latter.'

Silence. 'Tell me,' he said at last, his voice impersonal. He listened without interruption while she explained. When she'd finished, he replied just as she had expected. 'You know I can't intervene without being asked to do so by the Sevenoaks police, even if it has taken place on my patch.' Alex was the Yard's Detective Chief Inspector for this area of Kent.

Nell played her last card. 'There are lines of enquiry that the local police aren't investigating, and I do have evidence.' Even as she put it into words, this 'evidence' sounded even more flimsy.

Another silence. 'Perhaps Sevenoaks doesn't need anything more after Mr Briggs's confession. But tell me about this evidence,' he said. She did so, thankful that she had had the forethought to think of something, no matter how slender.

'I saw Mr Briggs there in the garden at about half past nine last night. The garden had been smashed up, but there was no body in the place where it was found early this morning, at about eight o'clock. So when Mr Briggs returned from Wychbourne to

Spitalfrith, no matter when that was, it could only have been in the hope of Freddie and Joe Carter having returned home. This morning his bed was unslept in, so he could have sat up all night worrying about the Carters returning to find the damaged garden and he probably returned to warn them early this morning.'

Yes, she thought, that must have been it. 'After all,' she finished, 'why on earth would Lady Saddler go to the garden at that time of night or early morning to meet a gardener or Mr Briggs or anyone else? It doesn't make sense.'

'What if Briggs met her elsewhere, killed her and brought her to the garden in revenge for the destruction she'd caused. *If* that was her doing.'

Nell was checkmated. Then she rallied. 'Lord Richard took Mr Briggs home when Lady Saddler was still alive – or at least not in the garden. The festival had recently closed, although there were still some people around. Why would Mr Briggs have come back earlier than he could have expected the Carters to be home? He couldn't have had any arrangement to meet Lady Saddler.'

Silence. 'I'll talk it over with the Yard and with the Sevenoaks police, plus the chief constable,' he said finally. 'It's possible I *might* point out that with such distinguished people involved, some of them foreigners, they wouldn't want to put a foot wrong.'

Nell was mightily cheered. 'Now that sounds like a great sauce for a Sunday roast.'

'Regrettably, a roast that is all fat and very little lean,' he rejoined. 'And, Nell,' he added as she relaxed in sheer relief, 'see that none of those guests at Spitalfrith vanish before I arrive tomorrow. *If* I do. *If* Sevenoaks agrees.'

FIVE

B ad news travels faster than spilt milk. Even so, Nell was surprised how quickly news of both the murder and Mr Briggs's arrest had reached Wychbourne Court. The kitchen was already buzzing in bewilderment and anger when she arrived after her telephone call to Alex.

'What's going to happen to Mr Briggs?' Kitty cried out, dropping her whisk so effectively that splashes of cream decorated the table, the floor and her hitherto spotless apron.

'It can't have been him that did it,' Mrs Squires chimed in, busy rushing to help clear up. 'He wouldn't hurt a fly.'

'What would he be doing murdering a ladyship?' demanded pageboy Jimmy, loitering in the doorway.

'That Robin Gurney's had a downer on him ever since Mr Briggs ran into his bike last month,' contributed scullery maid Muriel.

'Bet your boots his lordship won't like this,' Robert said with some satisfaction. 'He'll have to press his own shirts.'

All this and more was hurled at Nell, just as the other scullery maid rushed in to hear the latest news.

Time to marshal the troops. 'Cut the cackle,' Nell yelled over the hubbub. 'No use just shouting when the spuds boil over. We'll *do* something to help him.'

'What?' Kitty broke the silence that followed.

'For a start,' Nell said, thinking rapidly, 'we can't make omelettes before we get the frying pans hot. Translated, that means every single one of you who went to the festival yesterday needs to record where you were, who you saw and when you saw them, especially if you saw Mr Briggs. Agreed?'

She looked round at the dubious faces and registered the less than eager nods. Some of these youngsters – a few not so young – could barely read or write, so she realized she was asking a lot. Nevertheless, it was essential.

'Lady Saddler was murdered,' she continued firmly, 'late last evening or very early this morning, but if you saw her while you were there earlier, and if she was talking to someone, that would be very useful for the police to know.'

'I saw her with her clothes off, dancing,' Michel piped up.

Nell quelled him with a look. 'I expect we all did, but you should note the time nevertheless. Something might have happened during one of those performances that led to her murder later on.'

'Murder,' breathed Kitty. 'Poor lady, she only just moved here all the way from France and now she's dead. It's dreadful, isn't it?'

'It is, but we all know that Mr Briggs wasn't responsible,' Nell replied. 'Lord Richard drove him back here about ten o'clock, but for some reason he returned to Spitalfrith either during the night or early this morning. Did any of you hear or see him then?'

A low murmuring as they looked at each other. 'No, Miss Drury,' Kitty told her. 'We've been talking about that, but none of us did.'

'Did any of you go near the Carters' cottage, or see Freddie and Joe Carter at any point while you were at Spitalfrith? That's the cottage by the far boundary wall, set on its own within its own gardens.' More shaking of heads. 'The police,' Nell continued doggedly, 'might want to ask every one of you for any information, and so the quicker you write it down, the more accurate it's likely to be.'

'Why?' muttered Michel.

'Because,' Nell informed him, 'the more you talk among yourselves, the less clear your own memories will become.' Still some blank faces. She tried again. 'Suppose you piled all the ingredients for every menu of the day into a heap and then had to pick out the very one wanted. Ten to one it will be coated with flour or eggs or something. Remember that chestnut pudding when you forgot the rum to soak the macaroons in, Michel?' she asked meaningfully.

It was obvious Michel did, because he said no more. Nevertheless, the general reluctance over recording had registered, and Nell looked round the kitchen hoping for inspiration. She spotted it in the form of the easel carrying the daily menus and work schedules and pounced on it. 'I'll set this spare easel up with your names, times and columns so that you'll just have to tick whether you saw Mr Briggs or Lady Saddler or anyone else at Spitalfrith, plus fill in a figure or two. If there's a tick, then the police can follow it up by talking to you if they want to.'

There were slightly more positive nods in response, but at least it was a start, Nell thought. 'And now,' she added in her best marshalling voice, '*luncheon.*'

Far from practising what she preached, organizing luncheon came a poor second to her anxiety to hear from Lord Ansley. Surely he would telephone through to her? It was nearly midday and time for the servants' lunch, but she was on too many tenterhooks to stop for long. When the call finally came, she was in the middle of a hasty sandwich in Pug's Parlour. Pushing it aside, she sped through the Great Hall to his ground-floor office, fear increasing rapidly. The mere fact that he had returned to his office on a Sunday, rather than his private study, did not bode well.

One look at Lord Ansley's face and she knew it was bad news. He was pacing around the room in great agitation.

'There was nothing I could do, Nell, except thunder my objections to their carting poor Briggs off to Sevenoaks. I shall drive over there right away. Did you call Melbray?'

'Yes, Lord Ansley. He's going to telephone Inspector Farrell and the chief constable, although he isn't sure they'll agree to the Yard taking over the case.'

'But he'll try?'

'Yes. He said he might play the card of Sevenoaks not wanting the responsibility of a case with a foreigner's death and public names involved.'

'Very diplomatic of him. It depends on what Sevenoaks has in the way of evidence.'

'Do they have any – save this so-called confession?' Nell asked anxiously.

'They've only told me that they had asked Briggs what had happened and the answer was "I did it".'

Just as Constable Gurney had said, but Nell still could not believe it. 'Was Mr Briggs present when you spoke to the police?'

'I'm afraid he was. He didn't deny saying it. He just stared at me as though I was his commanding officer and would take charge,' Lord Ansley said bitterly. 'If only I could. Calling Melbray is all we can do at present, except notify my solicitors.'

'Inspector Melbray also confirmed that all the Spitalfrith guests should stay on,' Nell told him.

'Ah,' Lord Ansley said ruefully. 'It seems from what Richard tells me that we shall be entertaining them here. Anyway, the Sevenoaks police wouldn't budge either on letting them leave, as they might need fuller statements. Now I'll have to break the news to my wife that we will have five Artistes de Cler here for a day or two.'

'Perhaps they'll only need bones to eat, as they believe in reducing subjects to skeletons in their art,' Nell managed to joke.

That succeeded in bringing a smile to Lord Ansley's face, but only momentarily. 'I didn't take to Lady Saddler, and I suspect I'm not the only one, war heroine or not. Nevertheless, this horror is too much in itself, let alone with the factor that Briggs is involved.' He paused. 'You don't think—'

'No,' Nell replied quickly. 'I don't think Mr Briggs could have killed her, even supposing it might have been her who smashed his friend's garden to pieces.'

Before Lord Ansley could reply, they were interrupted by a thump on the door. Lady Clarice appeared and was clearly eager to talk, to say the least. Nell held her breath. *Not Jasper again*, she silently pleaded.

'Gerald, I must ask you—' Then she saw Nell. 'Miss Drury, I'm so glad you are present. You have evidence as you were there, which means I should tell the police, must I not, Gerald?'

Lord Ansley looked alarmed, which was hardly surprising. 'The police? Evidence about Lady Saddler, Clarice?'

'Miss Drury can confirm it, Gerald. I met *Jasper* last evening,' she replied, to Lord Ansley's visible relief – and Nell's, too. 'I was walking down the path towards the garden where this terrible murder happened,' Lady Clarice continued. 'The garden must be the one full of singing automata that Miss Saddler had told me about – so sad, and now all destroyed. I saw Lady Saddler on her way there early yesterday afternoon, when I was walking in the woods to find the dell where Jasper and I found such happiness. She had been most rude about him in the morning when Miss Saddler took me around the manor house, so when I glimpsed Lady Saddler in the afternoon, I wanted to explain to her what a wonderful person Jasper is. But she had already reached the gardener's cottage by the time I drew near to her, so I missed my opportunity. But in the evening, as dark fell, I went to meet Jasper and I *saw* him, didn't I, Nell?'

'You told me so,' Nell said gently. 'And I did meet you on the path, but that was only shortly before half past nine, and Lady Saddler was alive when I arrived a little later.'

Lord Ansley was clearly mustering his patience. 'Jasper is a ghost, Clarice, isn't he?'

'Of course he is, Gerald,' Lady Clarice rejoined indignantly. 'I do know that. But he was alive last evening. He was coming from the direction of the cottage, but he was making for our dell. He was approaching me through the bushes, and I sensed him immediately. He came out of the darkness, and I'm sure he reached out his hand to me, but something must have alarmed him because he melted away. But he was there. He *was*. He whispered my name. Then I saw you coming, Nell. Did you see him, too?'

'No, but it was a strange evening,' Nell said diplomatically. 'And he would have come to see you, not me, Lady Clarice.'

Lady Clarice turned to her. 'Oh, yes, it *was* strange. So should I tell the police? Jasper might have witnessed the murder, and we could hold a séance. Suppose he saw Lady Saddler?'

'He couldn't have done, unless they both came back later in the evening.' Nell glanced at Lord Ansley, who nodded, which meant she was taking the right line. Hopefully there'd be no more mention of a séance. 'I reached the Carters' garden about half past nine,' she continued, 'and I found it destroyed. But Lady Saddler wasn't there then. It wasn't until much later that the murder took place, at least eleven o'clock.' That's roughly what the police doctor had said, according to Constable Gurney, and that would certainly confirm Jasper's innocence, should the police become confused into thinking this Jasper was no ghost but a material witness.

Lady Clarice looked happier. 'Jasper would never have harmed her. I know that. Does that mean there is no need for me to tell the police?'

'Perhaps, Lord Ansley,' Nell said, fingers mentally crossed that she wasn't putting her thumb in the pie, 'you should just mention to them that Lady Clarice saw Lady Saddler early in the afternoon and where that was.' To her, that seemed an important clue to what might have happened yesterday. Why would Lady Saddler be visiting the Carters' cottage during the afternoon, though? If she was responsible for the destruction of the birds, surely that could not have happened in the early afternoon – there would have been repercussions of some sort before its discovery in the evening? Lady Clarice's story raised another question mark, too.

'An excellent idea, Miss Drury,' Lord Ansley said gravely. 'I'll take care of speaking to the police on your behalf, Clarice.'

Nell was sure they were both wondering the same thing, however. Who had Lady Clarice really seen last night?

With Lady Clarice reassured and luncheon over, Nell devoted herself to establishing the easel, with large sheets of cardboard duly marked with names and columns. She was fully aware that Alex might not approve of this initiative, but nevertheless she felt she was striking a blow on Mr Briggs's behalf.

There must be more she could do, though. How must poor Freddie Carter and Joe be feeling with Freddie's garden destroyed, a murder on their doorstep and Freddie's great friend arrested for the crime? Petra Saddler would be the only person at Spitalfrith who might be thinking of their plight, Nell thought, but she must have her hands full with looking after her father and organizing their guests leaving Spitalfrith for Wychbourne Court.

She would visit the Carters herself, Nell decided, and perhaps take them some supper. True, that might make her seem like a caricature of a Victorian lady doling out charity to the poor, but did she care a tinker's cuss about that? No. It did, however, guiltily cross her mind that it would be interesting to know where the Carters were last night and why. She dismissed any pangs of conscience. However charitable her intentions, Alex would most certainly not be pleased if he found out about this visit anyway, so she might as well be hanged for a sheep as a lamb.

Carrying her hamper, she braced herself onwards as she unlatched the cottage's front gate and marched up to the door. She half expected to be pounced on by Constable Gurney, but there was no sign of a police presence now, presumably because of the police's conviction that they had solved the crime. She had been able to glimpse the top of the colonnade over the wall, but no more. There had been no sounds of movement in the rear garden, and the terrible wreckage must surely still remain there as it was a crime scene.

By the time she rapped on the cottage door, she was beginning to regret her journey, feeling foolish as she stood here with her hamper of meats, fruit and bread. After all, Mrs Hayward might be looking after them. There was such a long silence after her knock that she was about to turn and go home, but then the door opened and Joe Carter stood there, eyes red-rimmed and looking very dour.

'I came to see how you and Freddie were after the terrible morning you must have had. I've brought you some food.' Her words sounded trite and inadequate, but to her relief he seemed to take them in good part, for he nodded and took the hamper from her.

'They took him, they did. They took away Charlie Briggs,' he said.

'He can't possibly be guilty of murder,' Nell said reassuringly.

For one tense moment she thought he didn't agree, but then he grunted. 'Couldn't lash out at no one, old Charlie.'

'It must have upset Freddie greatly. How is he?'

Another grunt. 'Come and see him, miss. Then you'll see how he is.'

She followed him into what was clearly their living room. She recognized the fair-haired Freddie from her brief glimpse of him on Thursday evening, and now that she saw him full-faced, she recalled having seen him in the village from time to time. He was sitting on the floor, hunched up by a window, and taking no notice of her or his father. In one hand he was grasping a wooden blackbird and stroking it from time to time.

'Is that the only bird that survived?' she risked asking gently. No reply.

'He don't speak much, do you, Freddie?'

There was no reply to his father either.

'I work in the kitchen at Wychbourne Court and we all want to help,' Nell said. Even as the words emerged, she thought how useless they were, so she tentatively squatted down at his side, putting out her hand to stroke the bird with him. At first, she thought he'd push it away, but he didn't, only continued his relentless movement.

She rose to her feet at last and tried another risky line. 'Once Charlie is back with us, he can help you restore the garden.'

This time she had gone too far, for Freddie jerked and turned his head away, and it was Joe who said, 'Best leave that a while, miss. We was away last night at my sister's up Mill Lane, and so it's all a bit of a shock to him. Dead bodies and police and all.'

'That explains why your cottage was in darkness when I came by about half past nine last night. Only Mr Briggs was here. The festival must have been very noisy earlier. Is that why you went away?' Had she stepped too far again? Perhaps, because Joe just stared at her.

'Went off as soon as we'd had tea,' he eventually said, 'about half past six or seven, it was.'

'And the garden wasn't damaged then?'

'Perhaps it was, perhaps it wasn't.' Joe glared at her.

She'd gone too far to draw back. 'Could Lady Saddler have done the damage, do you think?'

His face changed, and he growled, 'Maybe she did.'

'Did Charlie Briggs tell you so?' asked Nell quickly.

Another glare from Joe. 'You'd best be going now, miss. Ta for the grub.'

She was being given her marching orders. There must be more to be learned from them, she realized, but she wasn't going to receive any more answers to her questions now. As she left, she could hear Freddie's plaintive voice but could only make out two words: 'Marie-Hélène.'

'Well, my dears, from festival to murder to a majestic country house. And they say nothing ever happens in the country.' Lance Merryman glanced anxiously around their temporary home in Wychbourne Court. The Clerries had been allotted the blue drawing room for themselves alone, so that they could chat together. *So* kind, and here they were, all formally dressed for dinner as though they were taking part in a Noël Coward play, he thought. Gracious though it was of the marquess and his marchioness to accommodate them, it was *inhibiting*, however. It was true that as only they, the Clerries, were present here, they were free to discuss the horrors of the day, but this was a mixed blessing as far as Lance was concerned.

Poor Lisette had been brutally murdered, and frightful though this was, it did make one feel uncomfortable, given that all their livelihoods (save perhaps dear Thora's) had depended on her being removed from the scene. Once Gilbert was over the shock and could reassess the situation, the London exhibition might now go ahead, but none of them could as yet openly rejoice, even among themselves, at such relief while the murder was still so much the subject of the day. The future might look brighter, but the present most certainly did not. Policemen would be asking for witness statements at the very least, and not until this villain Briggs had been charged could they all feel truly at ease. After all, whatever reason he might have had for wanting to kill dear Lisette, all of them here in this *lovely* drawing room also had good reason to take steps to remove her. It was noticeable to Lance that everyone seemed remarkably eager to discuss dinner, not murder. Including, it had to be said, himself.

'A place this size must have a decent kitchen,' Gert observed after a long silence.

'A magnificent chef, so Miss Saddler assured me,' Thora said.

'Excellent – at least that's some compensation.' Lance tittered.

'For a murder having taken place?' Vinny asked quietly. 'She modelled for us all.'

Lance pouted. Why did Vinny have to spoil it all? He'd meant compensation for not being able to leave Wychbourne for his present Paris home, whereas Vinny seemed intent on bringing the conversation uncomfortably close to his own fears.

Then Thora had to have her say. She had been noticeably cooler in her attentiveness to Pierre ever since Lisette's outburst, so if, Lance thought, he judged the situation correctly, Pierre had better redouble his coos and caresses to undo the damage.

'She modelled mostly for you, Pierre,' Thora threw at him. 'Do you mourn her?'

Now, that was out of order. How splendid to openly raise such a delicate subject at that moment! Lance giggled to himself. How would Pierre respond when it was so clear that Thora was beginning to have doubts about her choice of fiancé?

'Do tell us, Pierre. We are all seekers of truth,' he said, smirking.

Pierre glared at him and then, as so often, surprised him. After a moment's pause, instead of his usual fawning subservience to his bride-to-be, he rose to his feet and stood there, the perfect Greek hero. Lance was transfixed. Pierre's stance made a perfect Landseer painting; he was 'The Monarch of the Glen'.

'*Mes amis, ma chère* Thora,' Pierre began, 'we Artistes de Cler are indeed seekers after truth, not just with our paintbrushes but in the inspiration that controls them. And now we have lost the key to our work, our model Lisette. Do I mourn her? Yes. I mourn the inspiration that produced my greatest work, "Eden", I mourn the inspiration for my masterpiece "Joy", for "The Dance" and for twenty other canvases that would not otherwise have existed. She was our path to the truth.'

Only Gert dared answer this. 'Path to the truth, perhaps. But what made Lisette such a good model – apart from her looks and figure – was that she had so many layers. Peel off one and there was the truth – or was it? The next day it might have changed. That's what was interesting.'

In view of last night's horrors, Lance considered it was good of Gert not to refer to her own Eden, which Lisette had destroyed just because she didn't think she was portrayed elegantly enough. In his own designs, he used Lisette's sinuous elegance to great effect. He, Lance Merryman, after all, was a member of the Chambre Syndicale de la Haute Couture. His tiered lace masterpiece with its diagonal neckline this year had revealed Lisette at her best, and his own favourite, the blue linen beachdress with Lisette stretching upwards to the sun in Cannes, was a triumph. Nevertheless, he would find another model easily enough when he moved to London – now that Lisette no longer stood in his way with her threats and demands.

'Lisette had many layers,' Vinny agreed. 'A singer who courageously risked her life to send intelligence to the British, a friend we all shared in Paris, enjoying cafés and restaurants after hours in the studio, the person who married Gilbert only two months ago and brought him happiness, the dancer who gave us Africa yesterday.'

'*Oui*, Lisette was a very special model,' Pierre said. 'But a model only, *ma chère* Thora,' he wisely added.

Thora did not respond, and Lance decided he could refrain no longer from his entrance on to the scene. 'Paths to the truth seem to be labyrinthine for you, Pierre. When I first met Lisette in Paris – when you had already founded the Artistes de Cler – dear Lisette posed merely for her lovers.'

The implication did not escape Pierre – or Thora.

Pierre moved first. 'That was the time I rescued you from being merely a failing artist and designer, Lance.'

'Careful, Lance. The whirligig of time brings in its revenges,' Gert warned him.

Perhaps, Lance thought ruefully, he'd gone a little too far, but no matter now. 'Three years ago, Pierre. That was also the time that Lisette became your mistress.'

How very satisfying. Lance had a moment's doubt, though. Was he making a mistake by antagonizing Pierre? No. Pierre wouldn't stop him participating in the exhibition next year if it took place, because he was the only designer among them, and Pierre needed the publicity that could attract. His only revenge would be to throw him out of the Clerries. But that was no problem; after the London exhibition, Lance calculated that he would not need their support. He would have taken the London fashion world by storm. Meanwhile . . .

'I assume that that is untrue, Pierre.' Thora was looking very icy.

'It was long before I met you, *ma chère*,' Pierre said desperately. No 'Monarch of the Glen' now. He was 'The Stag at Bay', Lance noted with glee.

'Before we tear each other to pieces,' Vinny intervened calmly, 'let us remember the importance of our exhibition next year, which we hope to resurrect. More importantly, remember that Lisette has been murdered, and although a man has been arrested, it is not long since we would all have cheerfully wished her dead.'

A polite cough, and Lance saw the butler standing in the doorway, which gave him an insane desire to giggle. 'Dinner is about to be served, ladies and gentlemen,' Peters announced.

Nell's Cooking Pot seemed even more of a refuge than usual on this gloomy Monday morning. It was also an excellent place for clear thinking. It was all very well being certain of Mr Briggs's innocence, but that did pose two questions for Nell. Why had he apparently confessed and, more importantly, who did kill Lady Saddler? The answer, she had to admit, could be Freddie or his father because she had destroyed their singing birds. The sister, Nell had now discovered from Mrs Squires, was Mrs Golding who lived in Chimney Cottage in Mill Lane. That wasn't far from Spitalfrith, and either of them could have returned to their home for whatever reason. If it had been late at night or very early morning, then that could have been why Mr Briggs came back to Spitalfrith from Wychbourne after Lord Richard had driven him home. It occurred to her that the Carters might not have gone to Mill Lane at all, but just lain low in the cottage until Lady Saddler returned late in the evening or in the small hours. Blithering bloaters, that didn't make sense, for why on earth would Lady Saddler come sneaking back around midnight to meet Freddie or Joe, especially if she had destroyed Freddie's garden? No, surely it was to meet someone else: her murderer.

Back to the drawing board. Why did she choose his garden for the meeting or was she killed somewhere else? 'Blither those bloaters yet again,' she muttered viciously.

'Menu playing up, Nell?' Peering through her open window was Alex Melbray.

SIX

'So Sevenoaks agreed?' Nell asked brightly, opening the
tradesmen's door into the yard for Alex. She had mixed
feelings, all churning themselves up. How could she be so
lost for words? She had met Alex in London since their last
encounter at Wychbourne, but here she was floundering like a
beached whale at seeing him here at Wychbourne Court, even
though she had so much wanted him to come.

She pulled herself together as she ushered him into the Cooking
Pot. Presumably, Alex was already at work here, judging by his
starched collar and Trilby hat. No casual blazers today. That meant
she could relax on one score, she told herself. No private matters
need be discussed for the time being. For the moment at least,
Alex in his role as a police officer was a mere face from the past,
or so she tried to convince herself.

It didn't work. He wasn't just one more policeman. He was
Alex with his shrewd eyes that could turn into loving warmth in
a jiffy and a laugh that could flip her heart over and set her giggling.
But not today. Although he was roughly the same height and build
as footman Robert, Alex's presence, especially when, as now, he
sat a mere foot or two away from her, seemed to dominate the
room. Or was that her fault for thinking that way?

'Sevenoaks, in the form of Inspector Farrell, did agree,' he told
her. 'That might have been because I pointed out that, in the
so-termed confession, your Mr Briggs's words were conveyed
verbally to them through just one constable, and the fact that Mr
Briggs is war-damaged is therefore a major factor. They disagreed.
However, my mention of my acquaintance with Lord Haig,' he
continued, straight-faced, 'who is known to be indefatigable in
his care for ex-servicemen, and also my observation that the
French ambassador would have to be consulted, might possibly
have been instrumental in their decision, agreed with the chief
constable, that the Yard should be in charge of the investigation.
Nevertheless, Inspector Farrell insisted on holding Briggs in

custody for another day at least while we assess the situation. That seemed reasonable.'

Nell struggled to bite back her instant objection. Alex was right, of course. The police had to be sure Mr Briggs was innocent, but even the thought of him in custody tormented her. With Alex now in charge, and Lord Ansley no doubt hard on his heels, insisting on his release, she realized bleakly that there was nothing she could do to help without treading on their toes. But how was Mr Briggs faring, locked up in a cell? She couldn't bear to think about that, especially as she had no way of helping him.

She quickly changed the subject. 'Are you staying at Spitalfrith?' she began cautiously.

He grinned. 'The Coach and Horses seemed preferable. Lady Ansley invited me to stay here in the Court—'

'But—'

'Quite. I'm told that the Spitalfrith guests are staying here, which, as they are witnesses, could be awkward.'

'How long will you keep them here?' Stupid question, she realized immediately, but he let her off lightly.

'I'll begin interviewing immediately. Lord Ansley has put two rooms at our disposal, and my team should be here at any moment now.'

'Are the Spitalfrith artists suspects?' Another pointless question. The cat had got her tongue and no mistake.

Perhaps Alex had a similar problem, it occurred to her, as he was formality itself when he replied, 'At present, the whole of Wychbourne is suspected, although it's surely no coincidence that Lady Saddler was murdered just after a festival starring her Parisian friends was held here at her home. But,' he added, perhaps foreseeing her frustration, 'I'm told that the rope used to throttle her came from one of the manor outhouses.'

'From the Carters' work shed?' Nell asked in alarm.

'No, it was one near the manor house itself.' Alex eyed her keenly. 'You said that very promptly. Any reason for that?'

'Of course,' she whipped back equally promptly. 'Because Mr Briggs wouldn't have access to outhouses near the house.' And, she reasoned, neither Freddie nor Joe was likely to have taken it from there.

'In *theory*, Mr Briggs could well have done so. Inspector Farrell tells me that anyone attending the festival and certainly the staff – including the gardeners – would have had access to the outhouses by the manor house. They aren't locked.'

'But taking it from there would need pre-planning,' Nell replied eagerly. Too eagerly.

'Possibly,' he said drily. 'But Charles Briggs, Freddie Carter and his father could have pre-planned it together. I'm told the Carters were away for the night, which also suggests pre-planning. They could also have slipped back to commit the murder.'

'I thought that too—'

'Did you, Nell?'

She ignored the warning signal. 'Yes, but if the Carters knew Lady Saddler had destroyed the birds and might be returning, they wouldn't have gone away, and Mr Briggs—'

'Nell,' he interrupted gently, 'we shouldn't be talking this way. I hope this case will lead to Mr Briggs being cleared, but this can't be a joint investigation.'

She stiffened. 'Of course not, but when I took them some food for supper yesterday, they told me—'

'Tell *me* exactly what they said,' he broke in. 'Word for word. And, Nell, you can't do my job for me. It's *my* case.'

'Agreed,' she managed to say, mentally kicking herself for rushing like the charge of the Light Brigade across the border into his territory. The private had to be distinct from the professional, and yet, suffering sausages, he'd asked for her help in the past, and furthermore she did have something to offer – even though she still had to work out quite what that was! 'We seem to have come to a curdling point,' she added lightly.

'You don't want *us* to curdle, do you?' Alex had looked alarmed. To her relief, he was her Alex again.

Only for a moment, though. She remembered mutinously that there had been no problem in talking about a case he was leading when she had met him in London a few weeks earlier, so why was there now? Reluctantly, she had to admit she knew the answer to that. This case in Wychbourne had barely begun and he didn't yet know where it was heading. *Did* she want the relationship between herself and Alex to curdle, fragile as it was? Lose it all? See him march away into someone else's arms just because she couldn't make up her mind between her love of her job at

Wychbourne and moving to London to be with him? What would her own life be without him? She'd be getting older and older and more set in her ways until she too curdled.

'No curdling,' she agreed.

'Don't stir too hard, then.'

Luncheon preparations and service took her mind off Alex for a while. All was now well. It had seemed so very easy to agree with him – she had meant it. Especially when she was in his arms and with his lips on hers. Of course, she now reflected happily, one can whip more and more oil into the egg yolks, adding more lemon juice until curdling point comes. The art of making a perfect mayonnaise comes in knowing when to stop.

Enough about curdling. She'd hit the right level in telling Alex exactly what Joe and Freddie had said, and now she had to keep that level steady. There were steps she *could* take, though – and surely she had to if they would help Mr Briggs. The fact that Lady Saddler had visited the Carters and almost certainly been the person who destroyed the garden might suggest that that was where she was killed. But suppose it wasn't?

Back to her earlier theory. If it wasn't, then why bring her back to the garden once dead? To cast blame on Joe, Freddie – and therefore, accidentally, Mr Briggs? Or the murderer could have been someone who had seen the damage and wanted to make a point by returning her body there. Lastly, she reasoned, it could have been put there because it would divert attention from Spitalfrith Manor and its guests.

Yes! And that threw the spotlight back on to Alex's possible suspects – the guests currently staying at Wychbourne Court, plus, she supposed, Miss Saddler and Sir Gilbert. The theory that someone from outside had murdered Lady Saddler was hardly viable considering the time she was killed – so back to the same conclusion: it must have been a rendezvous arranged with Lady Saddler. Which, of course, might have been with one of those Wychbourne guests, so perhaps there *might* be something she could do. Guiltily, Nell realized she was again slipping nearer that borderline and forced herself back to the matter of dinner.

'Nell, are you busy?' Jenny Smith was poking her head round the Cooking Pot door.

'Only with menus,' Nell replied as cheerfully as she could manage.

'Good. Petra Saddler would like to see you sometime this afternoon.'

Nell blinked. 'Why me?'

'She asked me first as I'd met her on Saturday evening with Lord Richard. She wanted me to go to Spitalfrith, but I told her you were the person to talk to if it's about the murder, which it is. She can't spell out what's worrying her to the police, but she only has some unanswered questions. Girls' chat.'

Only unanswered questions, Nell thought uneasily, although this unexpected invitation could well be useful. 'How can I help, though?' And how would this fit with her agreement with Alex?

'I haven't the foggiest. She must be worried about her father, though, not to mention the incidental fact that Lord Richard's making sheep's eyes at her. Have you noticed?'

'It's hard not to,' Nell said. 'As you know full well.'

Jenny laughed. 'He doesn't hold his horses. All in the cause of true love, of course, but true love can be short love with him, bless him. I could laugh it off when he had a pash on me, but Petra's not so worldly wise.'

'I'll go as soon as I can,' Nell promised, calculating the time with dinner preparations in mind. The sudden arrival of five guests yesterday had thrown out her menus, but the replacement Provençal mutton hash was already under way, so she could just about make a short visit to Spitalfrith if she drove.

The manor was a far different place to how it had looked on Saturday. It was silent and there was no one to be seen as she parked her Ford by the side of the house. It was hard to believe that monkeys and jazz bands had been in full swing in these grounds only two days ago.

The doorbell was answered by Miss Saddler herself, looking bleary-eyed and strained. 'Thank you for coming, Miss Drury. Miss Smith said you wouldn't mind too much.'

'Not at all. We're all concerned about you and your father.'

'He's up today, but very silent, which worries me even more. And this old house doesn't help. It reminds me of the unfriendly old boarding house I lived in for a while.'

She led Nell out to the terrace, which was still set with the chairs and tables of Saturday night. It made a desolate sight, bringing back all too vividly the horrors that had happened since. She could see the tents still there, but there was no movement. The heavy silence emphasized the gloomy atmosphere at Spitalfrith.

'Are the paintings and drawings still in the tents?' Nell asked.

'No. After they arrested that valet, the police said the artwork could be brought inside. Just seeing those empty tents, though, makes everything seem worse, especially with woodland behind them. There's something about it that's downright sinister.'

Nell agreed. 'Woodlands often are. When I walked along the track outside Spitalfrith – the one that borders Spital Wood – it felt as though a hundred eyes were watching me.'

'I know the track you mean. Those woods give me the heebie-jeebies, too,' Miss Saddler said. 'I didn't know whether it was imagination or whether it's because there are extra temporary labourers around for the corn harvest. I'm told most of them sleep in special outhouses, but there are also some tents in Spital Farm on the far side of those woods.'

Could that have been why she had that strange reaction on Thursday evening? Nell wondered. The Spitalfrith boundary wall was low enough to make its grounds accessible if the gate was locked. Could one of those labourers have killed Lady Saddler? Nell dismissed the idea, because Lady Saddler would hardly have come out to meet anyone so late at night or early in the morning? True, it was obvious that she and Sir Gilbert slept in different rooms; even so, such an expedition did not make sense. And then, of course, there was Jasper to consider!

'I know you've heard all about Lady Clarice and her ghost,' Nell said. 'She was very certain she met Jasper on Saturday night, but suppose that was a very human presence?'

That made Miss Saddler laugh. 'Yes, I feel as though I know Jasper after I introduced Lady Clarice to all the spectral possibilities in the manor. She hadn't set foot in here since her courting days in the nineties, so she loved every moment of it. There are all sorts of ghosts here, she informed me.'

'Including Jasper?'

'The possibility was discussed,' Miss Saddler said gravely. She hesitated. 'Have you met our guests yet now they're at Wychbourne?'

'Only by sight,' she said, mentally adding 'as yet'. That would be within Alex's 'rules', of course.

'Monsieur Christophe doesn't approve of such informality as calling them the Clerries, but that's how I think of them. Miss Drury,' Miss Saddler continued, 'I wanted to ask your opinion on whether I should tell the police that they all heartily disliked Madame Lisette – as did I. They had good reason to do so. The last straw was on Friday, when they discovered she had ordered my poor father to cancel a big exhibition of their work in London next year, which would put their careers at real risk – that's why she did it, of course.'

'Why would she want to, Miss Saddler?' Nell asked. She decided that she liked her hostess, and into the bargain it was already proving a fruitful visit.

'Do call me Petra. I'd like that, because I feel I can speak more freely.' She frowned. 'I'm not sure why she decided to do it. I've visited Paris on quite a few occasions and met them all, so I know what I'm talking about. From putting two and two together, she must have had a grudge against all the Clerries. Their prestige is beginning to grow, but they need to be internationally recognized, not just exhibiting in Paris, important though that is. The London exhibition publicity would make all the difference between starvation in a garret and a golden path ahead for anything they paint. My father is a Clerry, though, so her attitude is odd. I have a feeling that she disliked seeing herself in paintings and drawings – which is strange as she was a model by career. She particularly seemed to hate representations that could be said to come near to her true character. Snake-like. Now that the Clerries' work is more widely seen, she's making trouble. It could go back to the war – when she joined the fight against the enemy in Lille by passing intelligence back to England. She could have made enemies who were all too pally with the Germans. Does that make sense?'

Nell considered this. 'Some,' she said. 'It's all a question of scales and balances. The weights go down one side in that the Clerries must have admired her for her work during the war, but add their own careers on the other side and the scales not only balance but go down with a crash against her.'

'It would seem so, but there may be deeper waters, Nell. That's why I wanted to talk to you or Jenny just to help me think through what is relevant for the police to know. After all, they have apparently arrested the murderer, so it's not as though the Clerries are officially suspects.'

'Officially?' Nell picked up. 'You think they might be?'

'I can't see why a valet from Wychbourne Court should want to murder Madame Lisette in the middle of the night,' Petra said. 'Can you?'

'No, and knowing Mr Briggs makes me certain he couldn't have done it.' Thank goodness at least someone from Spitalfrith thought him innocent. 'He hasn't been charged yet, which is good news. So do speak to the police. They need to know there might be other suspects. Who are they?'

Petra looked relieved. 'I'm so grateful, Nell. They've been running around in my head like those rotating clock figures. Is it him? Is it her? And so on. Here goes, then: first, there's Monsieur Pierre Christophe himself, who clearly wishes to ensure his future by marrying money, in case the idiot public doesn't recognize his art for the masterpieces he considers them.'

'Are they masterpieces?' Nell queried, amused. She remembered them vividly, especially Monsieur Christophe's painting of the serpent in Eden. Good, but would it be so in a hundred years?

'Thora passionately believes they are, but she's head over heels in love with him. If she finds out for sure that he was Madame Lisette's fancy man, sparks would fly. She comes from a grand military family which eyes interlopers with deep suspicion and would never tolerate him. But I sense that love's glow has diminished these last few days, and her neat little poems reveal a less than tender feeling for Madame Lisette. Then there's Lance Merryman; he's a dear man but helpless. He was pinning everything on this exhibition. The news of its cancellation could have pushed pussy cat Lance into using his sharp claws, which he certainly has.

'Vinny Finch and Gert Radley are less definable,' she continued. 'Vinny is no self-promoter, but he believes in the Clerries wholeheartedly and no doubt saw Madame Lisette as their would-be destroyer. Gert Radley had a healthy dislike for her and makes no bones about it. For whatever reason, Madame Lisette destroyed Gert's portrait painted for the prestigious Paris Exposition Internationale des Arts Décoratif last year.'

'I talked to her at the festival on Saturday,' Nell remembered. 'She's an interesting woman – and sensible, too. What does she see in the Clerries?'

'Not sure,' Petra replied. 'A way forward perhaps. Belonging to a movement brings publicity, and she's getting on in years. Put together, all five of our dear Clerries had good reason to wish Madame Lisette dead. I've exempted my father, of course, because I doubt if he even knew what was going on half the time. He is much valued by the other Clerries as their passport to respectability – and it was for the same reason that she married—'

'My dear—'

Nell looked up and to her horror saw Sir Gilbert standing at the door. He must have overheard, and Petra naturally looked mortified. Sir Gilbert was grief-stricken enough already without hearing his daughter's wounding words. He didn't look angry, though, just tired, and thank goodness for that.

'I'm sorry, Father,' Petra said penitently.

'Do you think I was not aware of why Lisette married me, my dear? Of course I was, but there was more to our marriage than that. I wish,' he added querulously, 'that you had come to know her better.'

'Like Pierre?' Petra rashly asked, to Nell's dismay. Petra must have decided this was the time for truth, rightly or wrongly.

'Pierre had been her lover, of course,' Sir Gilbert said heavily. 'The Clerries all knew that – apart from Thora. But Lisette chose not to marry him. Nevertheless, her enemies have now struck.'

What did he mean by that? Nell wondered, but Petra was not daunted.

'She chose to come here, Father,' she pointed out gently. 'And she knew who the guests would be.'

'Indeed. We looked at many properties, but, although doubtful at first, she was happy with my choice. Lisette was used to living among enemies,' he explained simply. 'As you know, she fought for freedom in Lille, which was under the control of the German army during the war. Her parents were deported out of the city and died of starvation in the countryside, but she remained in Lille. She was a brave woman and was lucky to escape being captured and shot by the enemy.'

This time Sir Gilbert's composure did not hold. His face

crumpled and he looked his full age, Nell thought compassionately, creeping quietly out. He was totally bewildered at what life had thrown at him and needed to be alone with his daughter – who had given Nell much food for thought. The Clerries, who seemed a strange mixture, must surely be the prime suspects. There were strong reasons for why some of them might well have wished Lady Saddler out of their way.

Dinner at the Coach and Horses was a welcome change from the servants' supper. It was late, and Nell and Alex were the only diners in the dark-panelled dining room at the pub. Indeed, she suspected that was the only reason that she, a mere woman, had been permitted inside this hallowed sanctum.

'Roast mutton and cabbage must be a comedown for you, Nell,' Alex observed.

'Not at all. It takes me back to my youth. When I was pushing my dad's barrow to Spitalfields Market, mutton and cabbage would have been food of the gods. We did manage to gnaw the odd bone from time to time,' she joked.

'Very Clerrian. The truth of the mutton revealed.'

'Where will you begin tomorrow, Alex?' she asked, belatedly aware she might be treading on eggshells. She had probably already smashed a lot of them by talking to Petra, but there she had had no choice, which meant it didn't count.

'With the Carters,' he replied. 'They're central to this case. Among other things, I've been breaking the news to the Clerries that they have to stay on for at least another day. I trust that won't cause kitchen trouble.'

'Nothing causes kitchen trouble at Wychbourne,' she replied with dignity to this slur, despite the panic over the fish which had made the word 'crisis' seem inadequate yesterday. She couldn't hold back any longer, though. 'Is Mr Briggs—'

'Is the case against him dropped?' he finished for her. 'Not yet. I need more time with the Carters.'

'But if he is innocent and they were away—'

'Dearest Nell, I repeat that they are central to this case. The body was found in their garden. Their garden was destroyed, probably by Lady Saddler. They could have murdered her if they believed her responsible.'

So far so good. 'But if they didn't kill her?'

'As you must be aware, we have to ask why the body was there and whether she was killed elsewhere.' An artificial cough. 'I regret that the Coach and Horses doesn't run to wine. Cider?' he asked politely.

'Thank you.' She took the heavy hint meekly. No stepping over boundaries by accident.

'But first,' he continued, 'I'll examine the case against Charles Briggs,' and obviously seeing her about to speak, he added, 'and judge it.'

The words 'Can I help?' trembled on her lips, but she didn't voice them. If she had to continue treading on eggshells, surely, she reasoned, she could poach the eggs first?

SEVEN

Why no word from Alex? Was she expecting too much? The last thing he had said to her as he walked her back to Wychbourne after their supper at the Coach and Horses had been that he would keep her abreast of any news of Mr Briggs and there might be some tomorrow, Tuesday. Now it was well into Tuesday afternoon, and as yet Nell had heard nothing. Far from poaching those eggs, she couldn't even see where the chicken had laid them. Nor could she tell how the Spitalfrith guests were faring, having presumably all been interviewed by Alex's team.

Luncheon had been served to mostly silent guests, which probably indicated a far from united group. On her visit to the serving room, Nell could tell from Lady Ansley's muted tones that she too was on edge, which was hardly surprising. Small talk about Saturday's festival and the future of the Clerries could only go so far, when the murder of the festival's hostess was on all their minds, especially as the daily and evening newspapers were full of the story side by side with the tragic death of Hollywood's Rudolph Valentino.

Courtesy of Mr Peters, the kitchen was fully informed on both scores, and Nell had wisely not intervened in the hubbub and tears that the latter had caused, or joined the speculation over Lady Saddler. Luckily, Nell had gathered that the Haywards had done a good job of keeping the baying newspaper hounds from their Spitalfrith prey. Nell had her suspicions that the Clerries might have welcomed some publicity, but Lord Ansley had politely given the briefest of interviews. It was Lord Richard who had taken it upon himself to be a guarded spokesman for both Wychbourne and Spitalfrith.

Nell knew from Mr Peters that Lord and Lady Ansley had paid a formal call of condolence to Sir Gilbert and Petra yesterday, but she had heard nothing more of that. Indeed, why should she? She was a chef, she reminded herself, albeit one who had been able to help the family in previous times of trouble. Eager as she was to find out more about the Clerries, it wasn't that simple, given Alex's 'rules', her own duties and that they seemed to be keeping themselves to themselves, according to the servants' hall gossip. So far, she had only managed brief encounters which had produced nothing of interest.

Irrepressibly, though, she found herself guessing at what the Clerries might be doing with their time. Painting the 'truth' of the old dairy on the Wychbourne estate? Revealing the skeleton of the former Elizabethan banqueting house tucked away in the gardens? Painting Mr Fairweather's truthful lean figure? If so, perhaps she could just saunter out and have a word with them . . . No! Remember those 'rules'. First, she needed to be more up to date with the current situation, so *be patient*, she told herself.

She was rewarded half an hour later with a summons from Lord Ansley, but the tone of his voice on the house telephone told her it was not good news he had to impart.

'Chief Inspector Melbray came to see me about Briggs, Nell,' he told her as soon as she reached his study.

Her heart sank. Lord Ansley was well aware of her private friendship with Alex, so the formality of his 'chief inspector' was indeed ominous. 'Are they charging him?'

'Not yet, but it's highly likely they'll do so any moment now. Constable Gurney is quite clear that when he was there with Briggs, standing by Lady Saddler's body, Briggs said he was responsible.'

'But his words might have had some other meaning,' Nell said desperately.

'Such as?'

Nell scrabbled through a variety of possibilities, all dismissed. One last hope: 'Could he have been harking back to the war? Everything he normally says harks back to that.'

Lord Ansley brightened for a moment. 'That's possible – but to what would he have been confessing? A similar death during the war? No, how could it be similar? I'm afraid the police believe that Briggs returned to Spitalfrith after Richard left him in his room and stayed there until found by Gurney at eight o'clock. Perhaps having found the body – or, as the police have it, murdered Lady Saddler – he just waited for the Carters to reappear. They returned about half an hour after Gurney arrived. But there's no getting away from the fact that Briggs uttered those fatal words, Nell.'

Alex didn't arrive until gone half past four, by which time Nell had lost hope of seeing him and her anxiety had grown. When he finally arrived at the Cooking Pot, she could see that he too was under strain, but nevertheless she had to know what was happening.

'Has Mr Briggs been charged yet?' she threw at him.

'No, Nell.'

Tension subsided. 'He's coming home?'

But she could see from his face that he wasn't and her momentary hope vanished. 'Let's walk,' he said abruptly. 'How does your timetable look?'

Nell mentally skimmed through the dinner menu. The apple charlotte was on course, the consommé and Dover sole were under control, but the chicken *blanquette* was not. 'All done,' she nevertheless said brightly. Nothing wrong with a white lie in a good cause. She could catch up later.

The afternoon was still warm, and the August delphiniums and dahlias made an exotic show against the old red-brick walls backing on to the vegetable gardens. But she was in no mood to appreciate them. They walked down to the river, which, although not wide, would have pleased Rat and Mole, she thought idly. But this was no time for *The Wind in the Willows*. Even on such an afternoon as this, she supposed that romance had to come second to duty for Alex, but perhaps she was wrong, for he didn't launch straight into the Lady Saddler case.

'This ice house must have been vitally important at one time,' he reflected, as they stopped by the now rarely used ice house dug into the hillside close to the river. 'Time marches on, and now it's been replaced by a mere refrigerator and iceboxes. The glory has indeed departed. Is it used at all now?'

'Not in my time here,' she replied. 'During the war it must have been useful and until the Wychbourne generator grew more reliable.'

'Was Wychbourne Court a hospital during the war, or a military base?'

'Both, I'm told.' Nell struggled to seem interested in the past while the present was so urgent. 'The Ansleys moved to the east wing where we humble servants now rule the day. The west wing was a hospital, and the rest of the house an officers' HQ.'

'I know one of their sons was killed during the war, and I think their eldest son was something frightfully secret. Have you met him?'

'Lord Kenelm? Once, briefly, when he paid a stately visit to Wychbourne, but mainly he lives abroad as he's in the Colonial Office – Dominion Division, I think.'

'What's he like?'

'Poker-faced but quite pleasant. Not like Lord Richard, though. Definitely not a man of the people, in that he's more like Lady Helen than Lady Sophy.'

'Children?'

'Not yet. He married three years ago.' *Please tell me what's happening*, Nell silently begged.

But still Alex continued to ignore the main issue. 'What do you think will happen to Wychbourne eventually? Will he return here for good after Lord Ansley's death?'

Nell considered this. 'My guess is yes, but whether he does or not, I also guess he'd still want Lord Richard to run the estate.'

'Is that a good plan?'

She chose her words carefully. 'At present, not very, but Lord Richard is popular with the village, which is just as important.'

'I have the impression he's a lady killer – but not literally,' he added hastily.

Nell managed a laugh. 'He doesn't see it that way himself. He's convinced he's utterly faithful to the one and only girl in his life

– the current one.' She was beginning to fume. Delightful though it was to wander through the gardens with Alex and along the riverbank, watched only by Greek gods and their lady friends beaming at them from their picturesque stony plinths, it was time to concentrate on the modern world.

'Why did you really want to come outside, Alex?' she asked.

'It's easier to talk.'

Rebuffed. 'Gather ye rosebuds while ye may' was good poetical advice, but Alex showed no sign of wanting to gather any rosebuds. There had been no kiss, no embrace, and no 'Let me tell you about Mr Briggs'. Very well. Enough was enough.

'You mean that it's bad news,' she said flatly as they reached the river. 'Lord Ansley's already told me that Mr Briggs will be charged at any moment.'

Alex was gazing at the ripples on the water, not even looking at her. 'We've asked for an extension and Sevenoaks have been given one. There's nothing I can do about it, Nell, except—'

'You won't just walk away from us?' she burst out, aware of her childishness. She saw his lips tighten.

'Not yet, but I need evidence to the contrary, Nell. Unless Gurney is lying, Briggs told him he was guilty. The body was lying there. There can't have been confusion about what was meant.'

'And you've no evidence pointing towards other suspects?' Such as the Clerries, for instance? she thought, but managed to hold back the temptation to probe further.

He glanced at her. 'That's too near our dividing line, Nell. My job and yours again.'

Trust her to make a mess of things. Nell was cross with herself, and Alex must have picked this up because he took hold of her hand. 'You know, I'd rather be with you and anywhere but here.' Then he took her into his arms and there was nothing but the smell of the late roses from the gardens behind them, plus a slight whiff of the river.

'Do you know that age-old poem that ends "Christ, that my love were in my arms and I in my bed again"?' he said at last. 'It's with me all the time, and you don't make it easy, Nell. How hard do you think it is for me to be here pretending you're my sergeant so it's all right to talk about the case? But you're not, and I *am* here, so I have to steer my way through it as best I can. I suggest we sit here on the riverbank like two calm people, Nell, and I *will* talk to you as though you were my sergeant, but after that . . .'

'After that . . .' But that was the future and here they were in a suddenly glorious 'now'. 'Go right ahead, Guv,' said his newly appointed sergeant.

'It looks as though she was killed in the middle of the night rather than the early morning and, from evidence received, probably from around half past eleven to midnight. There was no evidence of a sexual attack, and it's agreed that it's highly unlikely that a stranger dropped by on chance and killed her. There's also agreed ground that Lady Saddler must have had some good reason to be there so late, whether it was to meet Briggs or not. *If* she destroyed the garden earlier, why would she go back? But there's no evidence that she destroyed it, only accusations and assumptions.'

Nell was silent, hearing nothing with which she could disagree.

'The Carters have told us that she came to see them in the early afternoon,' he continued, 'and ordered them not to let the automata sing during the festival. With the Carters' alibi holding up, it would seem the limelight is on the guests at Spitalfrith or some unidentifiable person at the festival who hid in the grounds and killed her. As Lady Saddler was a newcomer to the village, the latter seems unlikely. So, these guests. What can you tell me about them, Nell? And for once, not just the facts – I want your impressions.'

At last! She tried not to sound too eager. 'As a sergeant or witness?'

'Either. Valued chief witness or valued sergeant-in-training would define them more closely.'

Nell flushed. Was Alex just compensating for his over-strict application of the 'rules' or did he mean it? 'Who first?' she asked guardedly.

'Tell me your opinion of Sir Gilbert, Sergeant.'

An easy one. 'I've too little to go on,' she replied honestly. 'He seemed devoted to his wife, who ruled the roost. He looked' – she hesitated – 'a kindly man, but out of his depth as regards both her and the Clerries.'

'The what? Ah, you mean the art movement they belong to. I thought Pierre Christophe ran it.'

'He does, but Sir Gilbert seemed to be in charge of whether or not the exhibition at the Academy of Modern Art in London takes place next year. It was going to make their fortunes before Lady Saddler threatened to cancel it.'

'Why do that?'

'Goodness knows. Petra Saddler thinks she didn't like having her portrait on general show, although she was their model.'

'Is that likely?'

'In theory.' Nell warmed to her theme. 'But the little I saw of Lady Saddler suggested she wasn't a woman for such scruples.'

'And her stepdaughter, Miss Saddler? She told me she lived in London. Unusual for a young woman, even in this day and age.'

That fired Nell up. 'I lived away from home from the age of fourteen, and anyway Petra knows just what she's doing. And she disliked Lady Saddler to the extent she wouldn't think of her as a stepmother. Now she's very worried about her father. And then there's Lord Richard,' Nell added impulsively.

'How does he come into it?'

'Miss Saddler is his latest current choice for the only girl he'll ever love. I exaggerate, of course,' Nell said demurely. 'Oh, and she isn't a Clerry herself, by the way. I expect you've gathered that.'

'What of those who are? Monsieur Christophe, for example.'

'The Magnificent Pierre,' Nell murmured. 'Founder of the Clerries, and, as he sees it, top dog.' She tried to repress a mental image of a dog on its hind legs and wearing a top hat graciously receiving tributes while dancing on the top of an iced tiered cake.

'Does he deserve that rank?'

'I couldn't tell. Certainly he acts as if he does.' Her top dog took a bow on the icing. 'Some of his paintings have Lady Saddler as model, as do those of some of the other Clerries.'

'Reduced to a couple of eyes and a stick?'

'Not always. Wait till you see Gert Radley's. But she's a reasonable human being, whereas Pierre performs his role on a stage of his own. She does,' Nell added fairly, 'have an obsession where Lady Saddler's concerned. No love lost there. From what I've been told—'

'Third-party evidence not admissible, Sergeant.'

'From what I'm *told*,' Nell repeated firmly, 'for some reason Lady Saddler destroyed Gert's portrait of her apparently out of sheer vindictiveness because she didn't like the way she was portrayed. Gert isn't – I *think* – one to kiss and make up.'

'To the extent of wanting to murder her enemy?'

'If circumstances arose perhaps,' Nell said doubtfully, then added quickly, 'given that *wanting* isn't *doing.*'

'Humbled again. What about Theatrical Thora?'

'Passionately in love with Pierre,' Nell replied promptly, 'although there appears to be some doubt about that at the moment. She's passionately in love with her own work, though. Sees herself as reigning consort of the Clerries. She's not an artist in the painting field but a poetess.'

'In the Keats line?'

'Wordsworth at his worst, perhaps.' Then she reconsidered. 'This is unfair. I don't know them well enough to pontificate. How can I tell from short chats and observation alone?' Alex was looking disappointed, she realized, and that was promptly confirmed.

'That's all I need at the moment – thanks, Nell. How about Vinny Finch?'

'He's the most sensible of them. He should be top dog in my view, but he's content not to be. I didn't see any portraits of Lady Saddler in the work displayed in his tent, though she might have appeared in some form.'

'And the exotic Lance Merryman?'

'If you judge a man by his clothes, he's off his trolley, but I feel sorry for the Lances of this world. They can't fight their own battles.'

'Are you sure about that? If something upset him perhaps, wouldn't he lash out?'

Nell thought about that. 'Yes, perhaps he would, and perhaps quite viciously.'

'To the extent of murder?'

'That's unfair.'

'Think of Charles Briggs, Nell. You're helping him by trying to answer.'

She glared at him. 'Yes,' she said finally. 'But—'

'Thank you, Nell. One last question. What's your impression of them as a bunch? That's a permissible question.'

'It's an easy answer, though,' she said promptly. 'The jelly of

the group isn't working well, as far as I can see. I know there are
a lot more Clerries in Paris, but these six, including Sir Gilbert,
are the leaders, so there ought to be some kind of jelly all the
time, but they seem separate individuals, at present.'

'Why is that, do you think? The murder?'

Another puzzle. 'Possibly, though that might have brought
them together. Or it might be because of this exhibition, which
makes them think of their individual careers. The exhibition
might now take place, perhaps, if Sir Gilbert decides to hold it.'

'But if he doesn't, would that please anyone?'

'What an odd question,' Nell replied. 'Petra Saddler perhaps?
She might secretly be pleased if the exhibition remained cancelled
as it was planned as one devoted to the Artistes de Cler. I can't
believe she would murder her stepmother for it, though.'

To her relief, Alex didn't press her on this.

'Which means,' she summed up, 'that there are several people
who would be only too happy to see Lady Saddler out of the way.
But,' she added firmly, 'Mr Briggs had no motive.' Unless she had
destroyed the singing birds, she thought, deliberately holding back
on that.

But, of course, Alex had noticed the omission. 'You're forgetting that he might have known she destroyed those automata.'

That was the weak point on which she had no comeback. Or
did she? She saw a chink of light in his arguments, one she had
lost sight of. *Careful, Nell*, she warned herself. Don't turn the
gas up too high. 'You mean that it was a spur-of-the-moment
murder?' she asked innocently.

'Yes. The timings can be worked out.'

Deep breath, Nell. 'What about the rope? How could it be a
spur-of-the-moment murder for him if he remembered and fetched
a rope from a Spitalfrith outhouse?'

Alex stopped in his tracks, the muscles in his face working
furiously, as he thought this through. 'It might do, Nell. It might
indeed. But I doubt it.'

'Why?' she cried in anguish. 'The outhouse where it was kept
is a long way from the garden.'

The muscle in his cheek was working seriously overtime now.
'But it doesn't overrule what Briggs said: "I did it."'

*   *   *

'We are,' Vinny Finch observed, 'in a difficult position.'

Someone had to answer in the silence that followed, so Gert Radley decided it might as well be her. Her four companions were clearly struggling to make a suitable response to the obvious. Well, obvious to her, anyway. Surrounded by elegance in style, furniture and paintings that had nothing to do with her own art, she was resigned to such gracious living in Wychbourne Court for as long as it took to solve the case of Lisette's murder. Her companions seemed to have seized the arrest of Lord Ansley's valet with relief, but Gert was not so sure. She was well aware that Lisette's horrific death was not the tragedy to the Clerries that it must be to poor old Gilbert, who had been besotted with that witch.

'Agreed, Vinny,' Gert replied. No point beating about the bush. 'But now that Scotland Yard has been called in, just how do we get out of the polite prison that this oh-so-courteous inspector has put us in? It seems to me we have to stay here until he turns the key and lets us out. Country palaces like this are all very well, but it's a fortress, whether we like it or not.'

Not that this garden they were lounging in represented a physical fortress, but Wychbourne was a mental one, nevertheless. Were they cooped up like chickens because they were merely witnesses to the crime? Unlikely, surely. Lisette had been murdered, and it didn't take a Sherlock Holmes to work out that the Clerries could be involved. Gert was amused when she saw the opposition even her carefully worded comments on that had caused. She didn't care a fig. Whoever killed Lisette had acted for them all, whether any of them would have gone to such extremes or not.

She looked her companions. All decent enough as a rule, but today in this unusual situation they seemed like strangers. Sunday's squabble had only been the beginning.

'Are you suggesting that we are ourselves suspects?' Thora said coldly.

'Certainly,' Gert replied promptly. 'You heard what the inspector said – that he was only conducting a brief courtesy interview to check our movements. There will be more if and when this valet's set free.'

'But, my dears, was it so very courteous?' Lance asked anxiously. 'We are *forbidden* to leave.'

Gert looked round at the mutinous faces. Trouble lay ahead; she could see that at a glance. Lance looked like a scared rabbit, Thora was adopting her Queen of the Night stance, Vinny was playing elder statesman and Pierre was clearing his throat. That indicated he was about to mount his mental throne of superiority.

'*Mes amis*, when we see him next, he will merely confirm that this Mr Briggs is guilty. It is a formality only that he speaks to us.'

Lance leapt eagerly on this interpretation. 'You're right as always, Pierre.' He was making amends for yesterday, Gert thought, highly amused.

'You are *probably* right,' Vinny conceded. 'Though I fail to see why a valet from Wychbourne Court would wish to kill one of its neighbours who has only just arrived in the village.'

'Because it was obviously Lisette who destroyed all those wooden birds that someone built in their garden,' Thora contributed. 'She had no time for art or even my poetry.'

'Lisette was killed during the night,' Vinny pointed out. 'A strange time for her to be strolling through the grounds and worrying about damaged property.'

Gert snorted. 'She was a strange lady. Scotland Yard must be here for a reason. They must think there's doubt over this valet's arrest, and if so, that inspector will soon be digging his claws in everywhere.' Should she stop there or plunge into the heart of the matter now that Vinny had led the way? Gert made her decision. 'No doubt about it. We'd be suspects. We all secretly wanted Lisette removed from our lives, if not necessarily from her own.'

The instant uproar she had expected broke out.

Pierre was outraged. '*Mon dieu!* You too accuse us?'

'Quite idiotic, Gert, darling,' Lance cried shrilly.

'Why?' Gert asked flatly, as Thora and Vinny joined the protest. 'We were all counting on the exhibition Gilbert had arranged in London, and are hoping that now she's gone he'll resurrect it.' Facts had to be faced.

'Do you think he will?' Lance asked in excitement.

'We can hardly ask Gilbert at present,' Thora said icily. 'Do try to observe the proprieties, Lance.'

Vinny had remained quiet as usual. He'd had his say yesterday, and he was always the one who thought things through before he spoke. 'You're broadly right, Gert,' he said at last. 'But you're ignoring one avenue. Have we fully explored *why* Lisette was so opposed to our exhibition?'

'She told us that at length,' Thora snapped. 'Her unhappy experiences in occupied Lille during the war.'

'And that convinced you?' he asked.

'Of course. It was a terrible time for her.'

'There might have been more to her determination to cancel it,' Vinny said. 'We wish to establish the Artistes de Cler in England as a major step towards making ourselves a worldwide movement. But it's now clear that Lisette had no such desire. Why? Because she wanted Gilbert to take his rightful place in one of the new groups of English artists – the London Group, for instance. Then she could reign as a society queen. We are all fond of Gilbert, but I'm sure you'll agree that his genius lies not in Clerry art, excellent advertisement though he is for our group—'

'*Idiot.*' Pierre stood up dramatically. 'How can you say this? You do not see the truth.'

'On the contrary. I do. Gilbert's genius lies in his very present Englishness. He achieves his effects by noticing the details of his subjects rather than by stripping them away.'

Vinny was right, Gert thought, rapidly thinking this through.

'Even if that were so, Vinny, why should that affect us?' Thora asked coldly.

'Because if the exhibition were cancelled or replaced by an exhibition of Gilbert's English work only, the whole Clerry movement would not only lose Gilbert as its figurehead but wither away.'

'*Non,*' Pierre shouted. 'Gilbert would be a great loss. But it is *I* who founded *les Artistes de Cler. I* would rebuild it.'

There might be problems with that, Gert thought, as Thora kept noticeably silent, as did Vinny, while Lance merely giggled. She, Gert, was thinking most of all about last year's Paris Exposition and of coming into her studio ready to take her masterpiece to hang it, only to find it had been destroyed. It had had paint thrown over it and then been slashed with a knife by Lisette, its inscrutable model for her greatest work. And she had thought Lisette was her friend and admirer. It was true she had painted Lisette as a solitary figure (like Kipling's Cat that Walked by Himself in Vinny's opinion), but there had been something about the resulting image that Gert could not quite grasp. The portrait had had an extra dimension that seemed to have emerged from her paintbrush unbidden. Ruthlessness! Lisette had seen it – and destroyed the whole painting.

'I doubt if even you could rebuild the Artistes de Cler, Pierre,' she said. 'We might have to become yet one more vanished Parisian art movement. You may be thinking along the right lines, Vinny. She might not have been the only one who was prepared to spoil the Clerries' glory.'

Thora gasped. 'You mean darling Gilbert supported her and didn't have the courage to tell us? That cannot be so.'

'*Chérie*, it is possible,' Pierre declared, though Gert noticed Thora blenched at the endearment. 'Always he wishes to remain so British in his work. He does not see the wider world.'

'No, not Gilbert,' Vinny said. 'Someone else.'

'Someone who would have met her late at night to discuss it, Vinny?' Gert asked, seeing where this was leading. 'Someone who then killed her? But if so, why?'

'Perhaps,' he replied, 'it was someone who only pretended to share her views.'

'You can't think that is one of us?' Lance screamed.

Even Gert was taken aback. 'It's far more likely it was someone else whom she arranged to meet that night.' But even so, she was aware that the idea had been planted. It *could* have been one of them.

Kitchens took no prisoners. They demanded your attention at all times if they were to function properly. That was the ideal, of course, but at the moment Nell congratulated herself that hers was working admirably – because that was the only way to view it. Allow the possibility of error and one was on a slippery slope. *Eh bien*, as Monsieur Escoffier would have said, tonight the Dover sole was perfection, the *charlotte* a triumph, and even the chicken *blanquette* was a delight. Mrs Fielding was mercifully absent, and Mrs Squires had the servants' high tea and supper under control. All was well. This was her own kingdom and at present it was at peace.

Never take peace for granted. In a trice it changed as Jenny Smith came in en route for the scullery, carrying a tray from Lady Ansley and carolling out, 'Any news about Charlie Briggs?'

Nell was about to tell her the position when Kitty took her attention off what she was doing at the table. 'I don't understand why they think that Lady Saddler would have come out after dark like that to talk to our Mr Briggs.'

Fatal. She forgot about the stove, a saucepan began to boil over, Kitty raced to save it and Muriel collided with her. That caused Jenny just behind her to run into both of them, with the result that Muriel lost her balance and ended up on the floor surrounded by her newly peeled peaches and shelled peas. Nell counted to a quick three and dashed to the rescue, along with the rest of the kitchen staff, resulting in more minor collisions.

Once the last pea had been tracked down, and Kitty's and Muriel's tears mopped up, Muriel ventured to tell them why she'd been in such a hurry to rush in from the scullery.

'It wasn't Mr Briggs she was meeting,' she announced. 'It was someone else.'

'What are you talking about, Muriel?' Nell asked wearily, trying to get order restored.

'I heard her say so, Miss Drury.'

'*What?*' Nell summoned up her strength. 'Let's get this straight. You heard Lady Saddler talking about her movements? How did you know it was her and not someone else?'

'It wasn't someone else, Miss Drury,' Muriel replied indignantly. 'I was helping out with the sandwiches in the kitchen at Spitalfrith Manor, and I heard her ladyship talking to someone in the room next door. The windows were open, see? I knew who she was, and I'd seen her going into the room as I arrived. She was saying she couldn't talk about such things now, but they could have a word after supper at about eleven o'clock or so.'

Nell stared at her in disbelief. 'Are you sure of this, Muriel? Were they really inside the house or outside?' It would rule out Mr Briggs if it was inside.

'She didn't say, but inside, I suppose, as I'd seen her going in there.'

So far so good. 'And who was with her?' Nell held her breath. One of the Clerries? This was looking hopeful. 'And you're sure it was *inside* the manor house?' Outside, it could theoretically have been Mr Briggs.

'Don't know. I just heard her voice and a sort of low murmur.'

'From a man or a woman?' Nell asked eagerly.

'Don't know. They was in the next room, see, so I couldn't tell. But they was inside, all right. She was talking about a meeting later on after eleven o'clock.'

'Why didn't you tell anyone before?' Nell asked in anguish. She had studied the information on the easel that she had so carefully erected and there had been no sign of this.

'It didn't fit any of your columns, Miss Drury, and anyway everyone's saying Mr Briggs has confessed.'

Muriel looked at her in appeal, and Nell hadn't the heart to rant at her or anyone else. Instead, she counted to ten and then said, 'Will you tell the police this story, Muriel?'

'Oh, yes.' Muriel beamed.

This was more like it, Nell thought. At last she had something to present to Alex. *Evidence* – in the form of Muriel – that Lady Saddler had at least one appointment late that evening, and it wasn't with Mr Briggs.

She was almost singing as she strode down the drive to the Coach and Horses. The working day would be over for Alex, but she would surely find him there. Everything would be all right.

Not everything. She had yet another battle with Frank Hardcastle. 'The inspector's in the bar, Miss Drury,' the landlord informed her.

'I need to speak to him, *now.*' She wasn't going to give him the opportunity of pointing out that the bar was men only, as well as the dining room.

'I'll tell him that, Miss Drury, and you can talk to him nice and quiet in the snug. I won't let anyone else in,' he added smugly, as though she and Alex were going to throw themselves into each other's arms the minute the door was closed. If only that were so.

Nell surrendered. After all, she had no plans to seduce the entire Wychbourne male population, so she might as well be in the snug. She fidgeted there until Alex appeared, somewhat surprised.

'Delighted to see you, Nell. Not bad news, I hope?'

'Good news,' she said happily. 'I have *evidence* to clear Mr Briggs.'

He went very still and shut the door behind him very firmly. 'Tell me.'

'I've a witness who will swear that Lady Saddler was going to meet someone else that night after eleven o'clock, and it couldn't have been Mr Briggs.'

To her disappointment, his expression remained impassive. Couldn't he share her excitement for once? 'One of the artists?' he asked. 'And where were they to meet?'

'I don't know where or who, but it was someone Lady Saddler spoke to at the house, so it couldn't have been Mr Briggs.'

'Who's the witness?'

'Muriel, one of the scullery maids.'

'I remember her,' he said to Nell's relief. 'She's scatty but reliable, I'd have thought. It's a line to follow up. Well done, Nell.'

She grinned at him. 'And now I'll have to find Lady Clarice's ghost for you,' she joked.

'Dearest Nell, what are you talking about?'

'The ghost – this happened when I was on my way to the garden earlier on Saturday evening, and Lady Clarice came flying up to me to say she'd just seen the ghost of her lost lover, Jasper.'

He stared at her in disbelief. 'You know, Nell, Wychbourne is quite distinctive. It seems to be a place where the ghosts have to be considered as suspects. Who was it really?'

'I don't know. Of course, I thought later it might have been someone who had gone to the garden and seen the destroyed birds, or perhaps the person who had destroyed them.'

'But Lady Clarice was coming from the garden herself?'

She saw his point with alarm. 'Yes, but she can't have reached it. She didn't mention the garden and so she must have turned around when she saw Jasper.'

'Not Jasper. His ghost,' he reminded her. His smile was fading now. 'Did you see anything that she could have mistaken for a ghost?'

'No, the bushes and the trees could have hidden a dozen people.'

'So why did she think this one was a ghost?'

'Because she wanted to see Jasper.'

He sighed. 'Why the dickens haven't I been told of this?' he replied, reasonably mildly. 'True, I haven't interviewed Lady Clarice, but you haven't mentioned it before – only that you went to the garden.'

'But it happened so much earlier than the murder, making it seem irrelevant,' she said in dismay.

It was obviously relevant for Alex, judging by his set face. 'Could it have been one of the Carters?'

'The cottage was in darkness by then, but I suppose it could have been,' she admitted.

He relented. 'Cheer up. For the first time ever a ghost might be giving evidence in court.'

EIGHT

A summons to the Dower House was not something to be treated lightly. When Majesty calls (or in this case the dowager, Lady Enid), one obeys, even if the raspberry *bavarois* for luncheon was still unmade. Nell prepared herself for a gruelling encounter, glad that Arthur Fontenoy, the dowager's neighbour and arch enemy (in Lady Enid's view), was away in Scotland and would not be noting this out-of-the-ordinary occurrence. He would doubtless have been highly amused at this unexpected rapport between Nell and his neighbour.

The gruelling encounter began seconds after Nell rang the bell. Mr Robins, Lady Enid's butler, must practise this stately and forbidding stance as part of his ongoing rivalry with Mr Peters, Nell decided, as the door opened and she obediently presented her name to him. No matter that they must pass each other several times a week, the ritual had to be followed.

There was no competition with Mr Robins as far as Mr Peters was concerned. He reigned in Wychbourne Court unchallenged and, as far as Nell could tell, was oblivious to Mr Robins's struggles towards equal status. The pity of it was that robins were cheerful birds but Mr Robins seemed to think that a superior glare was essential for his role – or perhaps it just came naturally to him, Nell thought, as she followed dutifully in his wake to the morning room.

'Miss Drury, my lady.'

Feeling like royalty with such pomp and ceremony, Nell

advanced as Lady Enid rose from her armchair. She looked at her most regal today, but Nell had prepared herself for battle – needlessly, because the dowager was *smiling* in welcome. What the giddy geese was this about? Nell decided to tread cautiously. It was well known that Lady Enid *never* smiled.

'I am delighted to see you, Miss Drury.' The smile grew broader. It might even turn into a laugh.

This was really alarming. Should she grin in return?

'It seems we are colleagues, Nell – if I might so address you,' the dowager continued.

Was she awake or dreaming? Nell adopted an expression of great interest and indicated that nothing would please her more.

'Chief Inspector Melbray was most grateful for the information I have been able to impart to him. A mere snippet,' Lady Enid added modestly, 'but I trust it might help the plight of Mr Briggs.'

'That's very good news,' Nell said warmly, still recovering from the shock of her welcome. Whatever this information was, thank goodness for it, though. 'Are you permitted to tell me what it was?'

'I am. I have the inspector's permission to do so. It concerns the farmer's boy who brings our milk early each morning. I am not accustomed to conversing with him, but owing to the present unfortunate situation I decided to do so. He seemed to be under the impression that I was a kitchen maid, as he demanded to know where my bottles for refilling were. I was unable to help in this matter and directed him to my tradesmen's entrance, but he then informed me that the murder of Lady Saddler was a "rum do" – I believe those were his words – and that our Mr Briggs was a wrong 'un. I disagreed, to his surprise, and he volunteered that he must have "dunnit" because he saw Mr Briggs going out early on Sunday morning about seven o'clock. The boy thought he had a funny look on his face.'

Lady Enid sat back glowing with pride – and no wonder, Nell thought. '*Sunday* morning?' she repeated. 'But that means—'

'Yes, Miss Drury. I am told Lady Saddler died in the middle of the night in the region of half past eleven or twelve o'clock. Mr Briggs, it seems to me, is highly unlikely to have either walked or bicycled to Spitalfrith in the middle of the night to commit murder, returned to Wychbourne and then decided to make another visit to the gardens at seven in the morning to see if the unfortunate woman's body was still there.'

Sometimes salvation comes in the most unlikely of guises. 'Lady Enid,' Nell said gratefully, 'you're another Lady Molly of Scotland Yard.'

'Thank you. I am not a reader of cheap novels, but I understand her exploits are much admired. I'm told that Briggs's bed was unused last Saturday night, but as my grandson Richard saw him to his room, it is quite possible that he remained seated after the shock he had received. That would explain the unused bed and his early departure the next morning.'

'You may well have proved his innocence, Lady Enid. This will surely clear him.'

'Inspector Melbray refused to comment on that aspect, but there is no doubt that it must help. For that reason, Miss Drury, I have decided it is my duty to interest myself in this affair.'

Whoa! Nell saw a red flag waving vigorously. Diplomacy and enthusiasm required. 'That could be most valuable,' she said warmly. Provided disaster didn't lie ahead, she mentally added.

'My other reason for requesting your presence, Miss Drury, is to ask for your assistance on another matter.'

Red flag waving even more vigorously. Nell waited for the axe to fall.

'My daughter Clarice, as you know,' Lady Enid continued, 'is interested in the psychic manifestations of Wychbourne Court. She has recently taken an interest in Spitalfrith Manor for the same reason and has, in my view, misguidedly approached not only Miss Saddler but, worse, Sir Gilbert. As he is naturally distraught by the loss of his wife, he has asked if you would call on him as soon as possible. He is aware that you are sympathetic to my daughter's hobby and wishes to discuss it with you.' Another smile.

Spitalfrith, bereft of its guests, presented an even more forlorn appearance, Nell thought as she rang the bell. A fine thing. Here was the chef of Wychbourne Court doubling her role, with full permission from Lord Ansley, by stepping into Sir Arthur Conan Doyle's field as a ghost enthusiast. The door was opened by Petra whose expression brightened on seeing her.

'My father is so grateful, Nell. He has something he wants to tell you that he won't even tell me. Goodness knows what. He's going off his rocker at present, but I know you'll tread carefully.'

Nell followed her up to the first-floor lounge where Sir Gilbert was sitting by a low table covered with letters and newspapers. He looked shrunken within himself as he rose to his feet, and it was clear that it was an effort for him. What could be so important about ghosts for him to worry about at this of all times?

'Good of you to come, Miss Drury,' he greeted her. 'Had a word with his lordship to ask if I could purloin you. Jolly decent of him to do without his *coq au vin*, eh?'

'Everything's ready for luncheon,' Nell reassured him, with a vision of the still-unmade *bavarois* haunting her. 'And I've two very good underchefs.'

'That's the ticket, then,' he said vaguely. 'Youngsters, eh? Get everywhere nowadays.' A pause. 'Talked to that Chief Inspector Melbray yesterday. Recommended I talk to you. Lady Enid did, too. Can't talk to my daughter – not about this.'

Odd, Nell thought. 'Is it about ghosts?' she asked carefully, when silence fell.

He looked blank. 'Ghosts? Oh, you mean that Lady Clarice. No, this isn't about her – well, yes, it is, but most of the time I can't think straight. Keep wondering who killed my wife. Doesn't seem real – I ask myself who would want to? Lovely woman like that. Done so much to help others in the war; kept us Clerries going, then comes over here and someone kills her. There's a mystery here, Miss Drury. What was Lisette doing out at that time of night? I'd retired for the night – separate bedrooms, you see. I asked myself that, then I realized the answer.'

Steady the Buffs. Nell held her breath. Sir Gilbert seemed not so much to want her views as need a good listener. That explained Alex's and Lady Enid's endorsement of her, even if it suggested that Alex assumed nothing material would come of this meeting. It might do so for her, though. Anything she could learn about the late Lady Saddler or the Clerries might help clear Mr Briggs.

'During the war Lisette used to work in the late evenings,' Sir Gilbert explained. 'As well as passing intelligence about enemy train and troop movements, she'd sing at clubs, picking up the enemy's secrets while they were squiffy. She remembered being

out in the night air when all was silent and you could see the truth
blazing out at you from the sky. That's why she liked the Clerries,
she said. You saw things clear, like the stars. That's the only reason
I can see she'd be out that late on Saturday night.'

Lady Saddler had *liked* the Clerries? That's not what she had
understood, Nell thought.

'What's more,' he continued, 'Spital Farm had all those labourers
down here for the harvest, sleeping in huts of some sort. One of
them could have killed my wife. That inspector's been asking
questions about our Clerry guests, but I don't see any of them
killing Lisette. Must have been one of those labourers. A fishy lot
of fellows.'

Glad though she was to hear that Alex was himself making
enquiries about the Clerries, questions immediately came to Nell's
mind. If Sir Gilbert was right, it still didn't explain why his wife
had been in the garden or why a labourer would kill her. There'd
been no sexual assault or robbery detected.

'Did you tell Chief Inspector Melbray your theory?' she asked.

'Too intent on his own ideas to listen to mine,' he grunted.

Now she understood. She was indeed here as a listener, but one
with a purpose. Guesswork on her part, but surely Alex would
expect her to pick up any rambling comments about anything that
might be relevant. Very well. That gave her a freer hand.

'Your wife must have been a great admirer of all your work,
Sir Gilbert, not just your work with the Artistes de Cler. It seems
odd therefore that she wanted to cancel the London exhibition
planned for next year.'

To her relief, he replied after a brief hesitation. 'Lisette said
that was for my sake. I try to see things clearly in my portraits
and other work. Look at my portrait of Lady Enid. I painted that
in 'ninety-four and yet its subject's made clear enough for it to
be a piece of Clerry work. The point is made in my approach.
Nowadays, I suppose, I should take it one step further and paint
what isn't there.' To Nell's pleasure, he chuckled. He seemed
happier now that he was back on safer ground.

'What I mean,' he continued, 'is that an artist can see the truth
of a painting, but it's not always obvious to the viewer. That's
why we need the Clerries. That's what Lisette said, anyway.
Sometimes I wonder, though, whether Petra isn't right.' He looked

directly at Nell. 'So that's what I'd like to know, Miss Drury. Did I miss anything in my drawings of Lisette? Did someone see it more clearly than I? Something took her outside late at night. What was it?'

Deep water, Nell realized, with sudden alarm. How could she answer that in any meaningful way with his eyes fixed on her so hopefully? How to help? Tell the truth. 'None of us know that, Sir Gilbert,' she replied. 'But we can all remember her and what she achieved during the war. And somehow then the truth may emerge.'

Did that make sense? Whether it did or not, he seemed somewhat comforted. He nodded.

'They say it was that valet Briggs who killed her. Do you believe that?'

'No,' Nell said.

He sighed. 'Nor I, Miss Drury. Do you know who did?'

'I don't, but Chief Inspector Melbray will find out.'

'Thank you, Miss Drury, and forgive me. I grow old and ramble. You came here to talk about Lady Clarice and her ghost. I hear you met her on Saturday night, when she thought she saw one running around the gardens.'

This was safer territory. 'She thought she saw Jasper Montjoy,' she explained. 'He was her fiancé who lived here at Spitalfrith. He died in the Boer War.'

'Then why' – Sir Gilbert looked perplexed – 'did she think the fellow turned up in my gardens that night? It can't be anything to do with my wife's death because Lady Clarice said she met him about nine o'clock. She's asked me if she can wander around our gardens as soon as possible in case he drops in again. She's afraid if she doesn't do it soon, then the fellow will get discouraged and vanish. She also thinks it might help me if this Jasper appears because he might be able to indicate who killed Lisette. I find that hard to believe, although I don't wish to stop her from going on this wander-round, however dotty it seems. But I don't think she should go alone. I'd ask Petra, but you know her better.'

'When does she want to come?' Nell asked in trepidation. Surely not tonight when she needed to prepare the menus for tomorrow.

'Tonight. His lordship's agreed.' Sir Gilbert looked at her anxiously. 'Will you go?'

She summoned up as much enthusiasm as she could manage. 'Of course.' Never had she felt less like a run through the woods in the dark with Lady Clarice. 'If we're to take the same route as last Saturday, it might be wise to let Freddie and Joe Carter know,' she suggested.

He looked blank, then must have seen her reasoning. 'Rightie-ho. I'll tell Hayward to speak to them. Dusk – that all right with you?' A pause. 'I don't have to be there, do I?'

One possible problem solved. 'No, Sir Gilbert. The fewer the better.'

'I do believe Jasper will return,' Lady Clarice declared eagerly when Nell met her in the Great Hall to set off on the Great Adventure that evening. Indeed, dressed in her jodhpurs and sun hat (for no apparent reason), Lady Clarice could almost be one of those stalwart Victorian lady travellers or, more likely, a Hollywood lady setting forth across the desert to find her very own sheikh, her own Rudolph Valentino. His death was still being lamented in the kitchen.

'And if he doesn't?' Nell asked gently, bracing herself. 'It might not have been Jasper last Saturday.'

Lady Clarice showed her impatience. 'My dear Nell, of course it was Jasper. He came because I was there, but today is the anniversary of the day we plighted our troth. I know you are sceptical, Nell, but I have the advantage over you. I know Jasper is coming, you see, so you won't upset me, however much you believe I am wrong. He'll come to our dell, our own Ash Grove.'

She began to sing the old folk song softly. 'Around us for gladness the bluebells are ringing. Ah, then little thought I how soon we should part.'

Nell's annoyance at this evening madness vanished and there were tears in her eyes. After all, she told herself, crazy though it sounded, this venture might have something to do with Lady Saddler's murder.

'Shall I drive you there, Lady Clarice?' she asked.

'No,' Lady Clarice answered firmly. 'You motor there, but I shall walk to Spitalfrith as I used to do all those years ago. I want to feel as I did when I was twenty, to walk with a song in my heart on my way to meet Jasper.'

Nell felt humbled. Lady Clarice really believed that her sweet-heart would be there to meet her. If he wasn't present, so strong was her certainty that there would, Nell hoped, be something to convince Lady Clarice of his presence.

She left her motor car on the now-familiar track behind the Spitalfrith Manor gardens and walked in past the Carters' cottage to the path that led through the woods back to the manor house. Once she had reached the point roughly near where Lady Clarice believed Jasper had appeared, she stopped to wait. No sign of Lady Clarice yet. She shivered. Late August or not, she felt cold as she stood there on the path, transported back not to the Boer War but to last Saturday's horrors. No, think about Jasper and his possible ghost. She remembered the two Oxford ladies who had visited the Petit Trianon garden at Versailles and whose subsequent book recounted a detailed description not only of the gardens as they had been in Queen Marie Antoinette's time but of the apparitions they had seen. The ill-fated queen and her ladies-in-waiting were sitting on the lawns playing at being dairymaids. Imagination or not, here at Spitalfrith it was easy to think that Jasper might appear at any moment.

At last she heard movement ahead on the path and hurried towards Lady Clarice in relief, expecting to see her at any moment.

Lady Clarice wasn't there. Nell's heart lurched. What to do? How could she, a modern woman, be terrified of what must have been a rabbit or squirrel? Not a ghost, she told herself. Or was it? Or was a murderer still stalking these woods? Be a brave little soldier, Nell, as her mother used to say. Soldiers. An even crazier thought. Was Jasper really here, straight from the Boer War over a quarter of a century ago?

Think straight, girl, Nell ordered herself. First find Lady Clarice. She must be here by now. That meant she would already be in her dell – wherever that was. It couldn't be far away, but Nell dared not call out for fear she would frighten Jasper away (in Lady Clarice's imagination). She began to explore the paths around her, ducking under tree branches and brushing against the bushes. Still nothing, save the heavy atmosphere of a wood breathing at night. At last she heard a cry – of pleasure, not fear – from somewhere not far away. Pushing her way towards the sound, she reached a small overgrown glade and there, thankfully, was Lady Clarice.

She lifted an excited face up to Nell. 'I heard him, Nell. I heard him. No question about it.'

Thank goodness. 'That's wonderful, Lady Clarice.' Don't ask her if she saw him; don't ask *anything*. Leave it to her, Nell decided. She had probably only heard Nell's own movements.

'I saw him leaving, but I didn't mind.' Lady Clarice was stumbling over her words in her excitement. 'He reached out to me from the shadows, a dark figure emerging.' She pointed along another path – and Nell froze. *It was in a different direction from the path she had taken.*

'He wanted to come closer,' Lady Clarice continued, her face full of happiness, 'but he couldn't. He was summoned back. But he *was* coming. I ran after him even though it was so dark. I heard him moving, but he vanished, so I came back here, where we had been so happy. And, oh, Nell, I am happy again.'

Heard him moving? Did ghosts make a noise? Nell pulled herself together, and tomorrow Lady Clarice too would be her normal self. But tonight had to be dealt with first, bearing in mind Lady Saddler's murder and the need for Mr Briggs's release. Could this 'ghost' have been one of the Carters? she wondered. No, it was too late in the evening, and in any case he would not have retreated. He would have spoken to Lady Clarice. It could, she supposed, merely have been a late visitor to the Carters, but it was surely too far off the beaten track for that. Poachers? The grounds didn't seem large enough to attract them.

Nell steeled herself for action. 'Would you stay here for a little while, Lady Clarice? I'll follow Jasper if you'll point out the direction he took.'

Fortunately, Lady Clarice made no objection to this obviously pointless venture. She was so daffy, Nell thought affectionately, that it probably seemed quite natural to her that the Wychbourne Court chef should be rushing through the night looking for a vanished ghost.

'I'll be quite happy here in our dell,' Lady Clarice assured her as she pointed out the route her Jasper had taken. Nell left her perched on a tree trunk and clearly looking forward to being on her own with her memories.

Nell strode along the path which led to the woods where the festival had taken place. If this ghost was a human being, he would have rejoined the main path after his brief appearance at the dell, and if a trespasser – perhaps one of casual labourers Sir Gilbert had mentioned – he would be hurrying towards the rear gate and not wafting through woods like a ghost, if she understood spectral behaviour rightly. Satisfied with this deduction, she went out through the boundary gate and debated her next move.

Silence. No birds sang. Those words were used in that Keats poem – 'La Belle Dame sans Merci'. Was that ominous, given Lady Saddler's death? Nonsense, she reasoned. The birds are asleep, as you should be, not rushing through woods like crazy. Looking up and down the track, she could see nothing in either direction to indicate someone had recently passed through. Why should there be? This track simply led to the Wychbourne road in one direction and further along by the manor wall in the other. But, she noticed, there was also a narrow footpath opposite the gate she'd just come through, which must, she calculated, lead through Spital Wood to Spital Farm and the field where those casual workers must be housed. She took it, thankful that she had remembered to bring the pocket torch with her again – not to be used on ghosts, Lady Clarice had said firmly. Ghosts disliked torches as much as candles.

Shadowy bushes and tree branches moved in the breeze, and the last patch of dying sun vanished. What on earth was she doing stumbling on tree roots and brambles along this narrow path? No ghost had appeared so far. Then a sixth sense brought her to a halt. Animals sense danger – so do humans. And she had that feeling now. Just a pricking of her thumbs, as the witches chanted in *Macbeth*. But it wasn't just her thumbs that were pricking. It was her ears. As she stood there still, looking behind and around her, the shadows of the trees grew darker, forming themselves into shapes. No, just *one* shape which launched itself at her – or so it seemed as she backed with fear. No ghost. This was a man jumping down the bank on to the road beside her.

'*Bonjour, Madame.*'

Stout-hearted women don't faint. *You're not frightened. Not you, Nell.*

'*Bonjour, Monsieur,*' she rejoined, with a creditable performance of nonchalance despite her inner quaking.

He was standing only a foot or two from her. He was not a

robber about to sharpen his knife and stick it in her, she told herself. He was not about to place two hands around her neck and squeeze. Or was he? Someone had strangled Lady Saddler. She promptly turned the torch on him.

He smiled. '*Je m'appelle* Jean-Paul Girarde.'

He was slight of build, clad in dark trousers, dark farming smock, dark hair, and was somewhat taller than her own five foot six. His lean, alert face was studying her closely. He was waiting for her to speak, and so she would.

'*Je m'appelle* Nell Drury, the chef—'

'At Wychbourne Court. *Mes amis* Joe and Frederick Carter tell me of you.'

'And Lady Clarice tells me of you.'

'*Je m'excuse?*' He looked startled.

'Lady Clarice of Wychbourne Court believes you are the ghost of her former lover, Jasper. You aren't, are you?'

'Take my hand, Madame Drury.'

Do it, she commanded herself. The hand was firm, the fingers slender, even elegant, and she began to relax. 'I believe you are not a ghost,' she told him. 'What are you doing in the Spitalfrith Manor gardens that so deceived Lady Clarice with false hopes?'

'I saw you leave your motor car by the gate and wondered where you were going. That way lies the home of my friends, so I followed you. But I am sorry for the disappointment to this Lady Clarice.'

'She won't be disappointed. She believes in you,' Nell told him. So this was the Carters' friend and all was explained. Or was it? Was it sheer coincidence he was visiting them?

'Then all is well. I have performed an illusion of a ghost without meaning to do so, although I am a magician by trade. My brother and I, we work together, but now he has gone from Wychbourne so we cannot be ghosts for Lady Clarice.'

That explained it. 'You have a magician's hands,' she said.

He bowed. 'I thank you, Madame Drury. My life is made of magic and I travel everywhere with my brother Jacques. We travelling magicians do not earn much money so we work during harvests, but now my brother has gone because the corn harvest is nearly finished.'

She steeled herself to ask the all-important question: 'Was it you whom Lady Clarice saw in the Spitalfrith gardens last Saturday night?'

'Ah. The murder of Lady Saddler, madame. I talk to my friends Joe and Freddie about it. *Non.* I am not her murderer. I was there early that evening and I went with Freddie and Joe to Madame Golding's home, Joe's sister. There we talked of those damaged birds until night fell and then we slept. My brother came to Joe's cottage to look for us, he said, but could not find us – only Mr Briggs and the smashed garden. It made my brother cry, so he went back to our hut. But it was not dark then, so he too was not Lady Clarice's ghost. Poor Lady Clarice. This is a sad world, Madame Drury.'

NINE

'Are you busy, Nell?'

Her head shot up. The truthful answer would be yes. After all, who wouldn't be termed busy with merely the sirloin to keep her eye on, the salads to be supervised, the entremets to be finalized and a praline to be made for the soufflés? With Alex standing at the kitchen doorway and her kitchen staff gawping at him, there was only one answer she could give, but it wasn't 'yes' – especially as she had intended to seek him out as soon as her morning's work was under control. Not only was she bursting to tell him about the meeting with Jean-Paul Girarde last evening, but she was hoping to hear some good news about Mr Briggs, which there must surely be after the dowager's evidence *and* Muriel's pennyworth.

She and Jean-Paul (as, to her mild astonishment, she already thought of him) had talked for some time before she returned to Lady Clarice, who was blissfully unaware that Nell had been away for a good half hour or so. Jean-Paul had told her that he had no objection to talking to the police, but his chief worry was for Freddie. He had suggested she came with him this evening to talk to the Carters as they had appreciated her earlier visit. That was news to her, but she rapidly dismissed any misgivings as to what

Alex would think about another visit. This could count as a routine visit to neighbours, and she managed to quell her pangs of doubt.

'I can spare a few minutes,' she said graciously, sweeping past Alex to lead the way, no doubt to the accompaniment of many pairs of curious eyes. 'Come into the Cooking Pot.'

'That name always makes me feel as if I'm being sized up for a stew.'

'You are, saith the Cannibal Queen,' she retorted, waving him to his usual seat, 'unless you come bearing good news.'

'Who can judge that in the circumstances? But it's partly good, at least. Briggs might be released on grounds of insufficient evidence, although—'

'*Might* be?' she broke in, taken aback, 'even with the evidence that Muriel and Lady Enid have provided?'

'Despite that, Inspector Farrell has asked for yet more time, and although it's now my case, I don't disagree with that. Their doctor is concerned that if Briggs is released but then has to be rearrested, the shock would be too great.'

Reluctantly, she saw the point. 'You'll have to pacify Lady Enid. She sees herself as Mr Briggs's saviour.'

'No doubt. The problem is that he did confess, and as yet we've no clear evidence on any other candidates.'

Pleading would get her nowhere and Nell had to battle with impatience. 'I've a new lead,' she said firmly. Seeing Alex looking suspicious, she quickly added, 'And I'm not cooking up new lines of investigation. I really have found a new witness and possible suspect.'

'*You* have?' Alex sighed. 'Difficult, Nell. Be careful.'

Not another warning! Alex must see that the last thing she wanted was to overstep that wretched boundary line between interrogating witnesses and information she just came across by chance. After all, that had worked well in previous cases, so why not now? She had a dismal feeling she knew the answer to that. Just one word: love. They were closer to each other now. Even so, there had to be some way of making it work when she had vital information for him that he might not otherwise have gathered. And that included last night's encounter.

'I was ghost-hunting with Lady Clarice last night,' she began carefully.

That at least made him smile. 'So we may indeed have a ghost in the witness box.'

'A *live* witness. A Frenchman, Jean-Paul Girarde, and his brother, Jacques, whom I didn't meet. They're friends of Freddie and Joe Carter.'

Alex's face was impassive – always a danger sign – but she'd be blowed if she'd be put off by that. He remained impassive as she told him the whole story, adding, 'Jean-Paul went with Freddie and Joe to Joe's sister's home for the night – Mrs Golding's. He stayed there with them, so he's a witness that they can't have had anything to do with the murder. And similarly nor can he.'

At least Alex was listening, although she was rewarded by seeing a frown on his face. Well, be blowed to that, too. Mr Briggs's release was more important than frowns.

'This Jean-Paul was present for some time on Saturday?'

'Yes, he went to the Carters' cottage in the early evening and found the singing birds had been destroyed. Mr Briggs was there, though. Because of the shock, he suggested they should go away for the night, but Mr Briggs said he had to return to Wychbourne because Lord Ansley would need him. He probably didn't leave, of course, because he was there when I saw him later, and he wouldn't have rushed to Wychbourne and back again. Jean-Paul remained at Mrs Golding's home overnight, but in the meantime his brother Jacques had gone to the Carters' cottage to look for him at about nine o'clock and found no one there, save Mr Briggs guarding the remains of the wooden birds. He persuaded Mr Briggs to leave (or thought he had) and he himself went back to the hut he shared with his brother on the farm. It looks,' Nell concluded, 'as though Jacques could have been Lady Clarice's ghost that night.'

'Was he a talking ghost?' Alex enquired drily.

'No.' Wasn't Alex taking this seriously? 'Lady Clarice would have told me if Jasper had said anything to her either then or last night.' Nell hesitated. 'I'm going with Jean-Paul to visit Freddie and Joe this evening. They've asked to see me. Can I tell them that the news about Mr Briggs is hopeful?'

'No, Nell.'

Just what she had feared. 'You can't prevent me from talking to people,' Nell reminded him crossly.

'I can prevent you from telling them about Briggs, though. You and I always talk in confidence, and I can't prevent you from going about your daily life. But I do have to counsel you against talking too much about the case.' He broke off, then burst out, 'Oh damnation, Nell! This situation is becoming a pickle.'

'Pickles are supposed to cheer cold meat up.'

'You, my dearest love, are not cold meat. This situation is.'

Dearest love? Nell swallowed, thrown for a moment. Briefly Alex had seemed *her* Alex, not the chief inspector of Scotland Yard. All too briefly, though. 'But everyone thinks that Mr Briggs is a murderer. I have to do what I can,' she tried to explain – in her view reasonably.

'"But" is your favourite word, Nell.'

'Only when dealing with you,' she whipped back.

He was definitely back as Chief Inspector Melbray now. Very brisk. 'Give me all the details you can about this Jean-Paul.'

'And his brother – now departed?'

'*And* his brother. Seriously, Nell, I'm grateful for this information. It may or may not have anything to do with the case, though, because Lady Saddler was definitely killed several hours later than they claim to have been there. However, Jean-Paul is certainly material to the Carters' alibis, and his brother a witness to Mr Briggs's movements. Did Jean-Paul tell you how he came to know the Carters?'

'No,' she admitted.

'Let me find out, then.'

She noted there was slight emphasis on the 'me'. 'Of course, my dearest Alex,' she murmured sweetly.

A pickle indeed. Why, though? Once Mr Briggs was released, the pickle would end for her, wouldn't it? Possibly not, Nell realized. Mr Briggs would still be Freddie's friend, and then there were the singing birds to think of. Lady Saddler had seen Freddie in the early afternoon of Saturday, and it was likely that she had destroyed the birds either then or later that afternoon, and probably in the Carters' presence. How could they have stopped her? Lady Saddler was the new lady of Spitalfrith Manor.

Didn't she, Nell Drury, have a duty to Mr Briggs, she reasoned, to help prove who smashed his friend's creations, which was possibly (probably?) connected to Lady Saddler's death? Yes, she decided. If something relevant was said during this evening's visit, she must take note of it. That couldn't bring a frown to Alex's face. Besides, despite her news, his attention would surely be on the Clerries at Wychbourne Court, once Mr Briggs had been cleared. The murderer must surely be among them as Lady Saddler was not the most popular person in their midst, judging by what she'd seen and been told. That meant there was no harm at all in her talking to the Carters – and nor could there be any harm in her picking up any more information about the Clerries, provided she didn't actually go in search of it.

She didn't have long to wait. No sooner were luncheon and advance dinner preparations under control than an imperious rap on the door of the Cooking Pot revealed no less than the dowager herself, complete with her customary long skirts sweeping the ground, the huge old-fashioned hat, the regal stance and the elegant walking cane. Lady Enid had stepped across the threshold into the servants' east wing, ushered by Mr Peters who looked as horrified as Nell by this unannounced arrival. She was bereft of words to greet her caller. Some mistake? Some frightful calamity to the family had occurred that transcended their current crisis?

'Good day to you, Miss Drury. I trust I am not delaying you in your duties?'

'No,' Nell managed to stutter. 'Do please come in.' She gave an agonized glance at the piles of papers and files adorning the table, and quickly removed the cookery books on the visitor's chair, inviting her guest to sit there.

'Thank you, Miss Drury. I have some information to impart.' Lady Enid glanced around her. 'A most pleasant room.'

'Thank you. May I offer you coffee?' The dowager – to her amazement – having accepted, Nell rang the order through to the stillroom, thinking how times had changed. Here were a marchioness and a former barrow girl meeting on apparently equal terms.

'Thank you. Investigations are more arduous than I had imagined. Let me come speedily to the point, Miss Drury. Unless Mr Briggs is charged with Lady Saddler's murder before tomorrow – and from the evidence I have myself supplied to the police, that is highly unlikely – the inquest on the murder will take place tomorrow, Friday. I am most anxious that Mr Briggs does not have to undergo more ordeals.'

There was a pause as the stillroom maid struggled to deliver coffee to Nell's hastily cleared table, and then Lady Enid continued, 'However, an inquest might well lead to a verdict of, in effect, death by an unknown murderer, which leads to the supposition that one of our current guests here at Wychbourne Court is guilty. I have therefore decided to assist the police further.'

She sat back, and Nell almost applauded, since Lady Enid's proud figure seemed to demand it. This offer might herald trouble, however. Even the dowager couldn't directly interrogate the Clerries either about themselves or each other, though admittedly she was in a better position to do so than Nell herself. Nell might harbour her suspicions of the supercilious Pierre Christophe – too high and mighty not to be hiding something – but so far neither he nor any of the other guests seemed to be stepping out of the shadows into the role of murderer. Furthermore, she had to bear in mind that Alex would already be hot on their trail if they did.

'That's very generous, Lady Enid,' she managed to say.

The dowager inclined her head in acknowledgement. 'You are an excellent investigator yourself, Miss Drury, but I realize there are limits to how much you can achieve from a practical point of view. Time is of the essence, however, and the thought of the Ansley family sheltering a murderer under our roof is not a pleasant one.'

'Such work might be awkward, even dangerous, for you, Lady Enid,' Nell said doubtfully.

'You are correct, Miss Drury, but I do not propose to arm myself with a magnifying glass to pursue evidence in dark corners. I have other methods. I have checked our guests' movements on the evening and night in question. I believe the word is "alibis".'

'The police will be covering that angle,' Nell ventured to say.

'No doubt. However, I suggest that I am more diplomatic than they.'

Diplomatic? The dowager? Nell tried to look gravely approving, while battling with a mental image of Alex informing Lady Enid that she had no right to insist on checking guests' alibis. The glorious thing was that Alex couldn't do anything about it. She would do what she wished. A dowager marchioness, who was the mother of Lord Ansley, a valued member of the House of Lords and of every gentlemen's club in London, could do as she wished unhampered by mere chief inspectors.

'That's a very good point, Lady Enid,' she said.

'I am glad you agree, Miss Drury. Let me convey my discoveries to you so far.'

'You've already approached them?' Nell was astonished.

'Certainly. You may note down what I have to say. No doubt the police have much of this information but if there is need of it, then they may confirm it with me. Meanwhile, I trust it assists your own determination to clear Mr Briggs's name.'

'Thank you, Lady Enid.' Nell meant it. This was manna from heaven. Alex would have her guts for garters if she carried out direct investigation work on the Clerries, and she had been doing her best to hold back on that score in view of Alex's 'rules'. She had been hopeful, but not optimistic, that talking to the Carters would bring forth clues to what had really happened that night. Now she was a collaborator with the one person who could approach the Clerries without comment. Trouble there might be, but it would be unlikely to stem from Alex.

'First,' Lady Enid began, 'Mr Vinny Finch. He informed me he saw Lady Saddler leaving the manor house shortly after eleven o'clock that evening, when he himself returned there after a walk in the grounds. He thought this strange and mentioned it to Mrs Hayward, the Spitalfrith housekeeper, when he saw her clearing the supper dishes some ten minutes later. She had no idea as to why Lady Saddler should be going out as Sir Gilbert had already retired. Mr Finch then retired, too. Thus, Miss Drury, that establishes the time Lady Saddler left and Mr Finch's own movements.'

'That's very helpful,' Nell murmured, scribbling furiously, while Lady Enid studied her own notes with the help of her lorgnette.

'Monsieur Christophe and his fiancée were strolling in the gardens,' Lady Enid continued, 'and retired to their rooms some time before midnight. They saw no one while they were in the gardens. A vague alibi, Miss Drury, and perhaps suspicious in view of the fact that . . .' Lady Enid paused before adding, 'I confess, I am not certain of the etiquette of such frankness concerning one's own guests.'

'In these circumstances, normal etiquette should be abandoned, especially in the interests of helping Mr Briggs.' Nell crossed her fingers that this would be sufficient.

It was, for Lady Enid continued gravely, 'I agree, Miss Drury. I say suspicious where Monsieur Christophe is concerned as there seems to me to have been a change where he and Miss Thora Huntley-Doran are concerned. They are not the devoted couple they seemed to be at Saturday's festival. What, I wonder, has occurred to cause this?

'Then there is Miss Radley,' she continued, 'a most extraordinary lady who clads herself in *trousers*. She declares she retired to her room not long after half past ten on Saturday and did not leave it again that night. She claimed to have been reading *War and Peace*, which I consider most unlikely unless she has Bolshevik tendencies. She did, however, impart the news that she overheard quarrelling in the library as she retired for the night, and believes that the combatants were Lady Saddler and Mr Lance Merryman.'

'Did he confirm that?'

'Mr Merryman is a most strange person. Very *artistic*. At first, he denied being in the library, but under my persistent questioning he admitted he was. He discussed with Lady Saddler, he conceded, a matter that concerned all the Artistes de Cler. He was speaking for them all in declaring the importance of this exhibition that has apparently or would have been cancelled. He informs me that Lady Saddler was very reasonable on the subject and said perhaps she would reconsider. He was not sure what time she left. He thought about shortly after eleven, and he himself retired immediately afterwards.'

'Without breaking this good news to his comrades?' That seemed unlikely.

Lady Enid looked at her approvingly. 'Without doing so. Suspicious, do you not think, Miss Drury?'

'Everyone's a suspect until proven otherwise,' Nell said fairly. None of these alibis seemed watertight, but then wasn't that true of life? Innocent people didn't foresee having to keep notes on the exact time of their movements. Even so, it was very valuable information to consider in the light of having a complete picture of what happened that night. 'You have accomplished so much, Lady Enid,' Nell continued. She meant it. 'How did you persuade them to tell you all this?'

The dowager looked surprised. 'I spoke to them one by one, explaining that Wychbourne Court would not wish to be sheltering a murderer, and therefore I needed to be sure that no suspicion could fall on them.'

And what would Alex make of *that* approach? Nell laughed. 'You are a true diplomat, Lady Enid.'

'Thank you. Sir Gilbert was amused when I told him. Sir Gilbert is a dear man. Quite unlike my neighbour, Mr Fontenoy.' She fixed Nell with a gimlet eye. 'We are fortunate that he is still away in Scotland.'

Mr Briggs had confessed. '*I did it.*' Every time it came back to those three tiny words – and for all the tea in China, Nell couldn't think why he uttered them. *Buck up, woman*, she chided herself. *Get a move on*. Suppose a recipe didn't work. She would do her best to save it, wouldn't she? Then, if that failed, she'd go back to the beginning and start all over again. So what was the beginning here?

It was Constable Robin Gurney.

It was he who had heard Mr Briggs's confession, and like everyone else she had every faith in Constable Gurney. She knew he wouldn't be making it up or making a mistake over it. That would be exactly what he had heard. And yet she longed to hear him say it again. There just might be something she could gain from that. But if Alex discovered that she had sought him out for that reason, he would *not* be congratulating her on her initiative. So what could she do?

Think, Nell, think. Robin Gurney lived at home with his widowed mother. Nell knew Mrs Gurney as she sometimes came to Wychbourne Court. She took in needlework that was beyond Jenny Smith's skills or available time. There could be no harm in going to see Mrs Gurney – and perhaps take a few Victoria plums just coming into season or a peach or two with Mr Fairweather's grudging permission.

The Gurneys lived in Mead Lane. Robin's father had been a bootmaker, and since his death, Robin had used his light and airy business room at the front of the cottage for his own police work. His prominent position would then be off-putting for anyone with crime on his mind – or so he argued. Wychbourne had little petty crime, fortunately.

Mid-afternoon would be the right time to call, Nell decided – a time when Robin would be in his office, barring emergencies, Mrs Gurney would have finished her morning shopping and the Ansleys' dinner would be nicely advanced.

Mrs Gurney escorted her to the rear parlour where Nell duly handed over her gift, which was well received except for a slight snort over one over-ripe plum. 'You must have your hands full with the comings and goings over this murder,' Nell remarked conversationally, taking care that Robin could hear her from his office.

Mrs Gurney beamed. 'Quite the star he is, my Robin.'

Robin popped his head out of his office. 'Afternoon, Miss Drury. Did you see the photograph of me in the *Sevenoaks Times*?'

'My Robin was the first to find the body, poor lady,' Mrs Gurney said proudly.

'Apart from Mr Briggs,' Robin said rather reluctantly. 'But I was there. You remember, Miss Drury. You came along afterwards. I saw all them broken birds and flowers around and Mr Briggs standing in the middle, so I walked up to him to say, "What's all this?" And then I saw the body, dead. I knew what to do – felt for a pulse, checked if she were breathing. Nothing. She was a goner. Looked familiar, though I wasn't too sure. I said to Mr Briggs, "What's all this, then?" He didn't seem to be acting normal – looking all of a mizmaze, he was. Suppose he would be as he'd just strangled her. So I says to him again: "What's all this?" Says nothing. "How did it happen?" I asks. Says nothing. He didn't say nothing for a minute or two, just kept looking around as though I wasn't there and nor was the dead body. And then he says it: "I did it." "Did what?" I asked, being careful like. But he just said it again. "I did it." Poor chap. Not in his right mind at all. So I has to go up to the house to notify them of the occurrence in their grounds and telephone the guvnor at Sevenoaks. Then there was a lot of screeching when they realized who it was. Lady Saddler herself, poor lady. So I took off my cap in reverence.'

'You always was a good boy, Robin,' his mother said fondly.

So he was, and that meant there was no doubt about it, Nell thought dismally. That's just what Mr Briggs had said. 'Are you giving evidence at tomorrow's inquest?'

'I am,' Robin said proudly. 'So I ain't been telling you nothing you wouldn't hear tomorrow.'

Are we downhearted? Nell muttered to herself as she left. Yes, she was. She'd learned nothing new. Perhaps – hope crept back – she might this evening, though. Jean-Paul would be present at the Carters' cottage tonight, and she might even get a handle on who did kill Lady Saddler.

Seven o'clock dinner for the Ansley family (and guests!) had never passed so slowly. Nell watched on edge as the plum pudding received its rum zabaglione accompaniment, and finally she could leave. She motored up the track in the evening sunlight, her optimism returning. By the gate stood Jean-Paul awaiting her, and she had a sudden doubt. She had thought of him as a friend, but was he a foe? Could she trust what he said? There was no way of knowing, especially given his profession. Where conjurers were concerned, one concentrated so much on what that smiling face was telling you that one didn't notice the magic working. Friend he might be, she decided cautiously, but he was here with a purpose. From witness would he pass on to being suspect? Nothing like taking the bull by the horns . . .

'Why did *you* want me to come this evening, Jean-Paul?' she asked as he took his place beside her in the Ford.

He was clearly amused. 'To see justice done, Miss Drury. I am a magician. I am Houdini. I want to free Mr Briggs from bondage.'

Very smooth, she thought. Alex or no Alex, she could probe a little further. 'How did he seem when you saw him on Saturday night?'

'*Désolé.* Those poor birds, all dead, so sad. I tell Freddie and Joe they must go away for the night to recover from the shock and tomorrow we would find out who did this. But I told you that Mr Briggs would not come, and when my brother arrived, he was still here. The police are trying to find poor Jacques now. I know my brother will be scared if they do. I have given the policemen a photograph of us both together, so he will know that I have given it to them and that there is nothing to fear. That policeman *Monsieur l'Inspecteur* Melbray asked me for it. He is very polite, that one.'

'How long have you known Freddie and Joe?' she asked, as

they left her motor car on the track and walked through to the Carters' cottage.

'For some years now.'

'During the war?'

'After.' He held open the gate for her. '*Voilà*, Miss Drury, we are here.'

Was she imagining it or was he glad that he had to say no more as Joe opened the door and took them into the room she had visited before? Freddie was at the table, with a glass of what looked like cider before him. At first everything looked normal enough – but nothing *was* normal at the moment, Nell reminded herself.

'Freddie and me, we got something to tell you, Miss Drury,' Joe barked at her once they were all seated and he'd offered cider all round. 'Police been to see us, they have. You tell her, Freddie.'

Freddie nodded vigorously, reached out across the table and touched her hair gently, but he said nothing.

Nell sat very still. 'What did you want to say, Freddie? Is it about last Saturday?' There was tension in the room, but it wasn't coming only from her.

'Marie-Hélène,' he said.

His sweetheart, the one who had died, she remembered. She made a guess. 'Does my hair remind you of her?'

He nodded, then looked at Jean-Paul.

'Charlie Briggs, Corporal, Tenth Battalion, God Save the Queen's Own the Royal West Kents,' Freddie blurted out. Then he gave her a huge grin.

'What I have not yet told you, Miss Drury,' Jean-Paul said calmly, 'is that Marie-Hélène was my sister.'

So that explained it. That's what the connection was – and perhaps Mr Briggs knew her too if he was in the same battalion as Freddie.

'I heard about Freddie after the war ended,' Jean-Paul said. 'I was a prisoner of war and my brother in the army. When at the war's end we returned to Beaudricourt in northern France where our sister lived with our aunt, my aunt told us that Marie-Hélène was dead. She was killed some distance away in the ruined town of Bapaume in 1918. My aunt told us also of Freddie who wrote letters to her, and now we have met him.'

It sounded so matter-of-fact as Jean-Paul told the story, but Nell could well imagine the horrors that lay behind it. 'It's a tragic story,' she said soberly. 'I'm so sorry. Is that why you wanted me to come here this evening?'

'No,' Joe said immediately. 'It's them birds. Her ladyship Saddler destroyed them, didn't she, Freddie?'

No answer.

'She came here that afternoon to make trouble,' he continued. 'Said she didn't want no memories of war in her home, not like Freddie done for Marie-Hélène with those birds of his. Told us we'd have to go – she'd see to that. Them birds and us. We reminded her too much of what she'd gone through. Turned out of me own home, after I been here at Spitalfrith for forty years or more. I told her we'd talk to Sir Gilbert about that, not her. She weren't pleased, she weren't, so she told us she'd come back later and smash all the birds. Nothing we could do about it, was there, Freddie?'

'And she did come back?' Nell asked, the words dropping into a weird silence she couldn't understand.

Then the silence was broken. Freddie leapt to his feet, tears pouring down his face. 'No, Pa. It was me.'

'No, Freddie,' Joe shouted. 'You got it wrong, lad.'

'It was *me*, Pa. I smashed them up. I did it. All the little birds gone, gone.'

TEN

Nell sat bolt upright. Outside was a sky still full of stars, around her was the familiar combat zone of her bedroom, but her mind was crystal clear. She had come to bed last night dejected, puzzled and horrified. There had been no chance to talk to Jean-Paul further. He had slipped away even before she reached the gate of the Carters' cottage, and she had driven back to Wychbourne alone. Where lay the truth? *Had* Freddie destroyed the birds himself or was he confused? Could it even be that Mr Briggs had indeed killed Lady Saddler, because he *thought* she had destroyed the birds?

Now she knew the answer and it was, oh, so simple. Freddie had said 'I did it', and Mr Briggs had also said 'I did it'.

She tried to temper excitement with logic. Mr Briggs had been standing by Lady Saddler's body among the ruins of the garden, gazing around him, when PC Gurney had come across him. Gazing *around*, not down. Mr Briggs was still living partly at least in the past and the horrors of the trenches were still with him. Mr Briggs was used to seeing bodies, used to seeing his friends torn apart, as well as strangers. Lady Saddler was a stranger to him, and, in the light of his war experiences, her death, however terrible, might have meant little to him. He had been gazing not at her but at the garden he must have known so well, whose destruction he could see all around him. Freddie could well have told him that it was he, not Lady Saddler, who was responsible for it – and in all probability he had used those exact words – 'I did it.'

Could Mr Briggs therefore be thinking of the real crime being not Lady Saddler's death but – in his mind – the killing of those birds, and that's why he repeated Freddie's words to Robin Gurney: 'I did it'? He'd meant the birds, not the murder.

She realized she had already swung her feet to the floor, ready to dash out to tell someone, tell *anyone. Don't be daft, Nell*, she told herself. *It's the middle of the night and you might be muddle-minded. There's nothing can be done now. You need sleep before you tackle Alex.*

But sleep was fitful. Alex's image was uncomfortably close, leading to much tossing and turning, and by the time she was ready for the day and sufficiently free of her kitchen duties to go in search of him, she was on edge and already questioning her own theory. Perhaps this preoccupation with Alex was affecting her work too, because it seemed to her that the atmosphere in the kitchen held less than its usual amiable spirit, even though it was periodically laced with brief outbursts. Imagination on her part, surely. Anyway, she had to do her best for Mr Briggs. The inquest was to be held today, and Alex would pay short shrift to her story with that on his mind. Nevertheless, her theory refused to be banished.

By the time she reached the Coach and Horses, it was late morning. Kitty and Michel had cast mutinous glances at her for deserting the ship of supervising luncheon, and as she hurried down the drive to the inn, her theory seemed full of holes and spongy. As she arrived, she spotted Alex sitting at a table outside and was almost persuaded to abandon her mission, but she pulled herself together. After all, Wellington must have felt much the same when he was about to face Napoleon at Waterloo, but then she reminded herself that Wellington had required help before he won Waterloo.

And then Alex looked up and smiled, and Wellington charged straight into battle, help or no help. Words tumbled out in what seemed to her a disorderly and incomprehensible jumble, but remarkably Alex seemed to be considering it seriously.

Eventually, he said, 'If you're right and he was repeating Freddie Carter's words, how do you *know* that Freddie Carter was talking about the birds when he said "I did it" to you yesterday, let alone whether he said that to Briggs. He might have meant both the birds and Lady Saddler, or that he had killed Lady Saddler because he thought *she* had destroyed them, not Freddie.'

Nell fought for a reply. 'To Freddie, as well as to Mr Briggs, the birds would have been more important than anything else. You've seen how badly they're both war-damaged. And anyway, Lady Saddler's death took place about half past eleven at the earliest, when both Freddie and his father were absent.'

Alex sighed. 'To follow your line, we'd be relying on evidence from interested parties – Jean-Paul Girarde, Freddie's father and Joe's sister. And since presumably Mrs Golding didn't remain awake all night to count her guests in and out, any of them could have nipped back to Spitalfrith, killed Lady Saddler and have been back well before dawn.'

This was surely like King Alfred sitting twiddling his thumbs while the cakes burned, Nell thought crossly. Surely Alex could see how it all happened. 'There's Jean-Paul's brother Jacques, too. He might have seen more than Jean-Paul has told us.'

'I've talked to your Jean-Paul and set up a general search for the brother. We'll have plenty of posters around in the area with that photograph of them both. Even so, if Monsieur Girarde is correct in what he told us, the brother was also there too early last Saturday evening to be of much use in clearing Briggs. Therefore, on the whole, Nell, your evidence is helpful but it won't stand up before a judge.'

'Then the judge would be an idiot,' Nell declared and promptly regretted it.

Alex stiffened. 'I have to think of the law first. I'll certainly look into your theory and add it to the other evidence that makes it less likely that Briggs is guilty, but it's still a weak case. I'll talk to Freddie Carter again, too.'

'May I come?' she asked instantly. 'He must be scared of you. He's more comfortable with me.'

Alex hesitated. 'That wouldn't work,' he decided. 'I'll take my sergeant, if you're worried. He was in the war himself.'

'I won't intervene,' she pleaded. 'But I'm sure Freddie would be more relaxed if I was there.'

'His father will be present.'

'But he'll be prejudiced – he had no liking for Lady Saddler.'

'Very well.' Alex still looked very unwilling. 'But stay silent. We'll go right away and I'll drive you there in the Arrol-Johnston. I've parked it in their courtyard. There's just about time to get there and back before the inquest.'

When the stately old heap (Nell's opinion of Alex's beloved motor car) arrived at Spitalfrith, there was no sign of Freddie either in the workshop or in the front garden, but Joe came out of the nearest workshop, attracted by the noise and looking belligerent.

'I be working.'

'I too,' Alex said pleasantly. He was using his chief inspector's voice, Nell noted. 'I'd like to speak to your son.'

'He's not here.' Joe moved the fork he was carrying to his right hand as if ready for action.

'I can see that. Would you take me to him, please? I'd like you to be present,' Alex added.

That had some effect, for, with muttered grumbles, Joe led the way into the cottage.

'Freddie, where you got to?' he yelled. 'Copper to see you.'

There was no reply, and Joe lumbered up the stairs, reappearing to say, 'No sign of him, Mr Copper.'

'Try again,' Alex said.

This time a still surly-faced Joe reappeared with Freddie some paces behind. Freddie took one look at them and turned away to run upstairs again.

'He's a friend, Freddie,' Nell called out, despite Alex's glare at her. Freddie stopped, though.

'I want to ask you about Charlie Briggs,' Alex began.

'He be in prison.' Freddie came down a few steps.

Neither he nor Joe, though, showed any signs of moving away from the staircase – obviously Joe's method of getting rid of them quickly.

'That's right, Freddie,' Alex said. 'Do you want to help him?'

He brightened up, nodding his head. 'Yes.' He still looked nervous.

Alex tried again. 'Miss Drury tells me you said that it was you who destroyed all your birds – the wooden automata that you carved.'

'No,' Joe intervened, 'he never did. What you talking about, Miss Drury? He never said nothing like that. It were her ladyship.'

'You did say you'd killed the birds, didn't you, Freddie?' Nell asked him, forgetting her promise not to speak.

'Miss Drury!' Alex said warningly.

'I did kill 'em.' Tears were beginning to roll down Freddie's cheeks again. 'But she never done it.'

'Who, Freddie?' Alex asked sharply. 'Lady Saddler?'

Freddie stared at him in puzzlement. 'Marie-Hélène.'

'You keep your mouth shut, Freddie,' Joe shouted. 'I told you, didn't I, you was wrong. It's the birds. Her ladyship smashed them up.'

'Freddie?' Alex intervened, seeing him about to rush back upstairs again. 'Tell me about Marie-Hélène.'

Freddie stopped, and Nell had to struggle not to speak.

'Freddie don't know what he's talking about,' Joe snarled. 'You're on the wrong track, mister. It were her ladyship did for those birds. Threatened us in the afternoon, went and got a hammer, come back and destroyed it all.'

'What time?' Alex asked sharply.

'Maybe four o'clock.'

'Were you here then?'

'Had to watch her do it, didn't we? Nothing you can say to a woman like her.'

Freddie was sobbing now, but Alex calmly pushed on. 'I'm not here primarily about the birds, Freddie, but about Lady Saddler's death. Did you and Mr Briggs punish her for killing the birds?'

Nell let out an involuntary cry, quickly stifled.

'No, he didn't,' Joe yelled.

Freddie was looking very scared now. 'Her ladyship come here. Told me she done it,' he faltered.

Joe jumped in quickly. 'That's right, Freddie. She done it all right. Smashed all the birds.'

Nell saw Alex's face muscles working furiously, but his voice remained calm. 'What did Lady Saddler do, Freddie? And who is Marie-Hélène?'

Again, it was Joe who answered for him. 'Freddie's all mixed up. This Marie-Hélène's nothing to do with nothing. She was his sweetheart in the war and she were the sister of that Jean-Paul and his brother. Jean-Paul come here to see Freddie, and now Freddie's all mixed up over her ladyship. It was her done it, all right. Isn't that so, Freddie?'

Freddie nodded. 'Marie-Hélène never did it, but I killed the birds.'

'You said just now that her ladyship destroyed them,' Alex said.

'I did it,' Freddie said miserably. 'Because I thought she did it.'

No, no, *no.* There was something very wrong here, Nell thought, but Alex pressed on. 'Are you saying you killed Lady Saddler?' he asked.

Nell could bear it no longer. 'He's thinking about Marie-Hélène,' she cried.

'Miss Drury!' Alex warned her.

'Germans, spy,' Freddie wailed.

Marie-Hélène was a spy? Nell was horrified. Had Freddie been betrayed by her?

'I told you he was all mixed up over the war,' Joe shouted, glaring at them. 'The war ain't nothing to do with this, Freddie. That woman just didn't like your birds, did she?'

'Thank you,' Alex said quietly. 'I'll leave it there.'

What to say? Alex was silent as they walked to his motor car to return to Wychbourne. Very well, she would break the silence, Nell decided.

'Did it strike you that it was odd that Joe Carter kept insisting it was Lady Saddler who destroyed the birds, even though he gave himself and Freddie a motive for killing her?'

A silence, and then he replied, 'Perhaps he had some other reason. And perhaps he knew he and Freddie were safe.'

'How? Their alibi isn't very strong.'

'Because we know now that the body had been moved to the garden from the Spitalfrith grounds, we can be fairly sure that neither he nor Freddie could have killed her, weak alibi or not.'

'*What?*' Nell blinked. 'But is that established? Why didn't you tell me?'

Alex stopped the motor car with a jerk. 'Nell, we've reached an impasse,' he said at last. 'The answer to your question is that there's no reason I should have done.'

'But I thought—' Nell broke off, aware that this was dangerous territory, yet smarting at the realization that he hadn't told her, even though it must surely affect Mr Briggs's position.

'And I thought we'd agreed you should remain silent.'

'But Freddie was getting confused.'

'Only in your opinion – it's my job to work out what he means.'

'But you're a policeman and he's frightened.'

'Again, in your opinion.' He slumped back in the seat. 'It's not going to work, Nell.'

She knew immediately where they were heading. Make amends. 'I'll steer clear of your case once Mr Briggs is back.'

'Even if you did, it wouldn't work,' he said despairingly. 'I love you, Nell. No doubt about that, but you'll forever be wanting to go further in this case or any others that occur in the future. I'd have to shut you out completely, and we've gone too far along the road for me to do that, both in former cases and now this one.'

She tried to keep her voice steady. 'Too far? Are you saying goodbye, Alex?' Surely he couldn't mean that.

'I can't go on,' he said flatly. 'It's hard enough being with you without being lovers, but to fall out like this over a case is proof that our being together always wouldn't work. Don't make it worse, Nell.' He mustered a smile. 'You know the old poem: "Since there's no help, come let us kiss and part." Only I don't think today I can manage the kiss. I don't know where it would end. For some damned reason we decided not to marry or sleep together until we had solved the problem of trying to keep love and work separated, and we haven't done that. Perhaps that's just as well.'

Nell stumbled out of the motor car and ran back to Wychbourne Court, not looking back. Just reach the haven of home. Old poems? Yes, she remembered the one Alex had quoted to her, and now she never would be in his arms and in his bed. She'd left it too late. The stew had gone off the boil, the jelly had melted and the cocoa was cold. She felt like a dishcloth wrung inside out. Was she crying? She seemed to be. *Fight it*, she thought desperately. This was her own fault, and she had to face that. No, not fault, she amended. Decision. But now she had to live with it. Sweet heaven, how could she do that? Work? Cook? Yes, she could do that. And better, she could do her utmost to ensure that Mr Briggs was freed. She clutched at this straw and how to do it. *Concentrate*, she ordered herself.

She made the effort. Apart from Freddie and Joe Carter, Alex would be studying the case against the Clerries or the familiar line of the stranger wandering in from the street. Did Jean-Paul and Jacques Girarde count? If only she had – no! Back to the Saddler case. The brother had no alibi, though Jean-Paul did. Something to be looked at there. Was it a coincidence that they were working at Spital Farm at the same time as the Clerries' visit? She thought of Freddie's terrified statement that his sweetheart had worked for the Germans. Could it be that Lady Saddler had come to tell Freddie that Marie-Hélène was a traitor – and that's why he had smashed the birds he had so lovingly created in her memory?

Then she remembered the inquest due to begin shortly. How could she go now? But how could she not, if she was to continue trying to help Mr Briggs? Go, her head told her. Her heart disagreed but lost the battle, and Nell steeled herself as she went back down the drive once more. She comforted herself that the inquest would take her mind off Alex as she wouldn't be sitting near him. He would be talking to his fellow police officers anyway, and she could hide herself in the public seating towards the rear of the upstairs hall in the Coach and Horses where such events were always held.

Once she was tucked in there, the pain seemed easier to bear. The rituals of the arrival of the coroner and the formalities that followed were familiar to her, which meant she could watch with some detachment as the coroner's entry heralded the opening of the proceedings. Even the witnesses and speeches failed to engage her, although she was jerked into awareness when Constable Robin Gurney recounted his story.

'Why had you gone to the garden where you found the body?' the coroner asked him.

'Miss Petra Saddler telephoned me, sir, at half past seven in the morning to say that her stepmother was missing and her bed had not been slept in. I inspected the grounds first, sir, and heard a wailing sound coming from beyond the gardener's fence. "What's all this?" I asked myself, so I went in and there was Mr Briggs. Said nothing he did, when I shouted out to him, so I went up to him and saw the body. "Crikey," I said, "what's this?" He said he did it, so that was that.'

And on and on went the evidence, including the fact that, as Nell now knew, the body had been moved after death. There was no sign of Mr Briggs in court, though. A doctor gave evidence that he was not well enough to attend, which was bad news. He must be suffering torments in prison. She heard that a wheelbarrow had been discovered in the 'jungle' woodland, a piece of rope taken, a lady's sandal found – surely a rather obvious clue to be left, Nell thought. The police doctor gave evidence that Lady Saddler had died as a result of asphyxiation with a rope ligature. Joe Carter was called, but not Freddie (had Alex arranged that? she wondered). Joe's sister, Mrs Golding, a gentler version of Joe, was also called. Then the Clerries trooped to the witness stand, one by one.

So far nothing seemed to be helping Mr Briggs's cause, and Nell's depression increased. Then Jean-Paul Girarde came to the stand, and Nell was instantly alert. She hadn't noticed him in court, but there he was, formally clad in a lounge suit, looking quite different to the lithe, lean, unconventionally clad figure she'd grown used to.

He testified that he had stayed last Saturday night at Mrs Golding's home with Joe and Freddie, and that to the best of his knowledge his brother had visited the Carters' cottage that evening at about nine o'clock or perhaps a little earlier and, finding only Mr Briggs there, had returned to their farm accommodation. So far this was roughly what Nell already knew.

But there was more. '*Mon frère* Jacques returned to the manor gardens. He hoped still to find us as he was upset about the damage to our friends' birds. We were not there, but coming through the woods where the festival was held, he found Lady Saddler's body. She was dead. This was about twelve o'clock that night.'

Nell shared the general gasp in the hall. This was news, indeed. Jean-Paul had made no mention of this to her. Nor, it seemed, to Alex. By peering round the people in front of her, she could see that it was news to him, too. How would that fit in with the Clerries' alibis so carefully gathered by Lady Enid?

'My brother,' Jean-Paul continued, 'knew Lady Saddler, so he took her body to the garden of the birds and left her there.'

Nell couldn't believe she was hearing this. Nor, it appeared, did the coroner.

'Why would he do that?' he asked calmly.

'He did not like Lisette Rennard – Lady Saddler.'

'That,' the coroner said, 'does not explain your brother's actions.'

If this had been a trial, the coroner's questions would surely not be allowed, Nell thought, but here it was possible, even though – looking at Jean-Paul's face – it was clear he had planned to hold this back until now. This was no outburst of emotion. The emotion was being shown by the audience, particularly, Nell noted, by the Clerries, perhaps feeling protective towards Sir Gilbert.

'He – we – believed her responsible for our sister's death during the war in France.'

Marie-Hélène. The sister who had died and had worked for the Germans. Is that *why* she had died? Because Lady Saddler discovered and warned her fellow citizens? But Marie-Hélène lived in a place called Beaudricourt, not Lille where Lady Saddler was working. Nevertheless, that might have been the reason she had called on Freddie and Joe in the afternoon of the day she died. Nell felt dizzy with this new slant on the case – and with the realization that Jean-Paul seemed to have been holding back on her. Worse, it looked as though he'd been keeping information from Alex, too.

'And where is Mr Jacques Girarde now?' the coroner enquired in measured tones.

'I do not know,' Jean-Paul said. 'He is a wanderer. I shall find out what I can.'

'Please do that. And I suggest, Chief Inspector Melbray, that you do likewise.'

* * *

'Are you all right, Miss Drury?' Kitty ventured.

'Of course.' Nell managed a smile.

'It's just that you've put salt into the gooseberries, instead of sugar.'

Nell gazed into the saucepan with horror. Yesterday hadn't been the best of days, but at least she should be paying attention to her job. Her *real* job, as chef. A fine mess she was making of her detective efforts. What would Monsieur Escoffier have said if he'd seen her at work this morning? There was still time to change gooseberries for plums – or perhaps figs? That was lucky, but less fortunate was that, to her frustration, Mrs Fielding had bustled into the kitchen, obviously with the intent of conveying important news that only she had been worthy of receiving.

'The guests are staying on,' she announced. 'All five of them. They'll require luncheon and dinner.'

Down the drain went Nell's hopes of making today's delivery of fish suffice until Tuesday, with no fishing on a Sunday to provide a Monday delivery.

'Has Inspector Melbray asked them to stay?' she asked.

A tart reply. 'That I wouldn't know, Miss Drury. Perhaps you should ask him yourself.'

'Yes, perhaps I should.' If only she could, but there had been no word from Alex – only silence after a miserable, almost sleepless night. What sleep she had had consisted of nightmares in which Alex was intent on butchering Jean-Paul while she was apparently cheering him on.

No sooner had she rearranged luncheon plans than Mr Peters strode in with a summons to the Dower House. The collaboration! Nell had hoped the dowager would quietly forget this arrangement, but no such good fortune.

Lady Enid eyed her carefully on her arrival in her morning room, courtesy of butler Mr Robins who had announced her as though she were the Queen of Sheba instead of a mere cook. No, a fleeting thought reminded her, not the Queen of Sheba. Wrong comparison. Didn't she and King Solomon part after their few days of bliss?

'Miss Drury, it is high time we spoke about Mr Briggs's position. I take it we are still collaborators in this unfortunate case?' The dowager swept on without waiting for a reply. 'Now that the inquest has decided Lady Saddler died unlawfully, that is some relief. I had feared that Mr Briggs might be named. However' – she gave Nell a keen glance – 'I spoke to Chief Inspector Melbray last evening. He remained polite, but I was under the distinct impression that my efforts to solve this sad affair are not entirely welcome.'

Nell managed a smile. 'I fear that may be the case where I'm concerned, too.'

A keener glance now. 'That is unfortunate but not disastrous. It leaves us a clearer field.'

Did it? Nell hadn't looked at it that way, but perhaps Lady Enid was right. Provided they weren't too visible in their detection methods, the situation might have its advantages. 'You have heard, I trust, that the Artistes de Cler are to remain my son's guests for the time being?'

Nell rallied. 'Yes. At Inspector Melbray's request.'

'Not altogether, although he too is most grateful to my son for his agreement to his wishes. The chief inspector has returned to London for a few days to attend to other business, but will be coming back in due course. The Artistes de Cler are here for quite another reason. Sir Gilbert has asked them to remain, after having discussed the matter with my son.'

Nell was intrigued. 'Does he think that one of the Clerries is his wife's murderer?' With all the new evidence, it was vital not to dismiss the role that one or more of them could have played in Lady Saddler's death. They had reason enough.

'That I cannot say. His reason is more practical, however. I understand he wishes next year's exhibition to go ahead after all, albeit with certain conditions, which he will discuss with the Artistes de Cler.'

Nell was astonished. 'Given that Lady Saddler didn't like their work, I would have expected him to leave the exhibition cancelled.'

'Gilbert is a remarkable gentleman,' Lady Enid said complacently, as though taking the credit for this. 'I believe he has in mind some kind of tribute to her, although I cannot see how that suits Clerrian art with its triangles and circles and whatnots.'

'Does Miss Saddler approve of this tribute?'

The dowager paused for a moment. 'That is for her to say. But to our muttons, Miss Drury. With a murderer still among us, what are your plans?' she continued briskly. 'I am shocked that Mr Briggs is still in custody despite my evidence, and I intend to make every effort to acquaint myself more fully with the Artistes de Cler while they remain under our roof. One of them is undoubtedly guilty of murder.'

The dowager had echoed her own thoughts, but nevertheless for Nell another issue overrode it. Should she speak out and risk Lady Enid's displeasure? Nell made a quick decision. 'I agree, Lady Enid, and the alibis you obtained from them make that very possible, but I can't ignore the Carters' part in this story. It's true they both have alibis, and now I know that Lady Saddler's body was moved to their garden after her death, that makes their guilt even more unlikely. Even so, they still played a role I don't understand.'

'But I do, Miss Drury. As we now know, those two strange Frenchmen who come and go had a hand in events. They are mere distractions, as far as we are concerned, however. The mere fact that it has been publicly admitted that one of them moved the body makes it clear that he or they have been bribed by the Artistes de Cler so that suspicion does not fall on them. One Frenchman disappears, and the brother remains, obviously to divert attention from the artistes. Then he too will leave when the trail grows cold.

'Well, Miss Drury,' the dowager continued, 'what do you think of that? The chief inspector might not understand these artists, but I do. Among them I see fruit for the taking in the way of motives for Lady Saddler's murder.'

Lady Enid sat back in her armchair in triumph. Nell was still scrabbling her thoughts on this astonishing theory, when she was saved by Mr Robins's reappearance.

'Lady Clarice, your ladyship.'

'Thank you, Robins. Clarice—'

But whatever Lady Enid was going to say was swamped by Lady Clarice's declaration as soon as she came through the door.

'Mother, you will never guess what has happened. It's all so exciting.'

'Clarice, I do beg of you,' Lady Enid replied impatiently, 'to desist. We will discuss Jasper at luncheon.'

'Oh, Mama, not Jasper,' Lady Clarice replied.

'Then—'

'It's Mr Briggs. He has returned to us.'

ELEVEN

Where the dickens was he? Lady Clarice had told her that Mr Briggs had arrived at the main entrance to Wychbourne Court, not the east-wing servants' entrance. Nell found no sign of him. Mr Peters merely looked blank when she had asked him Mr Briggs's whereabouts, although Lady Clarice had said she personally escorted him inside. Puzzled, Nell returned to the east wing, but there was no Mr Briggs there either, and nor were there any signs of excitement. Perhaps nobody had heard the news? Back to the Great Hall and Mr Peters, then.

On her way there, she saw Jenny Smith running down the grand staircase and called out, 'I heard that Mr Briggs was back. Have you seen him?'

Jenny had apparently no time to spare and hurried by looking almost as though she didn't want to stop. Strange, Nell thought. Jenny did hurl back a reply, though. 'He's still with Lord Ansley, and his lordship was asking for you. He wants you to go to his study as soon as you can.'

Slightly puzzled, Nell obeyed. The study near the Ansleys' private rooms was personal to his lordship, unlike the estate office, so what could this be about? Mr Briggs? She hoped so. When her knock was answered, she found not only Lord and Lady Ansley present but Mr Briggs himself.

She barely recognized him, though. Even in these few days he seemed to have lost weight, and his face was pinched and yellow with fatigue. Even more alarmingly, he looked more vacant than usual. *Don't let him see that I'm alarmed*, she warned herself.

She put as much warmth into her voice as she could, as though all was now well. 'Welcome home, Mr Briggs.'

He made no reply but he seemed to recognize her – but, oh, what a change.

Lady Ansley looked as anxious as Nell felt. 'Mr Briggs is not well,' she said, 'and so we've arranged that for the time being he should have the former governess rooms nearer to the main house.'

This was surprising even in these circumstances. The governess rooms were positioned between the servants' wing and the main house, and harked back to earlier days when hierarchy was even more important than it was today. A governess was not quite a servant but not quite on a par with the family and its guests, and so what was Mr Briggs doing here? Even though he was ill, he would be better off in his familiar rooms in the east wing.

'Won't—' she began, until she caught a warning glance from Lady Ansley. Why, Nell had no idea, but she rapidly understood the message. 'That's splendid, Mr Briggs,' she added. 'You'll need to be looked after for a while until you are used to us all again.' She must be on the right path because Lord Ansley nodded agreement.

'Briggs will be carrying out his normal duties, won't you, Briggs?' he said.

Mr Briggs came alive for a moment. 'Morning suit, number one, single-breasted waistcoat. Buttons, six, *sir.*' Then he relapsed into silence.

'Shall I ask Mrs Fielding to arrange the change of room?' Nell asked.

Did she imagine it, or was there a hesitation before Lord Ansley replied? 'Thank you, Miss Drury, but Mrs Fielding will be looking after his meals and bedding and so forth for a few days.'

Nell was taken aback. His meals would normally be arranged through Nell herself and Mrs Squires, her plain cook. Still, she had no objection, strange though it was.

As if sensing Nell's bewilderment, Lady Ansley explained. 'We wanted to put you in the picture, Nell, so that you can spread the word to your staff. It will only be for a few days – a convenience to tide you over the effects of your ordeal, Briggs.' She smiled at him.

Nell returned to the east wing, still puzzled. There must be more to this than just concern for Mr Briggs's wellbeing. The servants' hall would have to be told, because all the staff would be looking forward to greeting him now that he was no longer under suspicion of murder. She'd talk about it at the servants' tea, now luncheon was over and dinner preparations were in hand.

Everyone was busy, true; nevertheless, something felt wrong this afternoon. It wasn't what was said that was strange; it was the fact that *nothing* was said. Even when they finally sat down for tea, total silence prevailed on the subject of Mr Briggs.

She'd had enough. Nell tried an exploratory gambit. 'Isn't it good news that Mr Briggs has returned to Wychbourne? He won't be with us here for a few days, though, because he's not too well.'

She saw Michel's and Muriel's faces light up, but there was no chorus of agreement. The opposite, in fact. Sullen expressions were turned her way. 'It's good news, isn't it?' she repeated uncertainly.

The mutinous silence continued until Robert broke it. 'Depends, don't it, Miss Drury. How do we know we won't be murdered in our beds, eh?'

Had she really heard him say that? Was it a joke? Nell looked around at the faces in astonishment. It was clear it was no joke.

'Dry up, Robert,' Muriel hissed. 'Mr Briggs has been cleared of murder.'

'How do we know? He's a looney, that one,' he retorted to murmurs of agreement.

This needed dealing with right away. 'He's Mr Briggs,' Nell intervened briskly. 'He's worked here at Wychbourne for six or seven years. We've always known that he's suffering from his war experiences, but he's far from looney.'

'We don't *know* the bloke.' Robert looked round the table, obviously seeking support. 'There ain't no knowing what a chap in that state might do.'

'That's enough,' Nell cried, appalled as everyone at the table burst into acrimonious argument. 'The police have released Mr Briggs, which means they do know he is innocent.'

Out of the corner of her eye she had seen Mrs Fielding sweep into the servants' hall with full housekeeper's superiority. 'I quite agree, Miss Drury,' she stated. 'Mr Briggs is one of us and should be treated as such. The police have released him with no stain on his character.'

No one replied. Once over the shock of Mrs Fielding being on the same side as she was, Nell realized the awful truth. Many of the servants around this table must believe that the police – Alex? – had released Mr Briggs because Lord Ansley – or perhaps even she herself – had urged them to do so? If only they knew just how little influence either of them had on Alex. Now the servants' hall was split over the issue. *Take control of this, Nell*, she ordered herself. *Quickly*.

'Chief inspectors of Scotland Yard,' she told them coolly, 'don't rise to the top of their profession by following their own wishes or those of others. They do it on the basis of what the evidence has proved. Is that clear?'

The murmured replies of 'Yes, Miss Drury' left her unconvinced.

Mrs Fielding too, it seemed. Her bosom swelled with indignation. 'Miss Drury is quite correct,' she informed them, somewhat pink in the face. 'And we'll *all* give Mr Briggs the support he needs. Is that also clear?'

The 'Yes, Mrs Fielding' that followed was also strained. It was obvious, Nell realized, that she and Mrs Fielding had a battle on their hands which had not yet been won. It would take more than the strength of hierarchy to solve this one.

She tackled Mrs Fielding as soon as they had left the servants' hall. 'Is this why Mr Briggs has been allotted the governess rooms?'

'I know that for a fact, Miss Drury. It seems best, Lady Ansley told me. Just till things settle down.'

'What about Mr Peters . . .' Nell stopped as she saw Mrs Fielding flush. What had she said amiss?

Then a frightening thought struck her just as Mrs Fielding blurted out, 'Mr Peters – he thinks Mr Briggs is guilty. I can't be having that. No, I can't.'

Nell stared at her in horror. 'Oh, Mrs Fielding, how terrible for you. But the police truly know that Mr Briggs had no motive for killing Lady Saddler. It was Freddie Carter who destroyed the garden. The police know that, and anyway Mr Briggs didn't leave here until after dawn.'

'Mr Peters says Mr Briggs *thought* Lady Saddler did all that damage and lashed out at her. Didn't matter whether she did or not.'

Mrs Fielding was in tears now, and Nell said impulsively, 'Come into my room for a cup of tea. We'll talk it over.'

That's a pocketful of hopes gone to kingdom come, Nell thought despondently late that evening. Talking it over had slightly cheered up Mrs Fielding, and a plan for dealing with the kitchen and household staff had been agreed, but Nell was left none the happier. None of the staff would be really convinced of Mr Briggs's

innocence until the true murderer of Lady Saddler had been found
– and he or she could well be here at Wychbourne.

Nell felt as though her own last pillar of strength had gone.
First Alex, and now her seemingly safe haven – Wychbourne Court
– had crumbled. It had stood guarding the village for centuries,
offering a path to settle others' problems, not produce some of its
own. If Wychbourne couldn't stand united, how could the village
do so? And how ironic that, apart from the Ansleys themselves,
Mrs Fielding should be her strongest ally. Everyone had assumed
that Mr Peters and Mrs Fielding would get married, after their
attachment to each other had been publicly revealed last year, but
still no wedding. And now perhaps there never would be – either
for Mrs Fielding or Nell Drury.

The trouble wasn't confined to the servants' hall, either. Mrs
Fielding had confided to her that Lady Helen had returned home
from London, disconsolate as usual, and, on goodness knows
what evidence, she too had decided that Mr Briggs was guilty.
Her admirer, Mr Beringer, believed him innocent, thus causing
ructions between them, especially as Lady Sophy sided with Mr
Beringer. Lord Richard was also stoutly defending Mr Briggs, but
it was hard even to guess what the rest of the village was thinking.

Everyday work presented a problem, therefore. Nell knew she
would be battling with mistrust, coupled with the fact that her own
mission to save Mr Briggs was not yet over, given the atmosphere
here. If all's lost, stand up and fight, her dad used to say, albeit
often staggering home with cut lips, bruised eyes and cheeks after
battles at the market. He had fought back and look what used to
happen. Still, it was a good attitude, she supposed. Keep on going
and you might be lucky one day.

How to keep on going in this case, though, was the dilemma.
Mr Briggs had been released, but not to everybody's satisfaction.
She could keep on going with that. On the other hand, Alex was
presumably still hunting for the real culprit but needed no help
from his former sweetheart, Nell Drury. His suspects were neatly
cooped up at Wychbourne Court, whether at his instigation or Sir
Gilbert's – she couldn't be sure which. Altogether the world seemed
a gloomy place. Perhaps she should keep on going through the
Looking Glass, like Alice, in which everything was the other way
around. Very well. Don't look at whether or not Mr Briggs is

innocent but whether the Clerries are guilty – and whether Alex would approve of her actions or not.

Now that she'd mixed the batter correctly, her spirits cautiously rose. The first opportunity through the Looking Glass came the next morning. A visit in search of Mr Fairweather, who couldn't be found in the kitchen garden, took her past the lake, where she found Lance Merryman sketching one of the young groundsmen lying posing for him. She seized the chance to speak to him.

'Such inspiration, don't you think?' Lance said merrily as she approached. 'Such grace. Such elegance. A pose I thought I might adapt for a ladies' magazine.'

'I'm sure it will look splendid,' Nell told him gravely, hoping that Jimmy the pageboy didn't present similar opportunities for him.

Lance giggled. 'One has to fill the daylight hours until that kind inspector says we may return to dear London town. He believes that may be soon, although as we do still hope to persuade Sir Gilbert to restore the plan for next year's exhibition, we might be trespassing on Lady Ansley's kind hospitality rather longer.'

'Are you still enthusiastic about the exhibition?'

'Indeed we are. Perhaps not the exhibition as previously envisaged but so disobligingly cancelled by the late Lady Saddler, but certainly one where the Clerries' art can be appreciated to the full. We await Sir Gilbert's announcement. It does so depend . . .'

'On what?' she asked out of curiosity when he hesitated.

'On whether this wretched murder can be solved. It does appear that now Briggs has been all but declared innocent, *any* of us might be found guilty.' He shot a coy look at Nell. 'But some of us are *therefore*,' he emphasized, 'not at all sure that Briggs is innocent, and so might I suggest – not my business, of course – that he should not be permitted to wander near the west wing where we poor emigrés from Spitalfrith are housed. Some of us' – another giggle – 'are just a spot nervous.'

'Completely unnecessarily, Mr Merryman,' Nell replied, trying to remain polite. It was a struggle. 'But I will pass your request on.' She decided not to clarify to whom. Mr Peters might even be sympathetic to such an outrageous demand.

'I've only spoken to that charming Peters – the butler, I believe – and he quite sees my point.'

Nell gritted her teeth. Of all people, Mr Peters, who had suffered himself in the past from such suspicions, had seemed the least likely to be so prejudiced.

'Not all we Clerries feel this way,' Lance added fairly. 'Dear Vinny believes Briggs innocent and darling Gert agrees. However, Pierre, our leader, is strongly of the opinion that he is guilty of murder. Of course, one must also consider those Carter people as suspects, despite their alibis. Dear me, I do sound quite like a policeman myself, don't I? And one must also bear in mind those mysterious French gentlemen, one of whom has disappeared from the scene remarkably quickly. Nevertheless, one cannot ignore the fact that Briggs was found with the body and appears to have no real alibi.'

Not again. 'He was here at Wychbourne Court during the night,' Nell pointed out.

'Of course. But for all of it?'

Hold on to your temper, Nell told herself. 'He was seen leaving Wychbourne Court long after the murder took place.'

'Ah, yes, so the delightful Lady Enid told us. She is investigating the case herself, I understand. Why would she trust the evidence of a farmer's milkboy, however?'

A *mere* milkboy was the implication. 'When you prick us, do we not bleed?' Nell murmured.

The sharp eyes gazed at her. 'Shakespeare, of course, and poor Shylock the Jew. We are indeed all flesh and blood. Quite the academic, aren't you, Miss Drury? I shall warn my fellow suspects that you are on their trail, as I sense you are.'

Nell was about to retort but disciplined herself. Instead, she managed a smile. 'I'm on the trail in the interests of your luncheon and dinner, Mr Merryman. I will cross you off my list as a suspect, though I'm told that you were talking to Lady Saddler until she left the manor shortly after eleven. Was the talk of interest?'

The bonhomie disappeared. 'A matter of work. An inspiration for *À La Mode* magazine, for which dear Lisette might have wished to pose.'

'It's slightly puzzling,' Nell said as casually as she could manage, 'because there's also evidence that she left a little earlier. Did you leave together?'

'Good gracious, no. I retired to my chamber,' Lance said airily. His eyes travelled to the groundsman now strolling away. 'Alas, alone,' he added.

Petra was in despair. She'd done her best but her father was adamant. Madame Lisette's funeral would be a very private one in London tomorrow. He had already made the arrangements. Despite his amiable and easy-going appearance, she knew he could be a man of steel when he put his mind to it. And it was clear he had done so over this issue. It was also clear to her that he had something else on his mind.

'What about Madame Lisette's family?' she had asked.

'She was estranged from them. She told me they had collaborated with the German occupiers in the city, and she could not forgive that, especially in view of her own magnificent work.'

'Won't the Clerries wish to attend?'

'No, Petra.'

No reason given. Not satisfied, she had managed to speak to the Frenchman, Jean-Paul Girarde, about Madame Lisette's family after the inquest. Surely they should be informed, despite their estrangement; he might know how to trace them, as he had told her he had met Madame Lisette after the war.

He had given her a charming smile. 'I do not think she saw her family again after they left Lille. So many people died. The influenza, of course. Thousand upon thousand. *Mademoiselle*, let me give advice, if I may. Stay in today's world. It is easier for all of us. Forget Lille, forget Paris, forget the sad days of war.'

She had tried again to point out to her father that the Clerries surely should be present at the funeral, as Madame Lisette had modelled for them.

He shook his head. 'Lisette saw life and its woes and pleasures more clearly than the Clerries did at times. When they painted her, they did not always like the results; they revealed the painter's own weaknesses. I don't believe they would wish to come tomorrow.'

She had plucked up her courage to ask, 'Could one of them have killed her, Father, now we know Mr Briggs is not guilty?'

A silence. 'No,' he said at last, and would not budge from that. Still convinced he had something else on his mind, she decided now to have one last attempt regarding the funeral arrangements. 'What about Lord and Lady Ansley? Should you suggest that they come? They have been very generous.'

'No, my pet. You may bring Lord Richard, if you wish. No one else.'

'But something is worrying you, Father. What is it?'

He smiled. 'I'm thinking about holding the exhibition next year despite what's happened.'

'*What?*' The very opposite of what she had imagined. Petra quickly recovered. 'That's splendid news.'

Her father looked mildly surprised at her enthusiasm. 'It won't be the usual Clerrian art, though that's part of it. "War into peace" is the theme. *Any* major artists would be able to exhibit, including the Clerries if they wish.'

This was breath-taking news, but she had instant doubts. 'Aren't people tired of thinking back to the war?'

'For many years that has been the case. But now, I believe, is the time to re-examine the past, which is not always as we thought. If we are to prevent another war, then we must know the truth about the last one.'

Nell was glad to have an excuse to walk down to the village. Not only was the atmosphere in the kitchen still very strained, with even a marked reluctance to prepare a breakfast tray for Mr Briggs on Monday morning, but the Ansley family seemed equally under strain. Lady Ansley had scarcely glanced at the menus when Nell brought them to her. 'We shall not be attending Lady Saddler's funeral tomorrow, Nell. We have not received a notification, and Richard tells me that it's a small gathering in London and that he will represent us.'

'Is that a relief?' Nell had asked boldly.

Lady Ansley had smiled. 'I'm afraid so, especially as I understand Sir Gilbert still believes Briggs guilty. Lady Enid is not pleased about that, as you can imagine. I believe she even expressed that to Sir Gilbert, pointing out that it was her evidence that proved he most certainly could not be guilty. Nor is Lady Clarice pleased. I'm afraid she sees her opportunities to search for Jasper in Spitalfrith Manor greatly reduced as a result.'

Nell was still meditating on the divided house and its guests when she reached the village. Were there any steps she could take to mend the situation? The Clerries were keeping themselves very much to themselves, and Alex would be looking very closely at them as his major suspects now. Lady Enid was still in a better position than Nell to pick up any evidence that had escaped his eye concerning them – not that that was likely. As Lady Saddler's body had been found in the grounds, the finger of suspicion certainly pointed at the Clerries – *if* Jean-Paul had been telling the truth. And yet the mystery surrounding the Carters beckoned her onwards in their direction.

She could see the police posters for the missing Jacques Girarde were now in evidence, and she stopped to study the one displayed outside the post office. Jacques was very recognizably Jean-Paul's brother, but he looked older and more serious than Jean-Paul. They shared their family nose, however.

'We are alike, are we not?' Without her noticing, Jean-Paul had come up from behind to join her. 'Jacques is two years older than I am. He is twenty-nine now.'

'It looks as though you have different characters,' she observed.

'He takes life with more difficulty than I. But then we all have two sides to us, do we not? But he is passionate where I am less so. He is open to the world where I am not, perhaps because I was a prisoner of the Germans during the war. Jacques was at the tragedy of Verdun. We both suffered.'

'And your sister Marie-Hélène in her own way perhaps.' Even traitors must suffer.

A silence. 'You are right, Miss Drury. She too was a victim of war.'

'Did you know Lady Saddler?'

'Not in wartime. Lisette Rennard was in Lille, where our family had lived, and Marie-Hélène, Jacques and I were born. When he and I returned after the end of the war, Marie-Hélène was dead and my parents also. My sister had fled from occupied Lille to our aunt's home in Beaudricourt. It is a village about twenty kilometres from Doullens, where the big conference was held in 1918 with all the allied commanders. Neither was in occupied territory, but Lille was about fifty kilometres to the north and quickly conquered when war broke out.'

'But if your family lived in Lille at one time, Marie-Hélène and

Lady Saddler could well have known each other during the war, even if you and Jacques weren't there,' Nell pressed. 'You said at the inquest that she was responsible for your sister's death, and I believe the reason she came to see Freddie and Joe on the day she died was what made Freddie destroy all the birds. Lady Saddler told him about your sister's role during the war. I'm sorry—' She broke off. 'This must be very painful for you.'

Jean-Paul did not reply – well, not directly anyway. 'This evening I shall be visiting Freddie again. I would like you to be there – and Mr Briggs also.'

TWELVE

To Nell's alarm, Mr Briggs seemed puzzled by her mention of Jean-Paul Girarde. By arrangement with Mrs Fielding, Nell had been permitted to deliver Mr Briggs's lunch. (This new-found goodwill between Mrs Fielding and herself would surely not last.) She had hoped to suggest to him that he might like to accompany them to see Freddie this evening. If he looked frightened at the idea – as he might, given the circumstances – no harm would have been done, but it could be just what he needed to break his solitary silence, without facing the whole of the servants' hall. In any case, that in itself would be a mistake at present. He had carried out his normal duties for Lord Ansley impeccably, so his lordship had told her, but afterwards he retreated to his rooms and remained there. When, earlier this morning, Jenny Smith had offered to escort him around the gardens, he had shaken his head vigorously.

'This may take a long time to heal, Nell, especially with the servants so divided,' Lord Ansley had added. Whenever he called her Nell, she noted, it was a sure sign that he was worried. Normally, the family kept rigidly to formalities unless it was a very much an off-duty matter. 'I gather,' he had continued, 'that even Peters and Mrs Fielding are at odds over their respective views on Briggs. Wychbourne has never been so unwelcoming during my tenure in charge of it. The presence of our guests, the Artistes de Cler, isn't helping either. I have to admit that I wish my son had not invited them here, especially as they are not only strangers to us but one of them possibly a murderer.'

'Guests can never arrive too early or leave too soon,' Nell quoted the old saying.

Lord Ansley laughed rather shamefacedly. 'I agree. One or two of them have taken over guest bedrooms in the west wing as makeshift studios. Gertrude was not pleased to hear it. I realize that my attitude transgresses the rules of hospitality, but no etiquette rules this situation. It was bad enough earlier this year when we faced a somewhat similar situation, but at least the guests were of our own choosing. Now we must try to treat these Clerries as honoured guests, but it is difficult to do so. Half the household apparently still believes that poor Briggs is guilty and that Gertrude and I are to blame for harbouring him, and my own family is divided on the issue. I trust Melbray will solve the matter quickly, but at present he is in London.'

Nell reflected on Lord Ansley's comments about the guest situation, as she made her way to the herb garden to secure some more basil. She had not pressed Mr Briggs about coming with her this evening and had decided she would tackle him again in an hour or two's time to see if he reacted differently. As she reached her present destination, she could see Thora Huntley-Doran and Gert Radley deep in conversation on the arbour bench. Even seated, they made a strange pair – one tall, looking like Edith Sitwell with her long draperies and soulful expression; the other stockier and clad in trousers, which amused Nell greatly. She'd often longed for her legs to be protected by more than thin stockings. Thank heavens corsets at least were on the way out of fashion, another symbol of women's new freedom. Soon, surely, they would all have the vote as well, not just those over thirty years of age. About time, too.

Miss Huntley-Doran rose to her feet and wafted up to her. 'Miss Drury – the chef, are you not? You are the very person we wanted to meet.'

Such patrician graciousness demanded acknowledgement. 'I'm honoured, Miss Huntley-Doran.' Nell mentally dropped a curtsey.

Miss Huntley-Doran inclined her head in acknowledgement. 'What news is there of Mr Briggs? Miss Radley and I are both concerned for his welfare.'

'We and Vinny seem to be the only ones who are,' grunted Gert Radley. 'Poor devil. Gets released and now he's sent to Coventry in his own home, judging by the servants' comments that we've heard.'

'*And* among our own number,' Miss Huntley-Doran pointed out with indignation.

How to handle this? 'At the moment he's happier having a retreat from normal life,' Nell said diplomatically. 'He needs time to become used to Wychbourne again.'

'Everyone needs a refuge in war, and it is war for him,' Gert said. 'Sounds as if he's found his refuge here. The innocent suffer most.'

'I have informed Monsieur Christophe of Mr Briggs's innocence,' Miss Huntley-Doran said vehemently, 'but he ignores me. I cannot understand this. I'm told you have some experience in such situations, Miss Drury. Mr Briggs's return must mean he is innocent, but the chief inspector has told us nothing. Does he suspect us instead? If so, we are all victims. Monsieur Christophe cannot see that Mr Briggs is therefore as much a victim as we are. The poet Lovelace was mistaken when he wrote that "Stone walls do not a prison make". This crime has undoubtedly created a prison for us here. I myself am seeking refuge in my poetry. Emotions are important, Miss Drury, but they must be skeletal emotions. The naked truth.'

Nell nodded solemnly, even as Miss Radley gruffly pointed out, 'It's Gilbert keeping us locked up here, though, not the inspector. He's coming up with another idea for the exhibition, and so we're allowed out to meet him at Spitalfrith for luncheon to discuss it.'

'Remaining here is another request of the inspector's, no doubt,' Miss Huntley-Doran said darkly. 'How could he possibly believe that the real culprit lies among us, the Artistes de Cler? I'm told you know Inspector Melbray's plans, Miss Drury?'

Nell stiffened. 'I'm not in his confidence, I'm afraid.'

Miss Radley cast a quick look at her. 'On a summer's day in a herb garden, murder seems a long way away,' she said briskly. 'Leave the police to their job, Thora.'

'I shall. After all, none of us is guilty,' Miss Huntley-Doran stated firmly. 'Monsieur Christophe and I walked through the Spitalfrith gardens late that evening, but there was no sign of Lisette, so we are indisputably innocent.'

'Unless you were in league with each other,' Miss Radley added cheerfully. 'And any of us could have leapt out of bed and rushed down to the gardens to kill Lisette. We all had reason enough, as only she stood in the way of our greater glory at the exhibition. Now it looks as though it will go ahead in some form or another. I must say, I admire old Gilbert. Not so under her ladyship's thumb as we all thought. Indeed, I often wondered . . .'

'What did you often wonder, Gert?' Miss Huntley-Doran asked coldly when she paused.

'Whether I should tackle the subject of the war and its results in my work,' Miss Radley replied blandly.

'That poses no problem for me,' Miss Huntley-Doran replied loftily. 'The results are that the future beckons us. Poetry is the leader; it marches forwards – that *is* the result of the war.'

Miss Radley snorted. 'While you're striding forward, Thora, you might remember that as Clerries we still have to know who killed that woman before we can join your jolly old march. Did the murder spring from our midst, and if so, was its motive generated by the principles of Clerrian art? You might well be wondering the same, Miss Drury, and so might the Ansleys. Did its motivation spring from the privileged life you lead here? You seem so concerned about the minutiae of what to do and what not to do.'

Nell gulped at this attack, although she was well used to such discussions with Lady Sophy, a passionate socialist. 'The system works,' she pointed out.

'The system glides over the question of who murdered Lisette,' Miss Radley retorted.

Miss Huntley-Doran now obviously felt on safer ground. 'At first, I thought Vinny or Lance killed her,' she declared bluntly, 'but not now. I believe I know who did kill her and I have informed the inspector so. It was that strange Frenchman's brother. One can tell from his photograph on the posters. There is pure evil in that face, whereas his brother Jean-Paul presents an unusual but different picture. Once the police have caught this scoundrel brother, we shall all be safe again.'

Nell hesitated but decided to speak. After Jean-Paul's appearance at the inquest, the Girarde brothers' involvement or otherwise was no secret. 'It's possible Jacques Girarde had a motive,' she said. 'Lady Saddler lived in Lille under the occupation, but the brothers, although born there, weren't there during the war. Both were in the army, one a prisoner of war. Their parents had died during the war.'

'From the famine or killed by the Germans?' Miss Radley asked mildly.

Or perhaps her parents were working *for* the Germans, Nell wondered, remembering her theory. Not just Marie-Hélène but her parents, too.

'Either is possible,' Miss Huntley-Doran answered Miss Radley. 'It was a terrible time, so Lisette told us. She was helping the intelligence services, of course, at first as part of the Alice Spy Ring, she told us; that was until Louise de Bettignies was captured, and then she worked as an agent for the La Dame Blanche network. There must be many collaborators still in Lille who would fear her revelations enough to kill her if she threatened them.'

'When our gallant Chief Inspector Melbray returns, I'm sure he'll still have his eye on one of us Clerries, despite your help, Thora,' Miss Radley retorted.

'Then he will certainly be mistaken,' Miss Huntley-Doran snapped. 'Pierre is foolishly misguided – that I admit – but he is not a murderer. Nor is Lance. And neither' – she glared at both Nell and Miss Radley – 'am I.'

Working for the Germans. Nell mulled this over as she duly picked her basil and returned to the kitchen. She was sure of her theory now. Marie-Hélène and perhaps her parents must have been working for the Germans in Lille before she left for Beaudricourt, probably because Lisette Rennard was passing the word about her around to her compatriots. Freddie was given the terrible news that Saturday afternoon that his sweetheart had been working for the enemy and that was why he had destroyed the birds he had so lovingly created in her memory. He would have told his great pal, Mr Briggs, not only that it was he who had destroyed the birds but why he had done so.

She forced herself to go a step further. Marie-Hélène's brothers would also have known the truth about their sister. But if so, didn't that give Freddie and the two brothers a motive for the murder? Wasn't it all too neat that Freddie, his father and Jean-Paul went to Mrs Golding's home for the night? Why not Jacques too in that case? But what was their motive for *killing* Lady Saddler? Because they still might not want the truth about their sister to emerge? The oppressed have long memories, and feelings must still be running high in their native town.

That didn't entirely satisfy her. There could be another reason. Revenge for Lady Saddler's having broadcast to her fellow citizens Marie-Hélène's name as a German spy? She would have had no choice, though, because for the citizens' own protection she would have been obliged to warn them.

Speculation, Nell reminded herself. Mere speculation. Nevertheless, she would tread gently this evening.

High tea for Mr Briggs. Nell carried a tray which she hoped looked enticing, with sandwiches and cake, together with a dish of peaches and cream. Mr Briggs liked peaches, and she had extracted these from Mr Fairweather with great difficulty. It took her away from brooding over Alex Melbray. While he was away, it was somewhat easier to pretend that he didn't exist, but that lump inside her still lurched every time she thought of him – proving that he very much did exist. Love was *very* indigestible.

She expected to find Mr Briggs alone, but to her astonishment she found Lady Clarice with him. Did he seem upset at that? No. He was sitting upright in his chair as though he was on duty, probably because this was his lordship's sister sitting with him. He genuinely seemed to be following what she was saying, however – although what he was making of it might be a different matter.

'Ah, Nell,' Lady Clarice greeted her happily, 'I've been telling Briggs all about Jasper, and he is most interested, aren't you, Briggs?'

To Nell's surprise and relief, he answered her, a sure sign that he was becoming used to Wychbourne again. 'Ghosts. There. Happy,' he said.

Nell hadn't a clue what Mr Briggs meant, but it was a step in the right direction. She was fairly sure he was not thinking of Jasper or of any of the Wychbourne ghosts, even though Lady Clarice could have been chatting about them as well as Jasper. It was, however, more likely that ghosts from his past filled his mind.

'I've promised Briggs that I'll take him on a tour of the Wychbourne ghosts – a special one that most people cannot appreciate,' Lady Clarice explained. 'I'm sure Briggs will, though. All the time he has worked here, he has never met the Ansley ancestors, but I have assured him it will be like meeting old friends.'

Would it? Nell wasn't so sure Mr Briggs would like to meet the unfortunate Sir Thomas, killed by a medieval minstrel, or the dairymaid who climbed up the ivy for a midnight tryst with the 4th Marquess, or the Victorian marchioness murdered by the same gentleman. Ghosts, Nell thought – if they existed – were created by unhappiness or unhappy events. There didn't seem to be many chuckling phantoms in Lady Clarice's repertoire, and the last thing Mr Briggs needed was a mournful ghost.

As if to prove her right, Mr Briggs unexpectedly burst into song: 'We are Fred Karno's army, the ragtime infantry . . .'

Camaraderie. Is that what he was thinking of? Marching songs or the evenings in the *estaminets* when they were at rest from the front line. Did he miss the company of his fellow infantrymen, most of whom would have died? Anyway, she was going to join the singing gusto, followed after a moment or two's surprise by Lady Clarice, who turned out to have a superb contralto voice. 'And when we get to Berlin, the Kaiser he will say . . .'

The moment was right, Nell decided. 'I've met an old friend who would like to see you this evening, Mr Briggs. Monsieur Jean-Paul Girarde. Shall we go together to meet him at Freddie's home?'

She held her breath, knowing it was a risk and hoping against hope that she wasn't making a big mistake. For a few moments it seemed that she had done just that, and her heart sank.

It was Lady Clarice, not Mr Briggs, who broke the silence. 'Oh, yes, Briggs, do go. Perhaps Jasper will appear if I come, too.'

No fear! Nell was horrified. What could be worse than another ghost hunt at the moment? 'Perhaps tomorrow, Lady Clarice,' she said tactfully. 'If we wait to see Jasper, it might make it too long a visit for Mr Briggs.'

Lady Clarice was quick to agree, bless her. 'Of course,' she said hurriedly. 'Perhaps Jasper will visit Wychbourne when you're well again, Briggs.'

*   *   *

Gert Radley was surprised to find Lance present. She'd intended to have a quick word with Vinny in the makeshift studio he had set up in the west wing. Unlike dear Pierre and Lance who had insisted on converting rooms inside Wychbourne Court, Vinny had chosen to erect a tented studio in the grounds. At least she wouldn't be interrupting Vinny's work, for when she looked inside, Lance was evidently doing that all too efficiently. Vinny was perched on a stool facing Lance with folded arms, obviously deep in discussion over Gilbert's great idea for next year's exhibition. At least there was going to be one, though she wasn't too sure that Gilbert's plan was going to work.

'Working on the "war into peace" angle already?' she joked, seeing a blank canvas at his side. Lance was waving a sketch of some monstrous dress, the sort that so many idiotic women seemed to favour but which made them look like caterpillars.

'A difficult project that Gilbert's given us.' Vinny grinned at her. 'Doesn't everything relate to war and peace?'

'Might as well paint bread and cheese,' Gert grunted. 'What with rationing and the need for survival, they make as good a symbol as anything else.'

'Why not, darling?' Lance said gaily. 'Matisse would be green with envy at the idea. Look at his "Dinner Table", after all.'

'True.' Gert laughed. What she had wanted to raise was the subject of Lisette's murder, and Lance was a distraction. You couldn't rely on a thing Lance said, whereas Vinny spoke from the heart. She'd have to revert to talking about the blasted exhibition again.

'I agree it's hard to see how the "war into peace" idea will work out,' she continued. 'I suppose I could paint my paintbrush,' she added idly. 'The tool of portraying war and the means of recovery from it.'

'Bravo, Gert.' Vinny grinned. 'Paint what's important to both war and peace.'

'My dears, surely that has to be beauty,' Lance said languidly. 'What for you, Vinny?'

'Weren't we fighting for the green fields of England? Freedom?'

'Yes, but how do we relate that to Clerrian art?' Gert said. 'It's all very well for Gilbert. He has his reputation to slide back into if the Artistes de Cler vanish. We don't, and there will be others besides us at the exhibition.'

'Our challenge, my dears,' Lance said.

'I'm too old for challenges,' Gert said flatly.

'Before we pick up our paintbrushes to face Gilbert's challenge,' Vinny said mildly, 'we have to escape this so delightful prison of Wychbourne Court by settling the matter of Lisette's murderer. I doubt if any of us still think that Briggs was guilty of it.'

Lance stiffened. 'That's the job of the police.'

'Ours, too,' Vinny pointed out. 'Since the murderer is quite possibly one of us.'

Here we go again, Gert thought, remembering Thora's theory. 'True, but there are those Frenchmen who were hanging around here. Lisette was French. Aren't they more likely to have killed her? We don't know much about Lisette's life before she became our model, except the stance she took during the war.'

'That is true, but don't forget,' Lance said smugly, 'that one of us Clerries knows Lisette a great deal better than the rest of us. The whole of Paris knows that Lisette was Pierre's mistress. Quite a little gadabout from gentleman to gentleman was our Lisette.'

'Quiet, Lance,' Gert said. 'Thora may still have her doubts about Pierre, and the last thing we all need is for you to give her any gory details.'

'And how I'd love to do that. I do wonder if, in the circumstances, poor Thora should be put out of her misery and be left in no doubt as to her beloved's amorous history – so conveniently curtailed for him.'

'Let's leave by the breakfast-room door, shall we, Mr Briggs?' Nell suggested brightly. She couldn't risk using either the servants' entrance or the main entrance with Mr Peters in attendance. Both doors might produce hostile reactions if they were seen, and Nell was well aware that feeling was mounting now that the news of Mr Peters's belief in his guilt had spread – much to Mrs Fielding's fury and distress.

'They'll have to answer to me if they treat Mr Briggs badly,' she had announced to Nell.

Mr Briggs made no objection to Nell's plan, although he did hesitate as they turned towards the door near the family breakfast room, rather than his familiar route. Then Nell realized what was really concerning him.

'We'll be coming back here,' she reassured him in case he thought he was returning to Sevenoaks Police Station. 'We'll be meeting Jean-Paul and then we'll go to Freddie's home.'

The walk, she hoped, would make him feel more at ease than driving him in the close confines of a motor car. To her relief, there was Jean-Paul walking up to meet them.

'*Mon cher* Monsieur Briggs.' Jean-Paul clasped his hand in his own, to Mr Briggs's obvious surprise – no, it was pleasure, Nell realized. And Mr Briggs did seem to recognize Jean-Paul. 'I am delighted to see you once more. I have not seen you since that Saturday night.'

This alarmed Nell. Was Mr Briggs ready for this? 'Take care,' she whispered to Jean-Paul, but he merely smiled.

'We remember it together, Monsieur Briggs,' he said. 'Freddie, his father and I stayed with the charming Mrs Golding, but you wished to remain at Spitalfrith. My brother saw you there later.'

Mr Briggs looked as blank as Nell felt. Why remind him of that unhappy time? she thought crossly. Brother Jacques was as hard to get to grips with as Jean-Paul himself. True, it was only just over a week since he had left Spital Farm, but he was a vital witness and even though he was in the garden of the singing birds even earlier than she had been that evening, he might have seen something very relevant to Lady Saddler's murder. Or, of course, he had returned late in the evening and was her murderer. It was hard to believe Jean-Paul could be guilty of such a crime, but the brother might be a different matter. Despite Miss Huntley-Doran's conviction that the missing Jacques Girarde was undoubtedly Lady Saddler's killer, Nell reasoned that the spotlight for murder must still be on the Clerries.

That was Alex's domain, though. Or mostly. Somewhere, she was sure, there must still be a missing ingredient that would turn this ordinary dish into a magnificent one, and until it was discovered, Wychbourne would not be itself again. It might remain as divided over Mr Briggs as it was now.

'Tomorrow at half past ten,' Jean-Paul said out of the blue as they walked along to Spitalfrith, 'I am to give a performance in the village hall at Wychbourne – it is for children, but perhaps you too would like to come? And Mr Briggs, too?'

Mr Briggs smiled, shaking his head, but Nell was curious. 'I'll be there if I can,' she assured him, wondering what had given Jean-Paul this idea, pleasant though it was.

'When did you meet Mr Briggs?' she asked.

'Not until after the war. Afterwards I went back first to Lille and then to Beaudricourt and my brother also, where we learned from our aunt about our sister's death – and about Freddie and Mr Briggs. They were in the same battalion, and Freddie wrote about him in his letters to my sister. He did not know till after the war that she had died.'

Mr Briggs came to life. 'Marie-Hélène,' he said abruptly.

Had he too known her? Nell wondered. And if so, did he also know about Marie-Hélène's traitorous role in the war?

Mr Briggs had stopped, staring at the cottage where Freddie lived. 'Dirty Half Hundred,' he pronounced. 'Corfe.'

What was this? Nell was taken aback. These were new words for him, and from the look on his face they were clearly important.

'Irregulars. Private Frederick Carter. Corporal, *sir.*' He saluted, and without a glance at them strode towards the cottage. Nell was about to follow, but Jean-Paul caught her by the arm.

'Now that I have met Mr Briggs again, it is good that we leave them alone. We are not needed, Miss Drury.'

'He's not well enough,' she replied, alarmed.

'But he is. He and Freddie both live in yesterday. They will talk, but not while we are present. Come, Nell, let us sit while we wait. We can sit on that tree trunk that leads to Lady Clarice's dell – who knows, Jasper might join us.'

'Or your brother,' she replied, as, still reluctant, she joined him on the tree trunk. He was right, but even so something might have emerged from their conversation that would be relevant to the murder. As it was, she had to admit that the evening sun made this a pleasant if not entirely comfortable perch.

'Indeed, Jacques might come this way. He will come in his own good time, though, not at our wishes. Instead, Miss Drury, I will tell you the whole story of Freddie, Marie-Hélène and

Charlie Briggs, if you wish, as that is what they share between them.'

'I do wish.' Indeed, she did, even if she did have to bear in mind that she wasn't at all sure of Jean-Paul's own story or his possible motivation in relating Freddie's. And why hadn't he told her the whole story before?

'In the spring of 1918, Freddie and Charlie were in the British Forty-First Division,' he began matter-of-factly. 'In the Tenth Battalion of the Queen's Own Royal West Kent Regiment, which long ago in your English history was called the Dirty Half Hundred. This was a joke. It fought in many wars, and in the big battles of this last war. It fought at the Somme, and at the Menin Road and Passchendaele, parts of the big battle for Ypres. It suffered much. Then the battalion was sent to Italy to fight there. It returned to France in the February of 1918.'

'What did Mr Briggs mean by Corfe? Is that where they were stationed?' she asked.

'No. It was the name of their colonel at the time when their battalion was nearly wiped out. He had been leading Eleventh Battalion, a very special one for the regiment, known as the Corfe's Irregulars, and joined the Tenth only a week or two before the German offensive began hoping to push the British line back past Amiens. When Freddie and Charlie's battalion came back from Italy, they needed rest, which was taken at Beaudricourt. It was during those few weeks that Freddie met and fell in love with Marie-Hélène. Our parents remained in Lille after the Germans occupied it. There was not enough food or money to feed so many citizens, our occupiers decided, so they sent many thousands into the countryside with no means of support. We never heard what happened to many of our friends.'

So the Girarde family hadn't been spies for the Germans, *if* Jean-Paul was telling the truth. 'Did your sister spy for the Germans in Beaudricourt?' she asked cautiously.

'*Non,*' he replied abruptly. 'Beaudricourt was behind the front line, and when the Germans began their fighting in March with such force, Freddie and Charlie's battalion was on its way to Albert, a town also behind the lines. Their train was stopped and the battalion was turned around to go back to Achiet-le-Grand, a

railway junction much nearer the front line. They were marched
to a village near Bapaume and during that night to a valley
near the village of Morchies, where they had to dig trenches on
the new front line, which was always moving backwards with the
Germans pushing on. The battle began at eight o'clock and
lasted all day, growing more and more fierce. Freddie and Charlie
were unlucky being in the Tenth Battalion. Orders from headquarters to retire reached the forces on their left and their right
but the Tenth never received them, which left them to face the
German onslaught alone. Freddie and Charlie fought until six
o'clock that night, by which time most of the battalion was dead,
and the survivors, including Colonel Corfe, had to surrender. That
was very sad. A very few of the battalion managed to drag
themselves back to the new British line and safety, and Freddie
and Charlie were among them. Both were wounded, physically as
well as mentally.'

'And your sister?' Nell asked, appalled at this story.

'Marie-Hélène heard about the battle and went to try to find
news of Freddie in Bapaume, which by then had been under
heavy bombardment. Our aunt received no news of her until after
the war, when she was told my sister had died there.'

Nell longed to ask more, but it would be painful for Jean-Paul
to talk at length about his sister, so instead she asked, 'What
happened to Lady Saddler after the war?'

'Lisette Rennard, as she then was, left Lille for Paris after
the war's end. She became a model, and the rest you know or
can guess. Nell, it is better to forget this story. Forget the past.
The present is where we live.' A long silence. 'Do you have a
lover, Nell?'

A blow straight to the heart and how it hurt. 'There is someone
I love.'

'*Quel dommage.* Does he love you, Nell?'

'I thought so. But he doesn't. Not enough.'

'Then you should love others. Should we love each other?'

That brought a smile to her face. 'In other times, Jean-Paul,
perhaps. Not now.'

'No,' he said. 'Not now.'

THIRTEEN

The village hall, where Jean-Paul's children's show was being held, was a recent addition to Wychbourne's institutions and new territory for Nell. She was used to local events being held either in the Coach and Horses or in a small building owned by the church and little more than an enlarged garden shed. Thanks to a bequest, though, some months ago a barn had been converted into a sizeable hall on the Ightham road, which branched off the village green past the inn and the north-eastern side of the Ansley estate.

With a stage at one end, the new hall was ideally suited for a children's show. It was still holiday time for them; school had not yet reopened. Not that it was much of a holiday as there was still plenty of harvesting and fruit picking to be done. With many farms around Wychbourne being family-run, children were fully occupied during the summer months.

Nell looked round the excited and chattering audience, expecting to see Mr Briggs, but there was no sign of him, although when Mrs Fielding had taken his breakfast to him, he had indicated to her that he would be attending. Perhaps at the last moment his courage had failed him at the thought of being surrounded by people laughing and cheering, or perhaps Lord Ansley's requirements had taken longer than usual. Even so, she was puzzled.

As the lights went out in the hall ready for the performance to begin, her unease was coupled with a childish excitement as the curtains were whisked back to a gasp of delight from his audience to reveal Jean-Paul in a wizard's pointed hat and long robes. Her own excitement mounted too, but nevertheless she wondered why he'd wanted her to come. Even if luncheon was under control, there was plenty of work for her to do at the Court, and yet here she was, watching a conjurer for no apparent reason save for his charm and her own curiosity. His charm, of course, might be outweighing other perhaps less desirable qualities.

Jean-Paul was working alone, not with an assistant, unless one counted the huge stuffed rabbit which looked about four or five feet high and was sitting upright, grinning broadly. In the wings, Tom Waites, a labourer on Wychbourne Home Farm, was acting as 'stage manager', although his only job seemed to be standing in the wings to draw the curtains to and fro.

Her moments of doubt about Jean-Paul disappeared as he looked out at his cheering audience with a smile.

'Watch me, *s'il vous plait. Je suis un magicien.* With this, my magic wand, I can make both beautiful and horrible things disappear, but it is important to believe in the beautiful things for they are always there to make the bad things go away. Shall we make them go, *mes enfants*?'

'Yes,' came the unanimous shout. Jean-Paul seemed to be looking at her, or was that pure fancy? Perhaps one of the bad things he was remembering was his sister's role in the war. It occurred to her to wonder whether brother Jacques had been a spy too, and not in the army, as Jean-Paul had said. No. That really was just speculation, as would be any suggestion that Jean-Paul himself had been a traitor. He was a magician and a good one, she told herself.

He proved that in what followed: birds flew out of an apparently empty hat and were promptly recaptured, only to vanish again; handkerchiefs all colours of the rainbow were whisked in and out; flowers appeared out of nowhere, were destroyed and miraculously restored; and the cheeky stuffed rabbit joined in with the conversational patter (with a French accent) which had the children roaring every time. Clearly Jean-Paul was not only a magician but a ventriloquist.

Hubert, for such appeared to be the rabbit's name, informed the audience that he was the master's proud assistant. His own speciality, he told them, was balancing cups on the point of a knife, thoughtfully provided for him by Jean-Paul. Unfortunately, Hubert was not as expert at this as his magician master, and a number of cups tumbling from the knife and escaping his paws were only saved by Jean-Paul's own skills in rushing to their rescue. Not a trick that Mrs Fielding would appreciate, Nell decided, much amused.

Finally, Hubert informed the audience that he was tired and wished to go home, whereupon the magician informed him that this was a nuisance, but if he really wanted to leave, the great magician would make him vanish.

'Sit on this chair, if you please, Hubert,' he said disapprovingly, indicating a plain armless wooden chair on which he helped Hubert to perch, looking most uncomfortable but still grinning. A large cloth was then thrown over Hubert and the chair.

'Are you comfortable, Hubert?' Jean-Paul asked anxiously, adjusting the cloth around him.

A muffled squeak implied that Hubert was.

'Then, *voilà, chez toi*, Hubert. Vanish, if you please.' He whisked off the cloth, throwing it into the wings – and no Hubert was to be seen. 'You have gone already?' Jean-Paul cried out. 'So I will join you. *Au revoir et merci, mes amis.* Where are you now, Hubert?'

The reply came from the far side of the stage. 'I am in my rabbit home. It is a long way away.' But Hubert spoke to thin air. Jean-Paul had vanished.

It was left to Tom Waites to come on to the stage, scratching his head in bewilderment. 'Bless my soul, he's gone,' he announced. 'Not a sign of him anywhere. But he whispered to me that his last trick had been to put lollipops and ice cream at the back of the hall for all you children.'

Nell did not join the rush for ice cream, still stunned at Jean-Paul's disappearing act. Was that because of her? she wondered, fuming with frustration and suspecting that he had not only vanished from the stage but had every intention of vanishing from Wychbourne, too. Curiosity sent her to prowl around the stage, but there was nothing to show that he had ever been there – no clothes, no props – and all that remained of Hubert was the cloth that had covered him. How on earth had Jean-Paul managed to get rid of Hubert? His own disappearance was clear enough. By using the age-old trick of misdirection, he must have speedily stepped into the wings, reached the back of the hall and taken the exit door. But Hubert? Where had he gone? Even Jean-Paul couldn't run off with a four-foot rabbit plus all the other items.

Why this abrupt farewell? Where Jean-Paul was concerned, Nell realized, she'd been taken in by the icing sugar and not paid enough attention to the cake underneath. She did manage to laugh at herself for having been so easily deceived, but where did this leave her?

Duty called, but this afternoon she would search high and low for him – and Hubert!

The search was in vain. Nell scoured the surrounding fields and then asked one of the labourers where the Girardes' hut was. When she reached it, the door was open and the hut was empty of all but two beds. No sign of clothes or any other belongings. She had been fooled and she had little doubt that this was what Jean-Paul had intended. Around her were fields, many of which were now only golden stubble. That might be good news for the birds, but it wasn't for her.

Why had Jean-Paul decided it was time to leave? Had he warned Alex Melbray he was leaving? She doubted that very much. She had the impression that Alex didn't regard him as a suspect, but was he right about that? It wasn't just this disappearance that seemed so planned. It was his whole presence here: the way he or his brother had appeared to her not once but twice when she was with Lady Clarice, with their 'now you see me, now you don't' game. Now both Jean-Paul and Jacques had taken planned exits. Was that because they had achieved their purpose in coming? Had they come to talk to Freddie about their sister – perhaps even to tell him she was a spy – or had they come primarily to see Lady Saddler? Had one of them killed her? If so, why?

All these question marks but no answers meant there must be a missing ingredient here somewhere, and Jean-Paul must surely know what it was. Did it really warrant this elaborate stuffed-rabbit exhibition? Last of all, and perhaps the most important question, why, oh, why should she still care so much about finding the truth behind Lady Saddler's murder?

Answer: still Mr Briggs.

She couldn't leave Mr Briggs and Freddie in uncertainty. Even when Alex untangled the ramifications of the Clerries' role in the murder, Mr Briggs might still be suspected by many at Wychbourne Court. Jean-Paul must have the key to all this, she thought in frustration. How dare he vanish?

What could she do about it? *Find* him.

How to do that? She took a deep breath. First step: pay a visit to Farmer Pearson, who ran Spital Farm.

*   *   *

Spital Farmhouse was an old Tudor building, much changed over the years but to something far less than its possible former grandeur. Nell only knew Farmer Pearson slightly, and their relationship was not cordial. Nor, to be fair, were his relationships with anybody else very warm.

'What do *you* want?' was his greeting.

'To ask about Lady Saddler's murder.'

'What about it? You invite a lot of barmy artists over here and look what happens.'

She ignored this. 'We think your temporary labourers Jean-Paul and Jacques Girarde know something about it, but they've both disappeared. Did you know they were leaving?'

'No. Told it to the bees maybe.' He sniggered.

'But they would have told you, too,' Nell said firmly. 'We need to know where they've gone.' Using this royal 'we' was a nuisance but necessary where Farmer Pearson was concerned. A mere chef would get nowhere, but the implication that the whole of Wychbourne Court was involved would convey a message.

It did. 'They're off together somewhere. Never saw much of them, only now and then. Out with the fairies, both of 'em.'

She seized on this. 'But do you have any idea where they might have gone?'

He rested a hand meaningfully on the door handle. 'No, I haven't, missis. Neither of them told me nothing.'

As Farmer Pearson was probably a tenant farmer, accountable to the Ansleys, she'd try the old-fashioned approach, Nell told herself, promptly adopting an anxious look. 'A pity. His lordship might be asking you the same questions because he needs to clear Mr Briggs of suspicion.'

Silence as he pondered this. 'That Jean-Paul said he'd another job to go to,' he replied at last. 'Maybe join his brother. Wanted a bit of sea air, he said.'

At last. Keep on digging. 'Harvesting at another farm?' she asked.

'They're no farmers, those two. Do their best, maybe, but they're a couple of those wizard fellows.' Long pause. 'Said something' – another long pause – 'about a booking.'

Nell drew a deep breath. 'Thank you – you wouldn't happen to know where?'

'No. And you can tell his lordship I did my best. Always pleased to oblige when I can.' He leered at her as she turned away to breathe fresh air. A booking – well, at least that was something.

And now *another* vanishing act. Mr Briggs too had apparently disappeared. Nell had hurried back to Wychbourne Court with two objectives. She needed to talk to Lord Ansley about taking time off to hunt for Jean-Paul, and perhaps his brother too, and she also wanted to find out how Mr Briggs was faring after his visit to Freddie yesterday evening. She and Jean-Paul had called for him at the cottage, but he wasn't ready to leave, so Jean-Paul had remained there while she had left in the interests of early-morning rising for work. Mrs Fielding had reported that Mr Briggs had eaten very little breakfast or lunch, and Nell's own duties had prevented her from speaking to him earlier.

Now there was no sign of him, and no one knew where he was – and no one, it seemed, cared. Even Mr Peters was dismissive when she tracked him down to Pug's Parlour – with Mrs Fielding. To be fair, it looked as though she had arrived at a tender moment between them. But tenderness vanished as soon as Mr Briggs's name was mentioned.

'I have no jurisdiction over Mr Briggs,' Mr Peters sniffed.

Mrs Fielding was instantly up in arms. 'He's one of us upper servants. You've a duty to look after him, Mr Peters. Well, it's my opinion he's gone to see that Freddie Carter again, Miss Drury. He was late back last night, and off he's gone again today.'

'Another of them murderers,' muttered Mr Peters.

'I don't know what's wrong with you, I'm sure,' Mrs Fielding shot back at him. 'They're innocent war victims, both of them.'

'Need their heads washing out,' was his reply, to Nell's dismay.

'I'm shocked, Mr Peters. I really am.' Mrs Fielding looked close to tears.

Mrs Fielding could well be right about Mr Briggs's where-abouts, Nell thought, after reassuring words that everyone was under strain. She just had time to drive to Spitalfrith before the stuffing for the timbales needed attention. If he was indeed there, she might be able to bring him home in good time for his early-evening duties for Lord Ansley.

As she reached the cottage, she could see Mr Briggs, to her

relief. He was standing with Freddie and Joe at the front porch. To her surprise, Vinny Finch and Gert Radley were with them. She could see that Freddie was holding what seemed to be a long piece of wood in his hands – was that a good sign? Apparently not, for he dropped it as soon as he noticed her arrival, which made her feel the unwelcome intruder she was. Brave it out, she decided.

'I wanted to tell you,' she said awkwardly, 'that your friend Mr Girarde has left Spitalfrith.'

By the look on their faces, this was not news to Freddie and Joe, nor to Mr Briggs, although it was to Mr Finch and Miss Radley.

'Are you sure?' Vinny Finch asked, surprised. 'He told me he was here for the whole harvest season.'

'I'm very sure. His hut was empty and Farmer Pearson confirmed he'd left. He performed a superb vanishing act at the end of the children's conjuring show. Presumably, he's gone to join his brother.'

'Did he tell you, Freddie? Or you, Briggs?' Mr Finch asked, and when Freddie nodded, added, 'Then he'll surely return.'

Mr Briggs, Nell noted, remained silent, just looking from one person to another, but then he marched past Joe to stand at Freddie's side as if to protect him.

'Corporal G/26420, *sir*!' he declared, saluting. Freddie tapped him on the arm.

'Come on, Charlie,' he said, leading him away, with Joe following after a caustic glance at the three of them.

'I seem to have walked into a real old stew,' Nell said, somewhat bewildered as to what was going on. 'I was only looking for Mr Briggs – it won't be long before he's due to attend Lord Ansley.'

'Stew or not, you seem to have settled the reason we came here,' Gert Radley said wryly. 'We wanted to know where we could find that Frenchman Jean-Paul. There's still no sign of that brother of his – all very fishy. It's my belief they knew Lisette long before the Clerries were honoured with her snaky presence and that's where our Chief Inspector Melbray might find her murderer.'

'It's a risky situation for Briggs being close to Freddie *and* the Girardes,' Vinny added.

'Risky? He's been cleared,' Nell said indignantly.

'But not, Miss Drury, of being a risk for the real murderer,' Gert Radley replied.

Nell shivered. She hadn't thought of that. The Girarde brothers might become very close to being included in Alex's net as he fished into the Clerries' part in Lady Saddler's death. The further he fished, however, the more the real murderer might well become trapped and fight his way out by ridding himself of dangerous witnesses. Or was this a red herring on Gert Radley's part to distract from the Clerries' own quarrels with her ladyship?

As if reading her mind, Miss Radley raised that issue herself. 'This matter is of some concern to us, Miss Drury. The exhibition that Lisette wanted cancelled might seem a small matter compared with the war, but there is no doubt that Chief Inspector Melbray has his eye on us because of that. Our artistic lives are, or were, at stake because of her. We have to *carpe diem* as best we can because the time for us to storm our way to recognition as a great movement is short. I'm still hoping that Gilbert might forget his new plan and revert to the forthcoming exhibition being for the Artistes de Cler only. Returning to war, no matter the angle, is looking backwards for art, whereas we must go forward.'

Vinny Finch nodded. 'It seems, though, that Gilbert is intent on his plan, either because he was an official war artist or because of Lisette.'

'Which brings us back to the Messieurs Girarde,' snorted Gert Radley.

Everything did come back to the Girarde brothers. Nell was sure of that. And tomorrow, by hook or by crook, she would be on a train to Folkestone. Why Folkestone? Because Farmer Pearson's reference to sea air, she had reasoned, was likely to imply that Jean-Paul's choice might not be that far away, even if his brother had gone elsewhere. Where would be a Frenchman's first choice for sea air? One of the ports accessible to northern France, where the brothers lived. Dover? Ramsgate? Both possible, but, she hoped, Folkestone would be their choice, since it possessed one great attraction: the Pleasure Gardens Theatre, renowned for its wide range of theatrical performances and variety shows. Was that where Jean-Paul would be performing? A mere telephone call asking casually what the current show was would suffice.

*   *   *

The kitchen at Wychbourne Court, that haven where everything and everyone used to have its own place and such wonderful dishes could be created, was once again disrupted. Dinner had to be served in precisely one hour's time, and at the moment there were no welcoming smells, no sign of her staff being intent on their own job. *And it was her fault.* Nell was in no doubt of that. She had taken her eye off the pot, and no matter how hard she had tried to organize everything before she left, she had failed. The entire kitchen staff were gathered around Mrs Squires, who was pink in the face with indignation and appeared to be verbally under siege.

'I've known Mrs Golding thirty years,' she was saying defensively. 'She's as honest as the day. If she says Joe and Freddie Carter were there all night, and this French chappie too, then they were. And they were there for breakfast.'

Half of Nell wanted to yell that dinner came first, but the other half wanted to question this statement of fact. The latter half won. 'How does she know?' she demanded. She had joined the group, intent on getting this situation solved as quickly as possible.

Mrs Squires stared at her as though she'd forgotten to boil the potatoes. 'Well, of course she knows, don't she? She lives there.'

'But she can't be certain.' Nell thought back to the inquest. Was this evidence challenged? She couldn't remember, but it needed to be. 'She could only be sure of what happened if she held the only key to the whole cottage so that no one could get in or out, and' – she held up her hand when there was an immediate protest from Michel – 'if they all slept in the same room.'

There was a hostile pause, and then Mrs Squires picked up the cudgel again. 'If someone's there for breakfast, it stands to reason they stayed the night.' She might just as well have added 'So there!' so belligerent was her tone.

Nell promptly examined this claim. *Did* it stand to reason? No. To a young man like Freddie, who had probably just found out that the great love of his life was a German spy, returning to Spitalfrith during the night wouldn't be a barrier. Nor would it deter a father anxious to protect his son at all costs. Nor Jean-Paul. As to brother Jacques, however, alone for the night in that hut, there'd be no one to testify to his movements unless there was a witness among the other harvesters. Had any of them come forward? Alex would know, but she hadn't heard of any.

The alibis provided by Mrs Golding, however much given in good faith, weren't as solid as they seemed, she reasoned. She would have to bear that in mind if – provided she had Lord Ansley's permission – she managed to track down Jean-Paul Girarde tomorrow, if not his brother, too. Even so, she also had to bear in mind that there were suspects other than the Girarde brothers, and any one of them could have murdered Lady Saddler in theory. Some detective she was, she thought crossly. Was Alex in the same boat? Somehow, she doubted it.

So much for her eager planning. Her telephone call to the Pleasure Gardens Theatre had been positive. Jean-Paul was performing there as the Wizard of France. Lord Ansley's permission had been obtained and the catering was organized for her to leave for Folkestone on the Tuesday morning. Then fate intervened. Lady Enid, so the note that pageboy Jimmy brought from the dowager, would like to see Miss Drury at eleven o'clock. What was this about? Nell thought wearily, as she made her way to the Dower House. Did Lady Enid want to reproach her for lack of progress?

Just as she was about to ring the bell, the front door opened. A visitor was leaving and the redoubtable Mr Robins stood aside as the guest walked past him and through the door.

It was Alex Melbray. He looked as startled as she was.

And to make the situation worse, here she was flustered and in a hectic rush to get this meeting over and catch her train. 'Good morning, Chief Inspector,' she heard herself say.

He raised his hat to her. 'Miss Drury.' Then he strode on past her.

FOURTEEN

'It seems to me, Miss Drury, that I have become the pivot in a see-saw.'

Lady Enid looked pleased with her new role, but it further unnerved Nell. What see-saw? She had a suspicion that this might be leading into a delicate subject.

'I refer, of course,' Lady Enid continued blithely, 'to the death of Lady Saddler. Nevertheless, although the paths of love are no longer mine to tread, I do still observe those travelled by others.'

She'd been right, but Nell managed to grasp this painful nettle. 'Thank you, Lady Enid.' The dowager was indeed referring to the see-saw between herself and Alex. That would not have escaped her eagle eyes. Nell's love affair with Alex, while not exactly a secret at Wychbourne Court, was never openly broached by the Ansleys or her fellow servants. Now it might be – at just the worst time.

'It does appear to me,' Lady Enid swept on, 'that the paths currently trodden by yourself and Scotland Yard – or, if I might express it more personally, Chief Inspector Melbray – are taking him in one direction while you are steadfastly following the other. Both of you no doubt have your own line of reasoning.' She adeptly changed direction herself. 'You have the Carter family in your sights, whereas the chief inspector appears glued to the Artistes de Cler.'

Nell seized the lifeline she had been thrown. 'Not so much the Carters as Mr Briggs, Lady Enid. Until Lady Saddler's murderer is found, the deadlock here will go on.' Mistake. Backtrack, she told herself. 'The kitchen is fiercely divided on the question of Mr Briggs's guilt but—' She broke off, realizing she could hardly mention the presence of the Clerry guests being a problem, but the dowager followed her reasoning.

'I agree, Nell. While the Artistes de Cler remain with us, nothing can be normal. To sum up, there are mysteries that need to be unravelled on both sides. The artistes are hiding secrets, but so, I believe, are the Carters. The appearance or otherwise of my daughter's former fiancé, Jasper Montjoy, in the neighbourhood of their cottage suggests to me less a spectral appearance than a very material visitor, such as this mysterious Frenchman. There are therefore clearly two lines of investigation for Lady Saddler's murder – most satisfying for an impartial investigator such as myself. Are there links between the two perhaps?'

Nell felt on safer ground. 'Post-war France perhaps. Also, the artistes had their careers at stake.'

'You may be correct.' The dowager sagely nodded her head. 'There are five suspects on the Artistes de Cler path, and four on the Carters' side, if one includes that poor young man who carved the automata.' She corrected herself. 'I should say seven, not five, if we include Sir Gilbert and his daughter. One cannot play chess without pawns.'

To her astonishment, Nell found herself smiling, and even her stomach seemed to be churning less strongly. 'Theoretically,' she agreed.

'We shall compromise on that. What is your next move on this chessboard of ours, Nell?' The dowager looked vexed at her use of Nell's Christian name. 'My dear Miss Drury, pray forgive me. I am too familiar.'

'But Wychbourne is my home.' Nell was amazed that this was the formidable dowager to whom she was talking. 'I like being called Nell. As for my next move . . .' She pulled herself together. No matter how much she was suffering over Alex, she had to move on for Mr Briggs's sake. 'The next move is for me to go to Folkestone this afternoon,' she declared.

The dowager's eyebrows shot up. 'An appropriate destination if you believe the answer lies in France.'

'No, Folkestone itself. The Pleasure Gardens Theatre,' Nell explained. 'That's where Jean-Paul Girarde is performing. I worked out his whereabouts with the help of Farmer Pearson and I want to get to the bottom of his relationship with the Carters.'

The dowager was watching her closely. 'Excellent, Nell. You are a splendid chess partner, and in chess I find one must often play boldly with an element of risk according to your opponent. I believe this also applies to the emotions. You may be putting your game in jeopardy of checkmate, but the queen must stand by the king, must she not? And the king is lost without her.'

For someone who had had a long-running feud with her neighbour, dear Arthur Fontenoy, Nell thought, entirely based on their joint but clashing love for her husband, Lady Enid seemed remarkably practical and knowledgeable about love. Her husband had died more than thirty years ago, and yet her hatred for Arthur was relentless.

At last she was on her way to Folkestone. The thought of the Clerries not having the benefit of her personal charge of cuisine for dinner didn't seem to upset them (or her) unduly, and by half past one she had been driving her Ford to Tonbridge railway station.

Only one change of train and she'd be there. Meanwhile, this was a splendid way to travel through the Kentish countryside, even if the odd cow did decide to wander across the line and delay progress.

How many soldiers had taken this railway route during the war, rattling through the Kentish hop fields and cherry orchards that many would never see again? All to reach the sea, which some might never have seen before, then to cross the Channel to France. It was said that the sound of gunfire from the trenches could be heard from the Folkestone clifftops. The town and nearby villages had suffered terribly from bombing during the war, especially from one raid by Gotha aircraft in 1917, when among many other casualties the shopping area of Tontine Street was obliterated, with more than ninety people killed and hundreds injured. Rebuilding it could not wipe out the memory of that.

From the central railway station, Nell walked down to the harbour, imagining what this would have looked like in wartime when Freddie Carter and Charlie Briggs would have seen it. She could almost hear the tread of marching feet on the road leading down from the cliffs where many troops had been stationed. In the harbour, which had welcomed so many Belgian refugees to England at the beginning of the war, endless columns of soldiers had boarded the ships awaiting them.

When she reached the Pleasure Gardens, she could see groups of small children everywhere, watched by parents and nannies, and the theatre with its towers and columned entrance stood grandly in its midst of the gardens. Outside it, she could see placards advertising the wizard she had come to see – with or without his brother and Hubert the rabbit as assistants. The matinee performance was still in progress, so she decided to make her way round to the stage-door exit and remain there until he emerged. Unless, of course, he spotted her first and promptly vanished. She was cheered by one aspect – the fact that he was clearly sought after for such billings as this confirmed that he and Jacques must have come to Wychbourne for a specific purpose that had nothing to do with harvesting corn. So what was it?

It was high time, Nell thought as she waited impatiently, that Jean-Paul told her the *whole* story. This pudding mix had to be stirred. The stage-door manager told her that the show would finish in half an hour, but although she duly saw the audience emerge from the front of the building and many of the cast from the stage door, there was no sign of Jean-Paul. She was on edge. Was he staying in the theatre for an evening performance? She crossed her fingers that he was just late emerging – and, indeed, a few minutes later he appeared, looking so very casual with a scarf knotted round his neck and a fisherman's cap on his head.

He was clearly startled to see her, but magicians move swiftly and he was quickly himself again.

'Madame Nell?' He took her hand, which she realized belatedly might be somewhat sticky from the sandwich she had eaten earlier.

'You look remarkably pleased to see me,' she said pleasantly. 'Do conjurers learn how to put on a brave face when things go wrong?'

'Do chefs flourish a sunken cake when cooking goes awry, madame?'

'They disguise it,' she admitted.

He smiled. 'Magicians, too. Let us take an ice cream together. It is good to honour the sun.'

'Is your brother with you?' She tried to make this sound a casual question as he bought two cones, presented one of them to her and waved her towards a vacant bench.

'He is not, Madame Nell,' he replied in between licks of ice cream. 'Did you come to see me in the belief that he would be? What a shame.'

'No, I came to see you.'

'Tell me why, please?'

'I believe there is something you are not telling me. Perhaps the reason you came to Spitalfrith. Something concerning your sister, Freddie Carter and Mr Briggs.'

'And if there were, why should I tell you, Madame Nell?'

'Because Mr Briggs will never be free of the shadow of guilt that lies over him until this murder case is solved and he is completely cleared.'

He considered this, continuing to lick the ice cream. '*Oui*, perhaps that is so, but how could a simple magician have the solution when I was not present in Beaudricourt where this story began?'

He wasn't going to get away with that. 'But you were born in Lille where Lady Saddler lived.'

For a moment a cloud came over his face, as the smile disappeared. 'Until I joined the army, yes.'

He was guarded now, and his eyes were watchful. Good. She would plunge into deeper water. 'There is still something you haven't told me about Marie-Hélène. I know she spied for the Germans and that Freddie probably discovered that from Lady Saddler, causing him to destroy the singing birds. But there's something else, isn't there?'

His face was blank, no sign of a smile now. 'Singing birds, you call them. Automata. I will tell you about *them* and then we shall see what else, Madame Nell. Singing birds can have two meanings, so what is true for us now? Most singing birds make our lives beautiful, fill our hearts with pleasure. Freddie's were carved with love. But how to carve and make them sing? That is a great skill. When Freddie grew to be a man, the owner of Spitalfrith was a gentleman who had lived many years in France. He worked for the Bontem family. Does that mean anything to you?'

'Yes.' Nell remembered Joe Carter telling her about that.

'Then you will know that in the last century the Bontem family were the leaders of the art of creating singing bird automata, and this gentleman learned the skills from them. When he bought Spitalfrith from the Montjoy family, he was old and he took pleasure in teaching Freddie the mechanisms necessary for the singing birds as Freddie was already a skilled wood carver. "I will give you a garden of singing birds," Freddie wrote to my sister with love. But singing birds has another meaning: betrayal of one's friends that can lead to their deaths. Singing birds build a prison of four walls around you, a prison of your own making that you cannot escape.'

Nell listened in dismay. Had Marie-Hélène regretted what she had done, built her own prison? How had her brothers felt, coming home after the war and finding their sister not only dead but despised for being a traitor? But having come so far, Nell had to continue. 'How did your sister and Freddie meet in Beaudricourt? Did he innocently pass on information which she passed on to the Germans?'

Jean-Paul sighed. 'This is difficult, Nell. You really want to know this?'

'Yes,' she replied. Unless she did, she had no way of understanding how this story fitted into what was going on at Wychbourne. And whether Jean-Paul was friend or foe.

'Then I will tell you. No, Marie-Hélène did not use information from Freddie or Charlie Briggs. It was in Lille that spying took place. I have told you that when Lille was occupied by the Germans, life became very hard there, and Jacques and I were already in the army. There were big taxes, no food, no money. My sister, like Lisette Rennard, was a singer, and worked often in the cafés that the Germans visited. There was much opposition to the German occupiers in Lille, led by great patriots like Léon Trulin and Louise de Bettignies, and later by agents for La Dame Blanche, the Belgian movement that spread to northern France. Everyone suspected their neighbours. My sister made enemies there because she was seen to be friendly with the German occupiers, and so, as you know, she had to move to Beaudricourt, which was not occupied and where no one knew her history. There she sang for the British troops in the village *estaminet* and that is where she met Freddie and Charlie Briggs, who were camped nearby. Freddie – who my aunt tells me was not then the poor invalid he is today – fell in love with her and she with him.'

'And presumably she wasn't known to be a spy there.'

'*Non*. Now I tell you more about how it ended. After the terrible battle where the Tenth Battalion was nearly wiped out, both Freddie and Charlie were wounded and were sent to different hospitals. Freddie then fought on with the Royal West Kents, ending the war in Belgium, but never fully recovered mentally from the fighting, as you know. In hospital for longer, Charlie Briggs met the brother of Lady Ansley. That is how, so I am told, he eventually came to Wychbourne as her husband's valet.'

So that was the connection. Nell had never known his story – but then, she realized, humbled, that she had never enquired. 'And your sister?' she asked quietly. 'You said she died in Bapaume.'

'Freddie and Charlie's battle was on the twenty-third of March, and the next day Bapaume was shelled and fell to the Germans. As I told you, Marie-Hélène, having heard that the English had retreated and not having news of Freddie, travelled there, hard though that was. No one knows her fate, save that she was listed dead.'

And now for the difficult question, determined as she was to find out the full story: 'How did Lady Saddler discover Marie-Hélène was a traitor?'

Jean-Paul seemed to be staring at passers-by rather than concentrating on her questions, but she was treading on delicate ground, so that was understandable. 'That is easy to answer,' he said. 'Suspicion travels quickly, especially in the world of the *estaminets.*'

She took a deep breath. 'And now I'm asking you why you really came to Spitalfrith, Jean-Paul?'

He took his time in answering her. 'I wished to warn Freddie.'

'Warn him?'

'That Lady Saddler was in fact Lisette Rennard, about whom Marie-Hélène must have talked to him.'

Nell was not convinced. 'Would your sister have talked to Freddie about life in Lille if she had had to flee because she was giving information to the Germans?'

'Stories get confused in wartime. Who knows what she told Freddie, but Lisette had known my sister for many years.' Jean-Paul buried his face in his hands. 'Forgive me, Nell, but I cannot speak of this any more. It is too painful.'

Nell was full of remorse. 'I shouldn't have made you tell me. I'm sorry.' She put her arm around him. It wasn't much, but it was all she could do.

'I will return, Nell. Soon. *Je te promets.* I promise.'

Nell smiled. 'Then there is one last question – not hard.'

'Tell me.'

'What happened to Hubert the rabbit?'

Gert Radley surveyed her fellow Artistes de Cler without enthusiasm. The sun might be shining, the late summer flowers of Wychbourne Court were undoubtedly beautiful, the hospitality they were receiving from the Ansleys faultless – indeed, over-generous – but nevertheless Wychbourne was still a prison in which they were all on remand. They were stuck here without a clue as to what was going on.

All that was clear was that neither Scotland Yard nor Gilbert wanted them to leave. Scotland Yard, in the form of Chief Inspector Melbray and an over-cheerful sergeant, paid visits from time to time, and, theoretically, the Clerries were free to go anywhere or paint as they pleased, provided they didn't leave Wychbourne. Even Gilbert had made it depressingly clear that he felt the answer to Lisette's murder was right here, close at hand, and until it had been found, he'd be most grateful if they stayed. That, Gert deduced, meant he thought that one of them was guilty.

So here they were, five Clerries, twiddling their thumbs and eyeing their comrades with deep suspicion. 'Is it you?' was in their eyes as they talked in such a friendly way to each other, when probably one of those pairs of eyes knew all too well who it was. Did that suspicion stem from Lisette's murder or about who might have supported her in her determination to cancel the exhibition? If, indeed, one of them had, the matter was immaterial now, as Gilbert had in effect had abandoned the Artistes de Cler by throwing the exhibition open to a wider field of approach.

'How much longer are we all to be kept here?' Thora asked plaintively.

'Darling,' Lance replied querulously, 'who knows? Until that polite chief inspector realizes that the valet Briggs is most certainly guilty?'

'*Oui*, you are right,' Pierre said quickly, to Gert's fury. It was all too easy to blame Briggs in order to avoid the more probable truth.

Thora wasn't pleased either, she noticed. She was glaring at her erstwhile beloved fiancé. So the poor things still hadn't resolved their disagreement. It was still stalemate. Thora believed in Briggs's innocence, just as Gert and Vinny did, but Pierre and Lance remained firmly of the opinion that he was guilty. Pierre's insistence on Briggs's guilt was strange indeed, considering his devotion to Thora's family coffers and his prospects. Of course, Lisette had once been his mistress, but Gert found it hard to believe that Pierre would endanger his comfortable life for that reason. With his intransigence over Briggs, he was merely adding to his problems.

'No doubt, Lance,' Thora said loftily, 'you consider Briggs guilty for reasons of your own. Why *were* you quarrelling with Lisette just before she went out to her death?'

Lance paled. 'It was merely a matter of the new season's hem lengths, darling. A light-hearted discussion regarding my latest designs. And, come to that, do you believe in Briggs's innocence merely because your upright sense of honour disguises the fact that you know perfectly well that someone else committed this crime – even you perhaps?'

Before Thora could reply, Vinny intervened. 'The more we argue, Lance, the less we achieve. We need to wait patiently until Gilbert is happy that everything is settled for the exhibition.'

'That's only an excuse, Vinny,' Gert said crossly. 'He wants us to stay until Lisette's murderer is found, although he can hardly expect any one of us to stand up and declare ourselves guilty.'

There was a silence, broken by Pierre. 'That is perhaps true, but for the future of the Artistes de Cler we need to be united in supporting Gilbert's new approach. I take it we are all working on that, and that I shall lead you into a new and exciting future? This is necessary for us to be saluted as the powerful movement we are.'

Gert broke the silence that followed. 'Certainly, Pierre,' she said briskly. 'However, the newspapers are currently providing us Clerries with the best advertisement we could ever hope for – and when Lisette's true murderer is unmasked, that will increase our fame.' She paused. 'Especially if it is one of us.'

'Miss Drury, how much longer are these guests going to stay?' Michel pleaded on Thursday morning. 'I do not like seeing my *Tournedos Mistinguett* returned on their plates. I am French. I know how to cook this dish.'

'We'll give them something new,' Nell said encouragingly. 'How about Imam Bayildi? We've enough recipes here for a thousand nights, like the stories in the *Arabian Nights*. Just be grateful that the guests can't cut off our heads because something isn't to their liking, like the Sultan's ridding himself of his wives. We'll try it as a dish for this evening, along with the Dover sole and mutton.'

Nevertheless, Nell was in full agreement with Michel, and it was clear that Mrs Fielding also shared their impatience. She had been especially tight-lipped about Miss Radley's attempt to assist the housemaids under the mistaken impression that they were downtrodden menials.

'Helping Lizzie with the beds indeed! It's a downright insult suggesting I don't know how to teach my girls bedmaking.'

Time was passing and nothing seemed to be happening, Nell fretted. Alex must surely be pursuing the Artistes de Cler to find his murderer, but there was no sign of it. Lady Enid had not produced any more information on any of them and Nell could not take any active steps herself unless Alex permitted it. And there was no hope of that. After her brief glimpse of him – it hurt that he hadn't even stopped as he marched past her – she was certain that nothing had changed. Their love affair was over. Once he had left Wychbourne, she told herself, she must begin her life again. A Prince Charming might even appear – a sort of Jean-Paul materializing out of the bushes. But somehow this did not comfort her.

The malaise in the servants' wing still continued. Kitty had taken luncheon to Mr Briggs and reported his absence. Nell assumed this meant another trip to see Freddie, so she was surprised to open the door to Pug's Parlour for her own lunch and find him sitting there. Unfortunately, Mr Peters was also present, looking stiffly disapproving, but luckily Jenny Smith was chattering nineteen to the dozen despite the frosty atmosphere.

Nell had only just sat down when Mrs Fielding arrived, but she stopped short in the doorway.

'I wondered where you all were,' she snapped.

As her eyes fixed themselves on Mr Peters, Nell inwardly groaned. Trouble was looming.

'I trust that I'm welcome here, Fred.' Mrs Fielding sniffed.

Mr Peters's Christian name was never used in public, a term that included the upper servants' lunch, so this, Nell thought, was a slip on Mrs Fielding's part, or perhaps she was making a point.

'Of course, *Mrs Fielding*,' Mr Peters retorted, as Jenny cast Nell a despairing glance. 'We take our meals together, even though Mr Briggs is present – and you, of course, Miss Drury.'

Nell was taken aback at the implication. Had the situation become so bad?

Mr Briggs leapt to his feet anxiously. 'Corporal—' he began.

'Sit down, Mr Briggs,' Mrs Fielding interrupted. 'And enjoy your lunch.'

Somewhat uncertainly, Mr Briggs obeyed.

'Pug's Parlour should be neutral ground, Mr Peters,' Nell said furiously, but Mr Peters did not reply, and the rest of the meal was finished in silence.

'What the blazes is happening to Wychbourne Court?' Jenny said to her as they left. 'It isn't just here in the servants' wing. Everyone's out of kilter. Lady Clarice is rushing around as if a hornet had bitten her.'

'Jasper again?' Nell asked resignedly.

'No idea. She was looking for you, though.'

Lady Clarice was beside herself with excitement when Nell reached her boudoir.

'There you are at last, Nell. I'm so glad. I knew you would want to be the first to know. I visited Spitalfrith this morning and, with Miss Saddler's permission, wandered through the grounds. I couldn't resist rambling through the woods as I used to do with Jasper, and – oh, Nell – Jasper was there. I know he was. He had come to tell me something.'

'I'm delighted,' Nell managed to say, searching desperately for the right words. 'But it was daytime. Are you sure it was Jasper?'

'It was he, Nell. He had a message for me.'

Tread carefully, Nell thought. This might be more serious than she had thought. 'Did he speak?' she asked cautiously.

'Of course not.' Lady Clarice smiled, though. 'He guided me. He was the gentle movement in the bushes as the breezes brought him to me; the sheer sense of his presence convinced me. I ran towards him, but he would not, *could* not, appear. Instead, he gave me this message. As I reached the edge of the woodland, I couldn't sense him any more, so I looked around me. And there were daisies, Michaelmas daisies, bluey-purple daisies, the very colour of the box in which I keep his letters from Africa. He guided me there. He was in the second battalion of the Queen's Own Royal West Kents, and his very last letter told me they had been fighting at a place called Wakkerstroom and were about to help free a beleaguered Guards battalion at Biddulph's Berg – I know these names by heart because I did not hear from him again, Nell.

'I can't show them to you,' she continued, 'but in that letter he told me this: "I shall return to you one day. I shall always be with you then. Never fear about that, my darling Clarice." It took six months for that letter to reach me, and I treasure it above all the others. Now my Jasper *is* always here. I have seen him.'

As she left, Nell was fighting back tears, partly for Lady Clarice and partly her own. Yesterday she had seen Alex with no such words as those that comforted Lady Clarice.

Lady Clarice's final words to her had been, 'I shall go again to Spitalfrith, Nell. That's why I wanted to see you so badly. I know you'll want to come with me.'

Of course she would go. Nell knew that. How could she not?

Gert Radley pondered her next step, tired of living in limbo. She needed action, and she wouldn't get it from Chief Inspector Alex Melbray, who was only too active but wasn't going to listen to her waffling on about Lisette Saddler. Miss Drury now – or Nell as she had come to think of her – was a different proposition. There was a whisper that Melbray was sweet on Nell, but Gert had seen no signs of that. Pity, although the Ansleys wouldn't want to lose their prize chef. A shame for Nell too if there was nothing to it.

Gert had just left Gilbert's so-called memorial tea for Lisette, although it was a strange one to say the least.

'Do you know why Gilbert's laid on this tea, Petra?' Gert had asked her beforehand.

'I'm afraid not,' Petra had answered – truthfully, Gert had thought, as Gilbert had always been one for playing the contented old man in the corner, until he decided to play his own cards.

Perhaps that had been today. All the Clerries had been there, of course, somewhat nervous to see if Gilbert had changed his mind again about the exhibition. He hadn't. The poor chap had really gone off his trolley, and Gert realized there would be no stopping him. She knew him of old. He'd wittered on, demanding to know how they were all planning to use the theme of 'war into peace' in their work for the exhibition. He'd listened carefully to all of their replies and then made his dramatic declaration.

'The Artistes de Cler stand for the truth, and yet I believe that none of us will tell the truth in our work. We all have secrets.'

That had silenced the troops, Gert thought with relish. Gilbert could be right, of course.

Then he had added something even more startling: 'I believe Lisette may have died because of hers.'

'What's your point, Gilbert?' Vinny had asked gently.

And then Gilbert had really gone off his rocker. 'If I knew my point, I'd tell you. But everything is all mixed up. *"You are old, Father William," the young man said. "And yet you incessantly stand on your head – do you think, at your age, it is right?"* No, I don't, but I'm incessantly standing on my head when I think of Lisette. Everything is upside down, back to front. She wanted the exhibition cancelled, and some of you think she had some support for that. But why did she feel so strongly? I am bewildered.'

Gilbert had spread out his hands to them in appeal. His message was clear. Help me, friends. But none of them could.

Gert's underlying fear had grown. She needed to talk – and Nell seemed her best hope. Clouds were gathering and the storm would shortly burst. Where or how, she could not tell, but it would happen.

FIFTEEN

What did Gert Radley want with her? Nell wondered, as she led her visitor to the Cooking Pot late on Thursday afternoon. Or was she becoming suspicious of *everybody* connected to Spitalfrith – save for Petra. Somewhere there must be a link to Lisette Saddler's murder.

'Nice room,' Gert remarked approvingly, although Nell had the impression this was far from being a mere social call.

'Not much room for easels and paintings,' she joked, as Miss Radley squeezed herself into the guest's chair.

'Each to his own.'

Perhaps Miss Radley was equally suspicious of her Clerry companions, rather than merely taking a look at the east wing. Nell remembered Mrs Fielding's tale of Miss Radley trying to help the housemaids out; perhaps she was now investigating why the servants had to be herded together in the east wing. An easy answer if so. They formed a family of their own here – even if at present that included a few squabbles and feuds.

Miss Radley grinned as though reading her mind. 'I'm here about Lisette Saddler, Nell.'

'About her, I hope, and not Mr Briggs,' Nell replied bluntly, noting the 'Nell' – just as well, since she always thought of her guest as Gert.

'Agreed on both. As to Lisette, the questions are who and why, as I'm sure you're aware.'

'Isn't that straightforward?' Nell replied, unsure where this might be leading. 'Either her death was due to her knocking your exhibition for six or it is connected with the destruction of the Carters' automata, which is how poor Mr Briggs became embroiled in this awful business.'

Gert took some time to answer. 'Probably. What about Lisette's life before she married Gilbert, though? We know her war record, but it's been nearly eight years since the fighting stopped and seven since Peace Day. Lisette had a life in Paris during those years. She was a model and she had lovers there, one of whom was our Pierre. We don't know much about the rest, save that when Gilbert married her two months ago, Pierre had not long since thrown her out. She turned her attention to Gilbert to spite him. Gilbert provided all she wanted. An English knight and a new country to live in, where any enemies she had picked up along the way wouldn't be able to touch her.'

'What about the war itself?' Nell asked, interested by this plain talk. 'We know she did much as an agent spying on the Germans, and that must have meant she picked up enemies somewhere. Is that the reason she left Lille to work in Paris?'

Gert shrugged. 'No idea. More work there, I suppose. I wasn't in her magic circle, but I'm an artist, and we study, sometimes subconsciously, the faces of those we draw. After that, we look at those painted faces and wonder.'

'What did you wonder about Lady Saddler?'

'What I hope I captured in my portrait of her – the one she destroyed before it could be exhibited. It showed all too clearly that this was a woman who, as Vinny Finch says, was the one who walked by herself. A Kipling cat. That's why I wanted a word with you. Chief Inspector Melbray looks at facts and puts them together like a kid's building set, but you're free to play differently. You can look at those blocks and take a leap away from them if you so choose. If you concentrate on Lisette, I hope you might spring to the right answer – and do so before Gilbert goes right off his trolley – or we all do. No aspersions on your hospitality, of course.'

Gert gave a light laugh but that didn't disguise her anxiety. Could she, Nell, really take leaps in this murder case? she wondered after Gert had left. Leaps were all very well, but they had to be in the right direction, and just at present she only had her instinct to choose what that was.

Concentrate on Lisette, Gert had said. Very well. Why had she been so eager to cancel the exhibition? She didn't like having her portrait painted and yet she was a model. She had lived in Lille, and Jean-Paul's reticence about Lille was noticeable. Sir Gilbert might be off his rocker, but perhaps she, Nell, was, too. The little she knew about Lisette's wartime life in Lille came from Jean-Paul when he was talking about Marie-Hélène. No. That wasn't entirely correct.

Break the eggs carefully, Nell warned herself. Those were the days when Marie-Hélène had been a spy for the Germans – so Freddie had said, and Jean-Paul had not denied it. Lisette Saddler had come to the Carters' cottage that Saturday afternoon and broken that news to Freddie, and in great distress Freddie had destroyed the birds. And Freddie had told Nell about his traitorous sweetheart.

Freddie!

What words had he actually used? She was dependent on them for working out what had really happened. 'Germans, spy' were the two words that stuck out, and they had referred to Marie-Hélène. But during the war the term 'spy' was used not only for enemy agents but for those opposing the enemy. At an earlier meeting Freddie had become very confused and used the words 'but she never done it'. Had Freddie made the same mistake as she had and assumed Marie-Hélène was a traitor when Lady Saddler came that afternoon, and as a result had destroyed the birds?

Steady the Buffs, Nell drilled herself. That was possible, but more probable was that Lady Saddler had either been maliciously lying about Marie-Hélène's activities or passing on what had been general gossip in Lille. But that didn't fit. Jean-Paul had never

denied that Marie-Hélène was guilty, and that implied her guilt
had been established. Yet Freddie had also said to Nell that 'she
never done it' – and *if* he was talking about his sweetheart and
not about Lady Saddler's destruction of the birds, who could he
have heard that from, if not Jean-Paul? *So why hadn't Jean-Paul
told her his sister was innocent?*

'Jasper will come to the dell, as he did before,' Lady Clarice told
Nell happily. Nell had driven her to Spitalfrith Manor to let Petra
know of their arrival before setting off on their evening mission.
'Or will it be on the woodland path?' she added anxiously, as
Petra opened the door. 'He came there once.'

And it was somewhere along there, Nell remembered wryly,
that she had chased the phantom who turned out to be Jean-Paul.
There'd been no sign of his return from Folkestone so far, and she
so desperately wanted to talk to him.

'I'll come with you,' Petra offered obligingly, 'and then we can
cover both possibilities.'

'Excellent,' Nell said with relief. Two could handle Lady Clarice
better than one. 'Perhaps I should remain on the path in case Jasper
comes there, and you could stay in the dell with Lady Clarice,
Petra? You'll be a better medium than I am.' She felt somewhat
guilty, not because she had any great love of dark paths in woods
at night but because she couldn't bear the idea of Lady Clarice's
disappointment. And if Jasper was keeping an eye open for them,
her doubts about his presence would hardly be encouraging for
him to materialize, she comforted herself.

Lady Clarice immediately warmed to Nell's suggestion. 'How
splendid. Jasper will enjoy the presence of someone whose family
dwells in his own ancestral home.'

Petra, with a slight quiver of her lips, agreed. 'I'd like that,' she
said bravely.

Nell was glad she had had the opportunity of filling Petra in
on the likely results (or lack of them) in the dell. As regards her
own patrolling area, she felt reasonably happy, especially because
she would be grasping a large torch in her hand, to Lady Clarice's
disapproval. Petra had brought one, too. Even if Jean-Paul had
returned, Nell reasoned, he was unlikely to be wandering around
these woodlands again, which might confuse the issue of Jasper.

Unless a stray poacher had chosen Spitalfrith for his prey tonight, there wouldn't be any rustling in the bushes to delude Lady Clarice that Jasper was around – and unfortunately her disappointment would be extreme tonight in view of the importance she had placed on this visit.

'Of course,' Lady Clarice chattered happily, 'Jasper used to tell me all about his childhood days here at Spitalfrith.'

'I can see why he loved it,' Petra assured her. 'Was he the son of Richard Montjoy – I think he was a member of parliament once, wasn't he?'

Bless you, Petra, Nell thought.

'Indeed he was!' Lady Clarice exclaimed with delight. 'Jasper's mother was from the Dorling family, you know.' Petra listened patiently as Lady Clarice led the way in the now fading light through the woods to the dell.

'They had many more servants, I suppose, than we've been lucky enough to inherit?' Petra pressed on.

'Many more,' Lady Clarice agreed tactlessly. 'At least fifteen. And gardeners, too. Six, I recall. They always seemed to be every-where, which is why our dell was so private and important to Jasper and me. We knew we would not be interrupted.'

Nell entertained visions of unbridled lovemaking amidst the tree roots. Brambles and nettles would be mingled with the daffo-dils and anemones. Like life, she thought philosophically. Even the sweetest pudding should have a dash of lemon in it.

'How long do we stay in the dell?' Petra asked politely, as they reached the junction of the paths.

'Until Jasper has left,' Lady Clarice informed them unhelpfully.

'May we talk to him?' Petra asked.

Lady Clarice thought this over. 'I need him to know I'm thinking of him first, but then I will do so. It does so depend on what mood he is in.'

The dusk birdsong had now almost ceased and it was growing much darker. Nell surreptitiously risked putting her torch on, but this crime was noted.

'Take care, Nell,' Lady Clarice warned her. 'Ghosts do not like candles, and torches therefore pose a real threat.'

So did the absence of light, Nell thought irrepressibly. She'd tripped over several tree roots on the way here. Jasper had a lot to answer for. Then she reproached herself as she parted from Lady Clarice and Petra when they reached the turning for the path to the dell. She had to take this seriously, hard though that was to do. There was nothing she liked better than a warm summer's evening in a damp woodland in the dark, she tried to convince herself. First of all, what should she do? Sit on that obligingly placed tree trunk and listen out for Jasper? Or should she patrol the path in case he was lurking in the bushes? *No, be serious*, she reminded herself.

She tried the tree trunk first. Damp, but not unbearably so. She waited there, feeling like a pixie perched on its toadstool. She could hear the murmur of voices from the dell, which made her wish she had chosen to go with them and patrolling the path be blowed. Here it was all silent. A whole army of wildlife would be waking up ready for their night sorties in search of food, but as yet there was no sign or sound of it.

After ten minutes she decided it was time to begin a patrol, *with* a torch. Jasper would just have to put up with it. Which direction should she take, though? What was she expecting? Answer: nothing, so rather than go backwards, she decided to turn left and march on. She had only walked fifty yards or so when she heard it. Footsteps? An animal's? Human? Must be the wind. She strained her eyes into the darkness beyond the torchlight. Were those moving shadows? Nothing that she could be sure of. She *must* be imagining it.

No, there was definitely a shape. A lurch of her stomach as she realized this was no ghost. Not Jasper. Was it Joe, Freddie – or Jean-Paul? Not *again*, surely? She relaxed slightly as the figure halted as the torchlight dimly caught him at the end of its range. Thin, wiry and tall. If it was him, she told her pounding heart, at least it was the known, not the unknown, and at dead of night that was reassuring.

'*Je m'excuse*,' he called out to her. It *was* him – no, it wasn't Jean-Paul's voice; it was harsher, harder. *Not* Jean-Paul? Then who? He must have heard her heart pounding for he called out, '*Jacques Girarde, Madame*.' He mockingly lifted his cap to her and turned to go.

The brother? The possible murderer? 'Where is Jean-Paul?' she yelled after him, but he was disappearing into the darkness of the track ahead.

His voice floated back. 'With Monsieur Carter and his son.'

'The police need to speak to you,' she shouted, and even as she did so, she realized how stupid that sounded.

But somehow she couldn't stop, determined to talk to him regardless of common sense. She broke into a run as he disappeared either around the corner ahead or into the dark undergrowth around them. Jacques Girarde could hold the key to the whole terrible situation, the key that might solve any lingering doubts about Mr Briggs's innocence.

She was near him now, she was sure of it, and the air seemed heavy with danger. She rounded the corner and immediately her arm was seized, making her drop the torch, as Jacques Girarde pounced on her, still gripping her arm tightly and leering at her in the darkness. So like Jean-Paul and yet so different. A rough face, full of menace. The grip grew tighter and she yelled out in pain. Then, just as suddenly, she was released as another shape materialized in the darkness and her attacker vanished into the woodland.

Her knight in shining armour was Alex Melbray.

'Are you hurt, Nell?' he asked grimly.

'Only my pride and a sore arm,' she managed to reply.

'I'm glad I could come to your rescue, but what the blazes are you doing here?'

'Ghost-hunting with Lady Clarice,' she said shakily. 'But that was Jean-Paul's brother, Jacques Girarde. Hadn't you better dash after him?' she added uncertainly when he didn't move.

'My men are watching him.'

'You *knew* he was back? Why didn't you warn us? And what are *you* doing here?'

'My job, my territory, Nell.' Softly softly.

Was that a comment on his handling of the case or a rebuke to her? she wondered as she picked up her torch and watched him walk away without another word, his own torch growing dimmer and dimmer. The pain from that really did hurt, but her arm did not. Still giddy with shock, she forced herself to turn back along the track and take the path to the dell.

All was silent there when she reached Lady Clarice and Petra.

'Jasper?' she whispered with some effort, although their faces gave her the answer.

'Not yet,' Petra said brightly.

Lady Clarice laid her hand on hers. 'He will come. Perhaps I mistook the date.'

Nell woke the next morning after fitful sleep. Where was Jean-Paul? If Jacques was here, then he would be here, too. She had to find him, but she wasn't eager to run into Jacques again.

She wrestled with this problem as she worked through the morning's agenda. She was longing to share her doubts about Marie-Hélène's guilt with Alex, but she would have to let him take the lead. Why else would he have had his men at Spitalfrith late last night if he didn't have the Girarde brothers in his sights for murder? Anyway, if she sought him out, he might think she was crawling back to him, pleading for another chance. She couldn't bear the idea of that – and anyway he wouldn't want to hear her as yet unproven ideas.

Mr Briggs, she muttered to herself. *Think about him* – no, first she'd begin her job. Think of dishes for future dinners, think about what she needed from Mr Fairweather and the butcher. Everyday things.

It didn't work. She hurried through the essential tasks for dinner, but Mr Briggs refused to vanish from her mind. Worse, so did Jacques Girarde. There was, she realized with a sinking heart, only one way out. She had to take the bull by the horns and find Alex. She had to talk to him, no matter what he thought.

Suppose he wasn't at the Coach and Horses, she thought as she made her way down the drive. Suppose he was lodging in Sevenoaks or had returned to London today. Was she right in her decision to talk to him? She didn't know whether to be glad or sorry to find that he was indeed staying at the Coach and Horses. He was in the snug, so Mr Hardcastle informed her once again, and, of course, a woman could not enter that sacred male territory.

She was pacing up and down with tension when Alex emerged, took one look at her and informed Mr Hardcastle that he was returning to the snug with Nell and no one else was to enter.

One up to Alex, Nell thought thankfully, but she didn't give much for her chances of a friendly conversation with Mr Hardcastle for a time.

The snug was a comfortable retreat, full of Toby jugs, tankards, prints of Sevenoaks and Tunbridge Wells, and leather armchairs ingrained with the smell of years of tobacco smoke. Alex, who didn't smoke cigarettes and only rarely a pipe, flung the window open. 'I take it this is about the Saddler case,' he said neutrally, taking a chair some distance away.

'Yes.' So he did think she might be crawling back again. She'd show him how wrong he was. At first words refused to come, but she took firm control of herself. 'Lady Saddler and the war.'

'Go on,' he said.

She did go on, and to her relief he listened carefully about the visit to Jean-Paul in Folkestone and her theory about Marie-Hélène.

'Could that affect the possible roles of the Artistes de Cler?' he asked when she drew to a close. Trust Alex to point that out.

'It could,' she said. 'And anyway, you know that Jacques Girarde is back now, and Jean-Paul, too – or will be shortly. You could talk to them – if you think there's anything to my theory,' she added hastily. 'You must know where they're living.'

'I do,' he said unexpectedly, 'but don't forget Jean-Paul Girarde has an alibi that has as yet gone unchallenged.'

'Do you believe it holds up? I saw holes in it,' she forced herself to say.

'No. I'm going off limits here, Nell, but I don't want you walking into a lions' cage, whether the lions are in it or not. Mrs Golding, as you no doubt deduced, is a simple soul. She retires at night and assumes that everybody currently under her roof does the same. She's now admitted that the bed Jean-Paul should have slept in was barely rumpled, although he was there at breakfast.'

'It was more likely his brother – he had no alibi and could certainly have returned and killed Lady Saddler.'

'There is no brother, Nell.'

'*What?*' She stared at him. 'We both saw him last night.'

'We saw Jean-Paul.'

SIXTEEN

Alex was regarding her almost compassionately as she struggled with this surely absurd notion. 'Did you see this brother close up, with light on his face?'

'No,' Nell admitted unwillingly, 'but you must have done.'

'I haven't. I called at the farm twice yesterday since Pearson said he'd let them the hut again, but, not surprisingly, I'd just missed Jacques, according to Jean-Paul. And no, Pearson couldn't actually swear he'd seen them together, and nor could anyone else. We had a lot of response to the poster we sent out around the country and to the ports – the photograph was faked, of course. Again, not surprisingly, all came from people who had seen Jean-Paul's act at their local theatres. That, incidentally, was a double act until they arrived in Spitalfrith,' he added.

'Well, that's proof that—' Nell stopped. There was clearly more to this.

Alex nodded. 'The *Sûreté* in Paris informs us that no such person appears on official French records. Nell, Jean-Paul Girarde is a mimic, a ventriloquist, a fine actor and, above all, a magician. His act is based on deception, of course, like those of all magicians. You think you're watching carefully, but you miss the vital actions.'

'Such as what happened to the giant rabbit in the show I saw?' Nell asked, still unconvinced. 'And in the case of the Girardes, it was two actual people, not just a rabbit.'

'The principle is the same. The magician and the assistant. The audience's attention is distracted. One person disappears behind the scenes, different voices are heard, and it seems that another completely different person appears, so speedily that one takes it at face value. Believe me, last night we were with Jean-Paul Girarde only, Nell. He was wearing his other face.'

'Doctor Jekyll and Mr Hyde.' She still found it hard to believe, especially in view of that merciless grip. She thought she had known Jean-Paul, but now she realized she hadn't known him at all. She had fallen for his patter, as he had fully intended.

'Yes. Do you believe me now, Nell?'

She had to do so, she supposed, difficult though it was. 'Were you following him or me last night?' she asked.

'You. Petra Saddler had told me about Lady Clarice's visit, and I guessed you'd be with her. Miss Saddler was worried on your behalf, and so was I. I knew Girarde was back and that you might be getting too close to the truth of what happened to Lady Saddler for him to risk. I'm sure he was hoping to scare you rather than kill you, though.'

'Thank you,' she said wryly. She swallowed her pride to add, 'This must affect your case, Alex. No Jacques to suspect. Was it Jean-Paul who killed Lady Saddler?'

'It looks that way.'

'But why?' she burst out. 'Even if I'm right about Marie-Hélène's innocence, why kill Lady Saddler?'

'Emotions run deep and they run for a long time.'

That didn't fit. There had to be some other reason. 'Did Lady Saddler *know* Marie-Hélène was innocent? Jean-Paul knew that it was Lady Saddler who had spread the rumours that Marie-Hélène was guilty? Why did she want the world – including Freddie – to think that Marie-Hélène was a traitor? If she was innocent, then perhaps she was indeed a spy but, like Lady Saddler herself, a spy for her compatriots, not the Germans. Didn't Lady Saddler like her . . .' *Like?* Like wasn't a word that applied to war. Hate perhaps. Jean-Paul could have hated Lady Saddler for spreading false rumours about Marie-Hélène. Still didn't fit. *Leap, Nell, leap*, she told herself, conscious that Alex was waiting, watching her.

She leapt. 'Lady Saddler, Lisette Rennard – was *she* the traitor? No heroine, but the opposite?' she threw at him.

Nell knew she'd landed safely. Everything fitted now. Why the goggling gurnards hadn't she realized that earlier? There were still questions – chiefly, why was Lady Saddler killed elsewhere and her body moved? – but the ground was firm to go ahead.

'That's the conclusion I came to,' Alex said. 'I've talked to people who were running La Dame Blanche and they were in complete agreement. Unfortunately, at that time there were powerful reasons why no one in Lille would publicly confirm that. Even so, Lisette Rennard had to leave Lille after the war.'

Nell pondered this, but question marks began to arise. 'But Marie-Hélène was in Beaudricourt when she met Freddie Carter, and Lady Saddler was still in Lille.'

'True. Marie-Hélène had to escape from Lille, because Lisette Rennard gave her name to the Germans. Even though she'd escaped their clutches in Lille, she was on the enemy's books as a wanted person, and I'm told it was Lisette Rennard who put her there. As a result, when Marie-Hélène reached Bapaume, she was caught, recognized as a wanted person and shot. That, Nell, was Jean-Paul's motive.'

Nell shuddered. 'Is Jean-Paul under arrest?'

Alex shook his head. 'We've no hard evidence yet, although he's as good as admitted his guilt through his silence.' He paused. 'Mr Briggs wasn't involved. The other evidence makes that doubly clear now, and once there's an arrest, you can ensure that everybody knows that.'

'Thank you.' Nell abruptly rose to her feet. She couldn't stand any more of this. She liked Jean-Paul, he liked her; there was a bond, an understanding between them. Or so she had thought. She had been wrong.

Alex looked concerned. 'Nell—' he began, rising as well.

She'd had enough. Alex was probably going to offer to walk with her back to Wychbourne, but she had to be alone. She had to come to terms with what she'd heard and as yet she still couldn't believe it.

A new day. A new start. Nell braced herself and tried to believe that all was well. Soon this would be over: Jean-Paul would be arrested, Mr Briggs would be completely cleared, the Clerries would leave and Wychbourne would be itself again. Life would be like Wychbourne's old Elizabethan banqueting house, the traces of which still stood in the grounds, incorporated into the Folly erected by the 2nd Marquess in the eighteenth century. Banqueting houses had signified a satisfying end to a wonderful feast for Tudor bon viveurs; they provided a pleasant stroll from the house on a summer's night to partake of the sweetmeats concluding the meal, after which diners could depart happily and sleep well.

Sleep well? How could she sleep peacefully having been drawn into the fatal attraction of Jean-Paul only to be told he was a murderer?

There were so many questions to ask, such as why he had not told Freddie long ago that his sister was innocent, or if he had only discovered that when he arrived at Spitalfrith, why he had continued to let her believe his sister was a traitor. The latter brought a depressing reply. If Jean-Paul had told her the truth, his motive for killing Lady Saddler would have been obvious.

She *still* found his guilt hard to believe, although this agonizing was on par with asking why the soufflé had sunk. At least there was usually a reason for sinking soufflés, whereas she might never know all the answers to her questions about Jean-Paul.

Look ahead. That was the only answer Nell could award herself. Ahead was her future. Her job, the Ansley family, Mr Briggs cleared – all positive, but it wasn't as easy as that. There were so many unanswered questions that lingered. Thankfully, the Clerries would be leaving shortly. She'd miss Gert and Vinny, but the others would be no loss. Life would move on even without Alex. At least Wychbourne was her home. It couldn't solve every problem, but it was there as a refuge. Like the banqueting house, it offered a resting place from the problems of the day.

By the early evening, though, Nell was still churning over the revelation about Jean-Paul, still wrenched between belief and disbelief. Fresh air, a fresh look at the situation. That's what she needed, and as soon as she had mentally ticked off the last item for tonight's dinner now being served, Nell made her way outside. A walk might help. Perhaps the banqueting house could provide some sweetness for her after the heavy meal of yesterday's news, she thought dejectedly. It was on a slight hill and had a dramatic view over the countryside, so perhaps it would put everything into perspective.

As that thought passed through her mind, it occurred to her that it had a familiar feel to it. Perhaps that was a sign that it could help her find a path to answer all the unresolved questions in her mind, although that was hoping for too much. Could it give the reason that Alex had been so set on the Clerries when he had now switched to the singing birds and the Carters? Could they be linked? The moving of the body to the garden must provide a link: was that to demonstrate the true motive for Lady Saddler's murder or, as Alex must have thought, to stop suspicion falling on the Clerries?

She tried to see things from Alex's point of view, as she found herself walking towards the banqueting house. True, he now believed Jean-Paul was guilty, but there had been no arrest yet. Did that mean he thought Jean-Paul might in fact be innocent or that someone else was involved, too? Who, then? Not his brother, who apparently didn't exist, nor Freddie, nor Joe, nor Mr Briggs, because they didn't fit the picture. Their priority was the singing birds, not the murder. If someone else was involved, she reasoned, it might explain Jean-Paul's reticence, his determination to mystify in order to keep the police away from the truth: the disappearing act, the non-existent brother, the alibi, and most of all why he hadn't told her of his sister's innocence. Was that to protect himself? Or someone else perhaps? Back to his brother – no!

There *was* no brother. Nell laughed at herself. She was going around in circles now, but this labyrinth surely had to lead somewhere. She could now see the banqueting house ahead at the top of its gentle incline. Well, at least that path was clear. Straight ahead and the answer might be there: would it be the story of the singing birds or the Clerries' quest for truth or the link between the two?

Perhaps neither she nor Alex had the complete answer. The singing bird story had ended in a pile of damaged wood; the Clerries' quest was displayed in their art. Very unhelpful. What about the link? She remembered the Eden and its snake, modelled by Lady Saddler; she remembered Vinny Finch's Harlequin and Columbine; she remembered Lance's fashionable lady; she remembered Gert Radley's portrait destroyed by Lady Saddler – the model who did not want her face so patently on display. Of course not. At the Exposition de Paris many people might remember and recognize Lisette Rennard, but – apart from Gert's – each of the Clerries' paintings revealed only one of Lisette Rennard's many faces.

Standing at the foot of the incline, Nell looked up at the banqueting house, torn between a determination to continue and an insane desire to turn and run, as almost forgotten words came back into her mind. 'Perhaps we all need a hill in life . . .' and – what was it? – 'the still and silent waters beneath' where no birds sing. She remembered with terrifying clarity where she had heard them now. The banqueting house was ahead, and below it were the still and silent waters of the lake.

She had to force herself to begin that climb, telling herself that she must surely be wrong, that no one would be sitting up there gazing down at the lake beneath. It was true there were missing faces at dinner this evening, but that was often the case. There was no reason at all why she shouldn't either continue up the hill if she really wanted to or else turn back to the safety of Wychbourne Court.

Safety? What could the unknown hold? Nothing to threaten her, she told herself. She would go on; she *must* go on. The nearer she came to the top, the easier it became, as she realized she had sensed the truth all along, ever since that day when she visited the Clerries' art festival. One image after another came to her: the snake, Columbine, the fashionable model, the blatant portrait. But one stood out, for it revealed the motive behind the murder. Every step of its story added up to the same conclusion. By the time Nell reached the top of the hill, it was without surprise that she saw what awaited her.

Vinny Finch was sitting on the bench on the far side of the hill overlooking the lake below and the fields that stretched out far into the distance. He seemed completely at ease, Nell thought. As though his mission was over. Almost as though he was waiting for her. He barely glanced at her as she came to join him.

They sat in silence for some time until he remarked almost conversationally, 'You find me alone and palely loitering, Miss Drury. The sedge has withered from the lake, and no birds sing.'

'*La Belle Dame sans Merci*,' she said quietly. 'Lisette Rennard.'

Nell realized with some surprise that she wasn't frightened of him, even though she now knew he was a murderer. Not as she had been frightened by the mythical Jacques Girarde.

'Look at that view before us,' he said. 'The birds *are* singing there and the lake is surrounded by green grass and flowers. Our own country. That's what people fought for during the war – for that and for their family and friends. Most people anyway. Jean-Paul did, I did, Marie-Hélène did. Lisette Rennard did not.'

'Why kill her, though?' Nell asked steadily. Such an enormous question, such a risk. Yet it did not seem so. Neither seemed to matter now.

Vinny smiled. 'To answer that, you needed to be there. Jean-Paul and I were, although we didn't know each other then. Why come here, Miss Drury? How did you know it was me you were looking for?'

'I've only just realized,' Nell said. 'It was your painting. The Harlequin waiting for his Columbine, separated by malicious people. It's Freddie's story.'

'We all suffer from the *Belle Dame sans Merci* called fate,' he said matter-of-factly. 'I told Jean-Paul late that Saturday afternoon that his sister was innocent and that Lisette Rennard had denounced her wrongly. When he returned to Lille after the war, he was told Marie-Hélène was a traitor, for that's the story that Lisette Rennard had spread to cover her own guilt. Jean-Paul is a kind man, and he had never told Freddie about his sister's supposed treachery. Lisette did that. Jean-Paul found out the truth from me too late to prevent Freddie's distress.'

'And' – Nell hardly dared ask this burning question, especially remembering Jean-Paul's vicious attack on her – 'did he help you when . . .'

She couldn't frame the words, but Vinny Finch took over. 'When I strangled her? No. I had long planned to kill her, and Jean-Paul guessed I had it in mind. He came by too late to stop me – had he wished to – but he was anxious I should not be arrested. For myself, I did not care, but he was adamant that we should move the body of Lisette Rennard to lie amidst the carnage she had caused in all our lives. He suspected I intended to act that evening, and he had persuaded Freddie and Joe to stay with Mrs Golding so that suspicion could not fall on them; in any case, Freddie was in no state to see the results of his own handiwork.'

'You planned it before you came here?' Nell struggled to ask.

'Long before. I made a point of getting to know Lisette Rennard. We met several times in Paris apart from the Artistes de Cler gatherings, and fate played into my hands when Gilbert bought Spitalfrith – knowing he was looking for a country house, I sent him the details. The time had come for action, and I let Lisette believe I fully concurred with her wish to ensure next year's exhibition did not happen. She was quite happy to meet me at half past eleven in the grounds to discuss our plans. I made her death as quick as I could and I told her why. I saw it as an execution, Miss Drury.'

But execution for what? Who was she to cast the first stone? Nell thought. She hadn't suffered during the war as they had. 'You said Lisette Rennard caused carnage in *all* your lives. So how were you involved?'

He smiled. 'Ah. The time for stories indeed. But I have time to tell you now, Miss Drury. All the time in the world – and out of it.'

'Then tell me, please.'

'My war was spent in British intelligence, stationed in Montreuil near Boulogne. Intelligence has many different operations. Information was vital, and as you know, there were many brave people who stood out against the enemy. In occupied territory this often took the form of sending information on railway troop movements. But by the time it reached us, it was many days out of date, and though it was of vital importance, it was not sufficient on its own, so we developed new methods, of which a major one was use of carrier pigeons. In 1917 there was a new initiative to send agents in by balloon; they carried with them baskets and homing pigeons, with the hope of building up a local network of new agents to use them. The balloons were not very successful, but I and my friend Armand Caron were chosen for one flight. We landed successfully in occupied territory near Lille, but the Germans were naturally looking for us. We were sheltered in the town by a patriotic family, but we were betrayed.'

He paused, and she could see what an effort it was for him to relive this. 'The family was shot,' he continued matter-of-factly, 'but I was not there at the time. My dear friend Armand was not so fortunate. He was arrested, tortured and shot. I miss him still. The person who betrayed our presence there was Lisette Rennard.'

'She betrayed you both?' Nell was appalled, dizzy with the enormity of what she was hearing.

'Yes. She did not know my real name, of course, but I knew of her. Her name is still whispered in Lille, which is why she disliked her full-faced portrait displayed.'

'How did you escape from Lille?'

'With much difficulty and only thanks to the Girarde family who sheltered me after Armand's death. Monsieur and Madame

Girarde would not leave their home and died as a result of Lisette's passing information to the enemy. I escaped with their daughter, Marie-Hélène.'

The war still cast its long shadow. The Clerries might be trumpeting their art for a new age, Nell reflected, but everyone who had endured it had to build on the mental rubble of the war, and many couldn't manage that. Including Vinny, including Jean-Paul. She stumbled her way back to Wychbourne, overcome with what she had been told. Vinny had quietly suggested she should go, and she had obeyed, leaving him a solitary figure still sitting on that bench, looking out into the fading light.

He had written to Alex Melbray, he had told her. They would be coming to arrest him shortly. Jean-Paul had suffered enough for him and it was time to make that clear. Nell had wanted to stay with him, so that he wasn't alone, but he had gently turned her offer down.

'I shall be here when they come, Miss Drury. Never fear about that,' he had said. 'Why should I run when I have chosen to have it this way? We Artistes de Cler see the true path, do we not? And this is mine.'

Nell slept badly that night, tossing and turning, wondering when Alex would be coming to Wychbourne as a result of Vinny Finch's letter. Perhaps he had already come; perhaps the kitchen would be agog with the news.

It was, but the news was not as she had expected when she arrived for breakfast, even though she couldn't face the thought of food.

Mrs Fielding was full of excitement. 'That Frenchman's back,' she said, beaming. 'I had it from the milk boy who saw that Inspector Melbray with him in his motor car. He's arrested him, that's for sure. I told Mr Peters the news *and* told him that proved Mr Briggs really is innocent.'

What was all this about? Nell thought aghast. Had Alex not received Vinny's letter? Did he still believe that Jean-Paul was guilty? No, she told herself. That couldn't be it. Perhaps Jean-Paul was with Alex but not under arrest. Simply to be questioned.

'Did Mr Peters say the police had come here, too?'

Mrs Fielding looked puzzled. 'No, all's well as far as I know. They'd have gone to Sevenoaks. It was at the Coach and Horses that the milk boy saw them.'

Something was seriously wrong, Nell knew, if Alex hadn't yet come here to arrest Vinny.

'I've told everyone,' Mrs Fielding continued happily. 'Now we can welcome Mr Briggs back properly and we'll make a special tea for him, with some of those fig tarts he likes.'

Nell made her excuses from joining the chattering breakfast table. Her stomach was churning, but not with hunger. Something was not right and she must find Alex, hoping that he hadn't already left for Sevenoaks. After checking again with Mr Peters that there had been no sign of him at Wychbourne Court this morning, she set off down the drive, full of misgivings.

'All quiet here, Miss Drury,' Mr Peters had told her. 'Nothing but the poachers out last night either. Jethro James up to his old tricks, eh?' He'd laughed. Lord Ashley turned a blind eye to Jethro James, who ostensibly hunted down poachers but was a keen poacher himself.

Mr Peters's words carried a new significance, as she quickened her pace and remembered with a shiver Vinny Finch as she had left him last night: 'I shall be here when they come. Never fear about that'. Hadn't he said he had all the time in the world – *and out of it*?

Alex was not at the Coach and Horses. He had been up at dawn, with all manner of police cars and vans, Mr Hardcastle told her with relish.

'Did you see him setting off for Sevenoaks?'

'No, Miss Drury. Along the Ightham road they went.'

Her fears grew. That passed the rear entrance of Wychbourne Court, she thought instantly. That was the gate nearest to the old banqueting hall. Thanking him, she turned back to Wychbourne Court. She'd rush straight through the grounds to the banqueting hall, but she dreaded what she might find there.

No vans were parked nearby when she arrived, only two motor cars, one of which she recognized as Alex's. She couldn't go up that hill to the banqueting hall, fearful of what she would find. Sickened, she watched silently until she saw Alex.

He didn't look surprised as he came down the hill to greet her; he looked tired and grey as he put his arm around her.

'He's killed himself?' she forced herself to ask.

'Yes. Shot.'

'Is he still . . .'

'No. The mortuary van's left. We're finishing here now.'

'He told me he'd written to you,' she blurted out.

'It seems we were both on the wrong track, Nell. I was so sure that the answer lay in the Clerries' art obsessions, and you that somehow those birds were mixed up with it.'

'But it was the shadow of the war that brought this about,' she finished for him. 'Will Jean-Paul—'

'I'll have to take that further, but' – he glanced at her – 'I hope not very far.'

'Thank you.'

'He's fond of you, Nell. Are you of him?'

She was standing on the cliff edge of her life. Pride, truth . . .

He helped her out. 'Harsh words have passed between us, Nell. They had to be spoken, but they don't have to remain. These last days without you have made me realize I'm not the strong force I thought I was. I love you, Nell, and I need you. For the rest of my life.'

There was no battle, no struggle. It was obvious really. He loved her, she loved him. It was that simple. They could work something out. *Very well, Life. Here I come*, she thought giddily.

She took the last step. 'We could always go to Paris,' she said.

He looked as though he could scarcely believe what he was hearing. 'With all that means?'

'It just means love, doesn't it?'

Seven days full of quiet contentment passed for Nell. She had never known such peace. A time of fear, horror and sorrow had been balanced by a happiness she had not thought possible. The future might hold sorrow too, but it would be shared with Alex, as would its joys.

The Clerries had departed, having made their peace with Sir Gilbert. Petra had arranged to move to the manor house, keeping her London flat for when she was studying at the Royal Academy of Dramatic Art; Lord Richard was delighted at this news, and

Lady Clarice was equally delighted, seeing the prospect of more appearances for Jasper. Lady Enid congratulated herself on her detective abilities, and the rest of the Ansley family had taken it upon themselves to smooth the path for a respectful burial for Vinny. And Mr Briggs had returned to the fold, although Nell noted he was often absent from the servants' lunch. Visiting Freddie? Other absences were often those of Mrs Fielding and Mr Peters, who, it was whispered, might at last be planning their marriage.

Only one concern remained. Nell had heard nothing from Jean-Paul. Was he still under arrest? *Had* he been arrested? Had he just left Spitalfrith without a word? And how were Freddie and Joe? How had Freddie taken the news?

A knock at the tradesman's entrance one afternoon took Nell by surprise. It was Jean-Paul.

He handed her a bouquet of sweet peas. 'For you, Nell. Will you walk with me?'

'Sweet peas mean goodbye in the language of flowers,' she said, taking them from him sadly.

'Au revoir, perhaps. I searched for hyacinths, but they cannot be found in late summer. They mean forgiveness, my mother once told me, and I need yours.'

'Your brother Jacques?'

'A noble brother in times of necessity, Nell. I know I hurt you and I know I lied to you, and Joe Carter did too, but while you all believed Jacques to have killed Lisette Rennard, you would not look too hard elsewhere. And especially not at Vinny.' He had followed her into the Cooking Pot while she found a vase for the flowers, and looked around appreciatively. 'I like this room, Nell. It speaks of warmth and love – love for more than just food.'

'You'll find them now perhaps.'

'Perhaps. Shall we walk to Spitalfrith, you and I, Nell? Don't be afraid. I shall not wave my wand and magic you away to France with me. I wish only that I could.' He led the way out of the door towards the gardens.

Nell laughed. 'You'd find me a poor companion compared with Hubert the Rabbit.'

'He is a faithful companion, indeed. He travels everywhere with me.'

She suddenly realized how that must be achieved. 'In that case, he must be . . .'

He placed his hand lightly across her lips. '*Chut, chérie*. If you speak its name, magic ceases to be.'

'I won't do that, then. You bring magic with you, Jean-Paul. It is a great gift.'

'It achieved little for Freddie or Vinny,' he said bitterly.

'You tried.'

'Vinny told you what happened? He told you of Marie-Hélène and his friend Armand?' When she nodded, he continued, 'When I returned from the war, I had no home to return to. My parents were dead, but I did not know why, and there were rumours my sister had been a traitor. I went to see my aunt in Beaudricourt who told me both of my sister's death and about this strange Englishman who had been writing to her and then came looking for her. He was creating a garden of singing birds for her in England, as he had promised her in his letters. The singing birds indeed had two meanings for him – his carved birds of love and the traitor that betrayed her. When I met Lisette in Lille after the war, she recognized me as Marie-Hélène's brother and confirmed for me that my sister was a traitor, so I told her about Freddie. I only learned the truth about Lisette from Vinny late that Saturday afternoon. He told me of my sister's true role in the war.'

'What brought you to Spitalfrith, then?'

'I had known for some time that Freddie was living here. I had met him before, when I brought my magic show to England. I never told him of my sister's supposed treachery, and so it was a great shock to him when Lisette spun her false story to him that afternoon. She did not know that he was living here and discovered only because Mademoiselle Petra mentioned it shortly after the Artistes de Cler arrived. And then you know what happened. Freddie acted so quickly, and by the time my dear Vinny had convinced me of the truth later that afternoon, it was too late. The vixen had spoken.'

'*La Belle Dame sans Merci*,' Nell said soberly. 'That's what Vinny called her. I was with him, Jean-Paul. I talked to him just before he died.'

'That must have meant much to him.'

'But I didn't know what would happen, I *didn't know*,' she said, anguished. 'I should have guessed, but I left him there alone.'

'As he wished, Nell.'

'Is there nothing I can do, Jean-Paul?' she pleaded.

'You can be Freddie's friend, as Charlie Briggs has been for so long.'

They had reached Spitalfrith now, and as they opened the gate and walked up the drive, she saw the door open. Joe emerged with Mr Briggs. Behind them was a bashful Freddie.

Freddie was stroking something, something he set gently down on the ground, then squatted down beside it. He glanced up nervously at his father.

'He just done it today, Jean-Paul, Miss Drury,' Joe said proudly. 'You go on, Freddie. Turn that key.'

Freddie turned it and stroked the wood lovingly as a singing blackbird carolled out his song.

FEB--2021